"I was warned," Garrick rumbled, "about creatures like you."

Maeve's skin tingled, for he had a deep voice that brought to mind lazy mornings and entwined limbs.

"Beware the spirits of the dead, I was told." He reached out and captured a tress of her hair rising aloft by the fire's wind. "And watch out for the fairy-women, who slip out between the veils this night to bewitch human men."

"It seems you need someone to take you in hand," she murmured. She swung up the hollowed-out turnip lantern she clutched by a leather thong. "Did no one give you a lantern?"

He rolled one massive shoulder. "Who needs a lantern with that moon and this fire?"

"Don't be losing it. You need it to ward off the dead who walk this night."

"I'll share yours."

The air she sucked into her lungs rushed tingling through her blood. "Then it's a bit of luck for you that you found me."

"More than a bit of luck." He thrust his hand past her cheek and into the fall of her hair. She reeled with the sensation of his hands curling against her scalp. He smelled of wood-fire smoke and sweet ale, the warm scents of a man's hard body.

"I was told there's magic in this night," he whispered as he traced the curve of her lower lip with his thumb. "And now I know it's true."

— from THE O'MADDEN, by Lisa Ann Verge

PUT SOME PASSION INTO YOUR
LIFE . . . WITH THIS STEAMY SELECTION OF
ZEBRA *LOVEGRAMS!*

SEA FIRES (3899, $4.50/$5.50)
by Christine Dorsey

Spirited, impetuous Miranda Chadwick arrives in the untamed New World prepared for any peril. But when the notorious pirate Gentleman Jack Blackstone kidnaps her in order to fulfill his secret plans, she can't help but surrender—to the shameless desires and raging hunger that his bronzed, lean body and demanding caresses ignite within her!

TEXAS MAGIC (3898, $4.50/$5.50)
by Wanda Owen

After being ambushed by bandits and saved by a ranchhand, headstrong Texas belle Bianca Moreno hires her gorgeous rescuer as a protective escort. But Rick Larkin does more than guard her body—he kisses away her maidenly inhibitions, and teaches her the secrets of wild, reckless love!

SEDUCTIVE CARESS (3767, $4.50/$5.50)
by Carla Simpson

Determined to find her missing sister, brave beauty Jessamyn Forsythe disguises herself as a simple working girl and follows her only clues to Whitechapel's darkest alleys . . . and the disturbingly handsome Inspector Devlin Burke. Burke, on the trail of a killer, becomes intrigued with the ebon-haired lass and discovers the secrets of her silken lips and the hidden promise of her sweet flesh.

SILVER SURRENDER (3769, $4.50/$5.50)
by Vivian Vaughan

When Mexican beauty Aurelia Mazón saves a handsome stranger from death, she finds herself on the run from the Federales with the most dangerous man she's ever met. And when Texas Ranger Carson Jarrett steals her heart with his intimate kisses and seductive caresses, she yields to an all-consuming passion from which she hopes to never escape!

ENDLESS SEDUCTION (3793, $4.50/$5.50)
by Rosalyn Alsobrook

Caught in the middle of a dangerous shoot-out, lovely Leona Stegall falls unconscious and awakens to the gentle touch of a handsome doctor. When her rescuer's caresses turn passionate, Leona surrenders to his fiery embrace and savors a night of soaring ecstasy!

Available wherever paperbacks are sold, or order direct from the Publisher. Send cover price plus 50¢ per copy for mailing and handling to Penguin USA, P.O. Box 999, c/o Dept. 17109, Bergenfield, NJ 07621. Residents of New York and Tennessee must include sales tax. DO NOT SEND CASH.

UNDER His SPELL

**ELLEN ARCHER
STEPHANIE BARTLETT
CHRISTINE DORSEY
LISA ANN VERGE**

**ZEBRA BOOKS
KENSINGTON PUBLISHING CORP.**

ZEBRA BOOKS are published by

Kensington Publishing Corp.
850 Third Avenue
New York, NY 10022

First Printing: October, 1995

Printed in the United States of America

Contents

Wishes

by

Ellen Archer

One

When Pandora Drummond was serenaded by clusters of eager-faced young men in evening wear, or sent expensive and frivolous gifts by men she barely knew, it never surprised her. Neither were such occurrences unexpected by her father, shipping magnate Hector Drummond, nor by her long-suffering Aunt Hesta, nor indeed by any man, woman, or child who had ever set an eye to the physical and social wonder which was Pandora.

It was also hardly amazing that since her official coming out two years prior, less fortunate girls in the San Francisco area had eagerly searched the society pages for images of Pandora Drummond, which they carefully snipped out with long-bladed scissors and affixed to the frames of their vanity mirrors before they copied Pandora's elaborate hairstyles, or practiced her perfect rosebud pout, or aped that certain haughty yet come-hither tilt to her delicate brows.

"She's so . . . perfect," they would sigh to one another after yet another less-than-successful group effort to achieve Pandora's coif of the moment. "Her lips, her eyes . . . just perfect. They say she has scores of suitors, and every single one is rich and handsome."

And then they would stare, frowning, into their mirrors, and wonder why fate had denied them Pandora Drummond's perfect honey hair or vaguely slanted eyes or tiny waist. Or her money. Or her social position. Or, by all accounts, her kind nature and impeccable manners.

And when the announcement was made of her engagement to Michael Crane—the richest man in the Arizona Territory, it was reported, and the most ideal specimen of mankind ever sighted on the California coast, it was whispered at parties— hundreds of young men were seen to weep openly because of their lost chance.

Hundreds of young women were secretly relieved.

Michael Crane, they said, lived in a fabulous hacienda the size of a castle—the seat of a huge Spanish land grant. They said he'd been educated at Harvard (some said abroad, at Oxford, or was it Cambridge?)—and that in the last few years an entire metropolis had grown up practically in his front yard. A rumor spread that he had saved his mining operation by single-handedly standing off half the Apache nations during the last days of the Indian Wars.

"What does any of that nonsense matter?" asked the more practical-minded. "The important thing is that he's wealthy and reasonably cultured. And enormously good-looking, of course."

Yes, Michael Crane was the catch of the season. At last, the city's social elders breathed in satisfaction, someone had come along who was good enough for "their" Pandora. The ranks of young suitors, formerly prone to over-mannered fisticuffs on her account, united in a common, quiet grudge against "that interloper, Crane."

The entire city was astonished and disappointed when Pandora's father announced that the ceremony would take place in far-off Arizona. Pandora Drummond's wedding would surely have been the highlight of any season, perhaps of a decade of seasons. But no other explanation was given, other than that the bride, the groom, and their families had all agreed upon it.

There was speculation, of course.

Some said it was the groom's whim. He was certainly handsome and rich, but what did anyone really *know* about him? Could one really trust a man who was so, well, *rugged,* even if he did look wonderful in evening clothes?

A few souls, meaner of spirit, hinted that the lovely Miss Drummond might be in a family way: the rumor picked up speed— and whisperers— once it was discovered that the wedding was to be private, with only immediate family in attendance.

Ridiculous! said the more romantically inclined. Why would the wedding have been put off for over a month if such an unspeakable thing were true? Wasn't it possible that Pandora and her young man were simply so much in love that they wanted miles and miles of privacy?

A handful of old family friends reminded each other that the Drummonds had always been a somewhat eccentric lot— *charmingly* eccentric, of course, they added hastily.

Roughly an equal number of old family enemies smirkingly decided that old Hector Drummond was just out to save a few dollars on a wedding which, if it were to be held with full pomp and ceremony in the city, would have been a staggeringly expensive affair.

When Pandora Drummond herself— slim and perfect and, as one society reporter put it, "the epitome of chastity and taste"— was confronted by reporters, she would only smile graciously and repeat, "No comment at this time, thank you."

The station was so crowded with admirers on the day Pandora and her entourage bade farewell to the city that two newsmen had to carry their equipment to the depot's roof in order to photograph the throng.

One fell off and broke his leg.

Two

Miss Hesta Drummond, spinster sister to Hector H. Drummond and aunt (also, of late, chaperon) to his only child, Pandora, marched down the wide, clay-tiled hallway amid a great deal of loud swishing: the sounds of her own perpetually black and voluminous skirts mixed with the frictive sway of the bright— if somewhat dusty— frock draped over her outstretched arms.

"Threw it out the window!" she muttered in time to the sharp taps of her shoes on the tiles. She often muttered to herself (and, in fact, frequently carried on quite audible solitary conversations): these past years she had found few people with sense enough to be worth talking to unless one was forced into it. And it looked as if she were about to be forced into a confrontation with her niece.

"Of all the selfish, empty-headed little— ." She found herself on the verge of uttering a word which would have propelled her, had she heard it on the street, to thrash the speaker with her handbag. She closed her mouth, biting down on the word so hard that her teeth clicked.

"Ungrateful . . . child," she said in its place,

just as she came to the main staircase, and started up.

We're in one of the grandest homes for hundreds— perhaps thousands— of miles in any direction, she thought, shoes beating a sharp tattoo on the steps, then the polished floorboards of the second story, *and all she can do is complain and throw her clothes out the window!*

She marched down the long hall of the upper west wing, skirts a-swish, then stopped before a carved and massive wooden door which might have looked more at home guarding the hacienda's entry instead of its master bedchamber. She tried the latch. It was locked.

"Pandora!" she called sternly. "Pandora, open this door immediately!"

"Go away!" came the barked reply, muffled somewhat by the door, but still clear enough to let Hesta know there was another tantrum taking place on the other side.

She took a deep breath. She pitied Michael Crane, who would have to put up with Pandora's shenanigans for the rest of his married life. Such a delightful man! Hesta seriously doubted Michael had witnessed even a hint of one of Pandy's tantrums; if he had, she was fairly certain he was too lovesick to have noticed. Pandora was always perfectly polite— perfectly gracious and perfectly charming, and, quite frankly, perfectly dazzling— in company. From the moment of her birth, she had dazzled men, women, and children with her smile, her grace, and her physical gifts.

But somewhere along the way— along about the

age of eleven, Hesta reckoned— Pandora had become acutely self-aware. So far as Hesta was concerned, that moment of realization had been her niece's downfall.

From that moment on, Pandora had ceased to settle for letting her natural charms shine through, well, naturally. She had actively dedicated herself to charm, and to perfection: perfection in all aspects of herself first, and then perfection in those surrounding her.

As furious as Hesta could be with Pandora, she also felt sorry for the girl. It must be a terrible burden to feel one always had to be so impeccable, so flawless. Although— as she was reminded by the locked door and the angry, mumbling sounds from beyond it— Pandora's perfection did have its limits.

That her niece could be such a model of decorum and feminine grace in public and such a harridan in private had been a great puzzlement to Hesta until she'd realized that being a paragon by occupation had to be quite a strain. Perhaps all that practiced flawlessness was like steam building up in a boiler, steam that had to be vented lest Pandora explode in even less becoming ways.

Michael's in for a surprise, Hesta thought with a sigh.

She leaned against the wall, letting the dress sag in her arms as she thought back to the first time any of them had met Michael Crane. She and Hector and Pandora had all attended a ball given by one of Hector's associates. There must have been at least a hundred guests, all chattering or dancing or both. But when Michael Crane entered the room, all heads— male and female— had turned. She had heard Pandora gasp softly, and Hesta admitted that even her own middle-aged heart had stuttered.

"Ah, that's young Crane," Pandora's father had announced to their little group. "Just in from Arizona. Mines, you know. Gold and silver. Met him at the club. I'll just go say hello."

"Do bring him over, Father," Hesta had heard Pandora say. And that, she supposed as she absently flicked dust from the dress in her arms, had been the beginning of the end.

If only they hadn't gone to that ball, if only Pandora hadn't seen Michael across that room— and more importantly, if Michael had never been exposed to her niece's prodigious charms— she would not at this moment be standing in the hard, tiled hallway of a rambling Spanish hacienda, and playing babysitter to the publicly acclaimed and privately spoilt ingenue in the next room.

From beyond the door came a crash. After years of standing witness to Pandora's crockery-breaking, Hesta had long since gone past being startled at the impacts. Instead, she had developed something akin to an ear for them, and her initial disgust at Pandora's tantrums had worn down over the years to a distanced, analytical annoyance.

Not glass, she mused, leaning resignedly against

the hallway wall. *Porcelain. Yes, that's it: porcelain on tile. That'll be a job to sweep up.*

What a shame, Hesta thought for perhaps the thousandth time, that her brother had been given such a self-indulgent ninny for a daughter. Oh, Pandora was certainly bright enough and pretty enough. Quite beautiful, actually.

Slim-waisted, full busted, graceful of limb and neck and motion, Pandora, with her thick and glossy honey hair and big green eyes and heart-shaped face had been, two years ago, San Francisco's favorite debutante: her picture had been in all the papers, invitations had flooded the mailbox. Just this past spring, she'd been voted "Most Beautiful Young Lady West of the Rockies" for the third year running by the boys over at some fraternity or other.

"Pandora?" she called again. She tried to remember which items, out of the few pieces of bric-a-brac in the room, had been porcelain. Two, she decided: the shepherd and shepherdess on the mantle. She wondered which of the pair had taken the brunt of Pandora's wrath. Another sudden explosion of porcelain on tile made the point moot, and she sighed.

"Pandora, those aren't your things you're breaking, you know. This isn't your house. Not yet."

From beyond the door came three more quickly spaced expressions of Pandora's displeasure: two small, sharp explosions, then one bright thunk followed by a small metallic bounce.

Two glass ornaments, one bronze figurine. Or per-

haps the inkwell . . . Hesta was somewhat comforted by the knowledge that the room's six vases had been removed earlier in order to change the flowers. For once, Pandora's perfectionism—the flowers had been slightly wilted—had prevented harm instead of causing it.

Everything had to be perfect for Pandora. And this, in Hesta's estimation, was the root of all her niece's unhappiness and, as a consequence, the family's. The hems, cuffs, every stitch of her dresses had to be just so, or back to the seamstresses they went. Her dinner had to be perfect in portion, scent, taste, and arrangement on the plate, or back it went to the kitchen. Her companions had to dress, speak, and comport themselves properly— properly, that was, to Pandora's etiquette of the moment— or they were no longer her companions.

It was indeed a fortunate thing, Hesta believed, that Pandora was such a strikingly beautiful girl. If her nose had been a bit askew or her ears a little large, she certainly would have badgered her father into sending her to the Continent for some extremely expensive surgery, and one did hear such horror stories about the outcomes. . . .

Poor Hector. Although Hesta supposed she really shouldn't be feeling so sorry for her brother. It was probably his fault as much as anyone's that Pandora was the way she was, though she had to commend Hector for at long last insisting that Pandora tidy up one of her own catastrophes, even if it meant banishing both herself and the girl—not to mention a manservant and two maids— to the wilds of Arizona and forcing Pandy to make good on her promise to marry Michael.

Hesta stood up straight and squared her shoulders. "Pandora Louise Drummond," she said firmly, "are you going to open this door, or am I going to have to go get the housekeeper's keys again?"

Three

"I will *not* put on that hideous rag!" was the first thing Pandora said when she opened the door and saw that wretched dress, in all its blood red and turquoise and bright orange obscenity, in her aunt's arms.

"It's not hideous, dear," Aunt Hesta said, peeping rather obviously over Pandy's shoulder as if to survey the damage. She frowned slightly before adding, "Michael sent it over so—"

Pandora planted her hands on her hips. Hesta could be so aggravating. "So that he could make a fool of me? So that everybody back home would hear about it and laugh and say, 'Oh did you hear? Pandy Drummond's gone native!' *Native!* Isn't it enough that I'm trapped here in this baked-out, sun-bleached, God-forsaken . . . well, I was going to say 'town' but Lost Arroyo isn't even a town, is it? Just a well and a plaza and a few mud huts! Oh, I wish we'd never come!"

"Pandora!" Hesta scolded. "I'm nearly at the end of my rope. Frankly, sometimes it's all I can do to keep from slapping you, and one of these days I'm going to—"

"Aunt Hesta! How dare you even think such a thing?"

"Don't try that hurt and precious look with me, Pandy," Hesta said as she picked her way across the room, through the glass and porcelain rubble on the floor—a little too dramatically, Pandora thought. She watched as Hesta draped the Mexican fiesta dress over the foot of the bed, then smoothed it.

"I know you too well," Hesta added, turning to face her. "I don't blame your father one tiny bit for sending you off. In a matter of days you're going to be Mrs. Michael Crane, and this will be your home. You'd best get used to it."

Pandora balled her hands into fists, then tucked them behind her back. It was an awful place, Arizona. This was an awful house. She wanted to throw something again, but settled for tapping her foot. "You're extremely rude, Aunt Hesta. I'm not a child anymore, and I won't be spoken to like this."

"Yes, you will, my dear." Hesta's dark eyes narrowed slightly but her expression was not unkind. "It's high time you had to make good on a promise. It's high time you paid the price for one of your caprices."

"Not fair," Pandora said, only slightly aware that her voice had trailed into a childish whine. "Daddy is so *mean!* He could have just taken away my allowance or something, couldn't he, if he were really that upset? But to make me actually marry Michael Crane? I wish I'd never set eyes on him!"

She sank down on the edge of the bed, shoving the wretched dress to the floor. "I mean, even if Daddy absolutely insisted on the wedding, it wouldn't have been so very awful if we could've gotten married in San Francisco. Maybe at home, in the garden. I could have had lots of bridesmaids and there would have been parties before and it all would have been terribly gay and the newspapers would have made a real show of it. I'd have had clippings to save. It might even have taken my mind off that . . . that . . . creature."

"Pandora!"

With the tip of one shoe, she kicked absently at the wretched fiesta dress, but succeeded only in fluttering the skirts. "If only he were more . . . interesting. Or something. He's so boring! He's too nice. Boring, boring, boring."

"I won't hear you speak of Michael that way," Aunt Hesta said firmly as she snatched up the gown before Pandora could aim another kick, and shook it gently. Two tiny shards of glass *pinged* to the floor. "He's perfectly wonderful, Pandy. Personally, I find him quite fascinating."

"You marry him, then," Pandora cut in.

Hesta ignored her. "He's kind and rich and intelligent and attractive, and he loves you. Although— may the Lord forgive me and watch over him— I can't understand why."

Pandora pursed her lips into a practiced pout before she said softly, "Well, he is rich." She trailed one finger over the bedspread. "And handsome."

To be honest, Pandora mused, "breathtaking"

would have been a more accurate description of Michael's looks— not that she'd admit that to Hesta, of course. On the night they'd met, her father had led him through the crowd at that party. Everyone was gawking at him— discreetly, of course— wondering who he was. And when he'd halted before her, he'd stared at her in a way that, strangely enough, hadn't seemed even slightly rude. When Michael looked at you, you were the only two people in the world. And then he'd said, quite simply, "My God." The way he'd said it had made her knees wobble.

She looked up at her aunt. "I never *really* meant to marry him. It's just that it was so . . . romantic. So perfect." She closed her eyes for a moment, recalling the night he'd proposed. It had been a matchless rose-scented evening, exactly three weeks and five parties after their first meeting. There had been a ball at her father's mansion and she and Michael had danced all night and sipped too much champagne, and when he'd taken her into his arms on the terrace and proposed . . .

She made herself open her eyes, forced herself to stop thinking about Michael and the effect he had on her when she wasn't on her guard.

"It was the ambiance, Aunt Hesta," she said, once again working as hard to convince herself as anyone else. "It was the ball and the music, and the evening and everything. That was all. I don't see why he couldn't have been polite about it, like the others."

"Like the others you jilted, I assume you

mean?" Aunt Hesta sat down in a leather wing-back chair, the twice-rescued dress draped across her lap. It looked to Pandora as if Aunt Hesta meant to make a siege of it. How boring.

"Jilted is a harsh word," Pandora said evenly. "I hardly think a little flirtation is— "

"Five engagements, Pandora," Aunt Hesta broke in. "Four of them broken in just the last two years, and your poor father having to disentangle things every time. Your father is a great man, Pandora, a powerful man; a dignified man. Imagine what a fool he must have felt, explaining to those young men and their families that his only daughter was such a brainless, vain, flibberty-gibbet that she seemed to have made a hobby out of collecting— and accepting— marriage proposals?"

"Aunt Hesta— "

"Why do you always have to accept them, Pandy? Other girls just tally up the proposals, like savages counting coup. Why do you always have to say yes?"

Pandora snorted softly. She was really quite bored. "I don't *always* say yes. I hardly *ever* say yes! I could make a list for you of the ones to whom I've said no."

She cocked one brow at her aunt, whose small but regal face was currently arranged in one of her most irritatingly patient expressions.

"It would be a very long list, Aunt Hesta," she added before she shrugged. "I suppose I just get caught up in it. The romance of it all. Moonlight, flowers, soft lights, sweet talk, all that. But it only means I'm soft-hearted. I made those boys very happy."

Hesta pressed her fingertips together, tenting her hands. "For a day or two. Until your father had to send for them and explain. I don't have to remind you that it got a bit messy a time or two, especially with that Upton boy's family."

Frowning, Pandora flopped backward on the bed and spread her arms wide at her sides. The winter of her tenth year, she had accompanied her father on a trip to Scotland. She hadn't cared for the trip or Scotland much either, to tell the truth. The whole country had seemed cold and drafty and covered in snow, and everyone talked oddly. But she had learned to make snow angels. She moved her arms slowly upward over the coverlet, then down, then up. She didn't suppose she'd ever see snow again. She wondered if the natives here made sand angels instead.

"Pandora, I do wish you'd pay attention." Aunt Hesta was on her feet again.

Pandora sat up. She crossed her arms over her chest. "I'm tired of this discussion."

"Aren't we all."

Pandora began to thump her heel against the bed frame. "Now you're being mean, Aunt Hesta. *Both* you and Daddy are mean. If he had to make me accept somebody, why did it have to be somebody who lives practically at the end of the earth? I feel like some banished princess in a nursery book! I won't live here, you know. I hate this town. I hate this house. I hate everything about it."

Tired of drumming her heel, Pandora rose and went to the window. There was nothing green outside it, nothing civilized, either. Just squat adobe buildings, a few donkeys and chickens and a peasant or two. And that strange woman cloaked in pale blue and half hidden in the shadowed arch of the tobacconist's courtyard across the plaza. Pandy rubbed at her arms. The woman had been there for hours, and Pandora had the most annoying feeling that the filthy peasant was watching her.

From behind her came Hesta's voice. "You honestly don't understand, do you? About why you've been . . . what did you call it? Banished."

She turned her back on the shoddy vista— and the woman in blue— to face her aunt. "Daddy said he had to go to Boston. He said it wouldn't be proper for me to make all my own arrangements without his presence. I think that's a lie. I think he's doing this just to punish me."

"That's partly right, Pandy my dear," Aunt Hesta said, a strangely piteous look on her face. She looked down at her hands. "He *is* doing it to punish you. But you might as well know the rest of it."

"What?" Pandora demanded impatiently.

"He's . . . he's ashamed."

"Ashamed! Ashamed of what?"

Aunt Hesta walked to the door and rested her hand on the latch before she turned and softly said, "Ashamed of you, dearest."

"What?" Pandora exclaimed. "Ashamed of *me*? But I'm the prettiest girl in San Francisco!"

Aunt Hesta's brows knitted slightly before she added sadly, "And I'm afraid that's just about all you are. I feel mightily sorry for Michael Crane. And for you."

Four

Ashamed? Ashamed of me? Pandora's first reaction, as the door closed behind her aunt, was to grab the nearest piece of crockery and throw it. Having used up everything within range, she stomped instead on the shards of the pieces she'd already ruined, gratified when they crunched and popped beneath her shoes, powdering into the hardwood, scarring it. And then she threw herself onto the bed.

She did not cry, however. It hurt too much to entertain the notion that her father might actually be ashamed of her, and so she refused to think about it. Instead, she lay on her back, fingers locked behind her head, and began to try to plot a way out of her predicament. Michael Crane was something of a catch, she had to admit that; she also had to admit that sometimes, when she let her guard slip, she found herself thinking kind thoughts about him.

He really could be awfully nice, couldn't he? He was tall and blond and had the most wonderful blue eyes and a deep, silky voice. She supposed that was what had possessed her to say yes to him more than anything else that night on her father's terrace— Michael's voice. When he'd whispered to her there in the dark . . . well, what girl could have resisted a voice that vibrated right through her body like that, a voice that made her feel as if her insides were about to boil over?

And he was a wonderful dancer, wasn't he? The way he'd held her had made her feel—

"I'm doing it again," she said angrily, and sat up. "It doesn't matter that he's a good dancer when there's not a ballroom within two hundred, three hundred, maybe five hundred miles, for all I know. I wish I was back home in my own room instead of here in *his.*"

It was a nice room, though, she had to admit. Largish and pleasingly proportioned, the room was furnished in Spanish Colonial (which Pandora, much to her irritation, was surprised to discover she liked), and was flooded by light from several windows and a set of French doors which led out to the long balcony.

Ever the gentleman, Michael had moved out until the wedding, leaving behind his staff, most of whom spoke nothing but Spanish— an impossible language, Spanish, if you asked her— and his invalid mother, whom she had never met.

"She's feeling too ill for visitors at the moment," Michael had explained the day before, as they passed the door to his mother's private apartment. The only contact Pandora or any of her party had had with the elderly Mrs. Crane was the annoying clang of her bell, which she seemed able to ring quite loudly— and frequently— despite her infirm health.

Michael was temporarily staying across the plaza at the hotel, and Pandora and her entourage had taken over the old hacienda, about which, Michael had told her, the town of Lost Arroyo had grown up.

"Town," she snorted. "There can't be more than three hundred souls in the whole place—donkeys included—and practically all of them work for Michael. I might as well be in prison."

Someone rapped at the door. "Miss Pandora?" It was her personal maid.

"What is it, Constance?" she snapped.

"Miss Hesta says you should dress for dinner. Mr. Crane's going to be here in a half hour. Would you like me to help you—?"

"Go away!" Pandora shouted, automatically reaching toward the night table for something throwable, and remembering only when her fingers came up empty that she'd already broken the little glass bird which had once perched there. She settled for pounding one fist backward, into the headboard, immediately cursing under her breath and tucking her stinging hand under one armpit before she added through clenched teeth, "I can dress myself!"

As Constance's shoes scuffed away down the hall, Pandora threw her legs over the side of the bed in what Aunt Hesta would surely have called a most unladylike motion, and went to the window. Shaking the fingers of her sore hand—drat that headboard, anyway, for being so hard!—she gazed out over the wide plaza again.

The sun, already dipped halfway beneath the

horizon, had painted the sky pink and lavender and orange, and cast eerie fingers of color and shadow over the circular plaza, which was perhaps half as wide as a city block was long and paved in cobblestones. At its hub stood a large, round well surrounded by a waist-high stone wall. Pandora squinted at the buildings across the way, searching in the fading light for the little tobacconist's shop and its courtyard. So far as she could tell, the woman in blue was no longer there. Odd that the woman's absence should flood her with such relief.

Her hand had, for the most part, stopped hurting. She flexed her fingers. "I wish Daddy would come to his senses," she muttered as she crunched back across the floor, glittery with glass fragments, and stopped beside the chair where Aunt Hesta had left the fiesta dress. "This is all Daddy's fault."

She knew she was supposed to wear this horrid Mexican atrocity to dinner to please Michael. What in the world had possessed him to think she'd ever consent to be seen in such a thing? She picked it up with the tips of her fingers, arms outstretched. Incredibly *gauche*.

On impulse, she gripped it in both hands, and crying out, "I can't bear it!" ripped the bodice.

"Drat!" she whispered through clenched teeth when she realized what she'd done. She hadn't, until this moment, noticed the delicate embroidery work— thousands of tiny stitches that formed a pattern of entwined roses— red, pink, and orange— upon the black bodice. Now their broken threads trailed from either piece like impossibly fine multicolored fringe. The needlework alone must have cost a small fortune. Even if the dress was repulsive, the perfectionist in her had to admire the artistry.

She let it drop from her hands. "It's not my fault," she said softly. Then, more firmly, "They drove me to it."

On impulse, she snatched up her shawl and strode past the window to the French doors and stepped through them, onto the balcony. A soft breeze made the outdoors cooler than she'd expected, but she was sick of the house and sick of Michael's room.

I'll run away, she thought as she moved down the long balcony, toward the spiral stair at its end. *I'll show them. I'll get on a train. . . .* But there was no train, she remembered. Barely even a stage line: just two stops a week, they'd told her.

She went down the stairs carefully in the dusky light, and once on ground level she walked out onto the plaza and toward its central well. The place seemed deserted. The only sounds were soft snatches of music and laughter from some unseen cantina, and the occasional cry of a night-hunting bird.

When she reached the well, she picked up a pebble and dropped it over the edge. The small, echoed *plop* of stone hitting water came back to her almost immediately.

Boring, she thought. *Boring, boring, boring. If I were back home, I'd be at a party. I'd be dancing. Handsome men would be saying witty things to me and*

*telling me I'm beautiful, and at the end of the evening
they'd fight over whose turn it was to see me home.
And kiss my hand goodnight at the door.*

"I hate this place," she muttered under her
breath, and snugged the shawl over her shoulders.

"*Señorita* Drummond? Miss?"

Pandora whirled, bumping her hip against the
old stone well. "Wh-where did you come from?"
she whispered, steadying herself.

It was the old woman, cloaked and cowled in
blue. Close up, in the last rays of the sun, she
seemed incredibly wizened. At least the flesh
about her eyes did. That was the only part of
her face visible to Pandora, the rest being con-
cealed by her cowl-like shawl and its shadows.

"How did you come up behind me?" she stuttered. "I didn't hear you. What do you want?"

The old woman stood her ground. "No need
to be afraid, *Señorita,*" she said softly.

The accent was different from the others Pandora had heard spoken here, and the woman's
voice had an odd quality— abrasive yet soothing.
For some odd reason, it made Pandora think of
clear cold water moving languidly over the shifting pebbles of a brook. She tried to move her
feet, and found she couldn't.

"You seem so unhappy," the woman continued.
"I have watched, and I know. It is not right that
the intended of *Señor* Crane be sad. *Señor* Crane
is a very big man in Lost Arroyo. Without him
there would be no Lost Arroyo, no?"

Pandora heard herself say, "I have to go now." Had her own voice ever sounded so small?

"I have for you a gift," the woman continued, as if Pandora hadn't spoken. "Please to hold out your hand?"

Pandora was about to announce that she certainly would do no such thing, then realized the woman had already taken her hand and placed something in it.

"A coin," the woman said, her voice washing over Pandora, simultaneously soothing and frightening her. "But no ordinary coin is this. Much magic."

She stopped for a moment, then shrugged. "Well, not so much. But enough. When you hold this coin and make a wish, it will come true. As many times as you want. But it cannot be such a big wish. Small things. You cannot say, 'I wish I had a giant hacienda,' and *poof,* it is there. No. But you could say, 'I wish my shoes did not hurt,' and that would happen. You see?"

Did the coin burn her palm, or was it just her imagination? Pandora found she couldn't open her fingers, couldn't drop the filthy thing. It was probably full of germs that would make her just as crazy as this old hag obviously was.

Or perhaps it was too late already. She couldn't seem to take her eyes away from the woman's, which appeared to be gradually receding deeper and deeper into her cowl, yet brightening, almost burning.

"The coin will only work when you hold it, like you hold it now. And remember, no big wishes, just small ones. The things that come to you from this coin, they are my wedding gift to you."

The woman moved away slightly, as if to leave, and Pandora sagged against the lip of the well. But then the woman turned back. "I forgot the most important thing. If you take back a wish, any wish, the coin takes back everything. If you do this, then it is the last wish for you. Be careful. Even small wishes can be great magic."

The woman took a step away, at last severing eye contact with Pandora, whose knees were suddenly so weak that she had to catch herself on the well's rim with one elbow. Vaguely registering that the sun had set and the plaza was now lit by the soft, silvery light of a three-quarter moon, she looked down at her hand and slowly opened it. On her palm lay a single gold coin, glinting dully in the moonlight, irregular and hand-stamped by the look of it, and crudely pierced, near the edge, with a hole for stringing on a necklace or bracelet. A Spanish doubloon? No, too small, she thought. Roman, perhaps, or Greek?

"But what am I supposed to— ?"

The woman was gone. There was no trace of movement anywhere, no sound of retreating footsteps.

Pandora shook her head. *This is silly!* she thought. *Preposterous!* She nearly turned and dropped the coin down the well, then thought better of it. It was probably worth something— not that she needed the money— but perhaps worth more in the story she could tell about it if she ever got out of this backward hamlet and home to civilization.

She stood up straight. She took two steps toward the hacienda. She stopped. She looked down at the coin in her hand. What if it worked?

You're as crazy as that crone! she thought, then laughed out loud.

But what if it really did work?

"Oh, all right," she said to the coin. She closed her fingers over it and said, "I wish I were home in San Francisco." She opened her eyes. Same grimy plaza. Michael Crane's hacienda, windows glowing with lamp light, still loomed before her, a golden-eyed behemoth guarding the plaza and the town.

Lips tight with irritation, Pandora lifted her hand as if to throw the coin like so much smashable crockery, but stopped herself. "Was that wish too big?" she muttered. "A small one, then." She closed her eyes. She didn't know that it would make any difference, but it seemed the thing to do. "I wish . . . I wish that the dress I tore this evening was mended as good as new."

She opened her eyes and was a little disappointed when the sky didn't suddenly fill with lightning.

"I am an idiot," she said, as she jammed the coin into her skirt pocket and started toward the balcony stairs.

It wasn't possible. Her maid must have done it.

Yes, that's it, Pandora decided. *Constance mended the dress while I was outside.*

Still, she was almost afraid to touch the garment let alone examine it closely. And when she mustered the nerve, she could not, for the life of her, find any trace of mending. The embroidery, all the intricate stitching, looked complete and perfect, as if it had never been damaged. Still *gauche*, still too bright and too . . . well . . . too heathen. But perfect.

Constance had never sewn such fine needlework in her life. The woman could barely hem a dish towel.

A chill raced up Pandora's spine, and she let the dress slip from her fingers. Twisting her hands, she took a step back just as someone pounded on her door.

She jumped, gasping.

"Wh-who is it?" she called, her voice breaking slightly, her eye on the crumpled dress.

"Dinner, Miss Pandora," came Constance's voice.

"Dinner. Of course. Constance, did you mend my dress?"

"Which dress is that, miss? I haven't mended— "

"Never mind. I'll be down in a minute."

As Constance's muffled footsteps faded, Pandora gingerly reached into her skirt pocket and took out the coin.

It didn't look magical at all. It looked old, of course, but it was dirty and dull, and she was fairly certain that a magic coin ought to glow or something. She looked back down to the floor and the dress, puddled in its bright skirts.

Impossible! she chided herself. *One of the other servants must have mended it.*

Shoes softly crunching porcelain and glass fragments into the floor, she strode to the bureau and checked her hair in the mirror. Perfect. She smoothed her skirts. Perfect.

And then she opened the top drawer. "I've had enough of you," she said to the coin. But then, just before she dropped it into the drawer, she added facetiously, "Magic, eh? Well, here's a wish for you: I wish that nobody at dinner notices that I'm not wearing that horrid dress!"

"Darling." Michael stepped forward and tucked her hand into the crook of his arm as she entered the parlor.

"Have you been waiting long?" Pandora wished he wouldn't touch her. His touch made her feel oddly weak, as if her bones were melting. It made her forget how badly she wanted to be away from this place.

"Only a few minutes," he said. His smile, totally infectious, was a broad inverted triangle framed by a strong, clean jaw. "Although any minute away from you seems like hours." He dipped his head, brushing a warm kiss against her temple before whispering, "How beautiful you look tonight!"

As usual, Pandora fought the urge to sag against him.

Aunt Hesta, waiting in the doorway, cleared her

throat as if to remind them of the proprieties, and Pandora was grateful.

Pandora on Michael's left arm, Aunt Hesta on his right, he guided them into the dining room and pulled out their chairs.

"What have you ladies been up to today?" he asked as a servant slid a shallow bowl of soup in front of Pandora.

"Clam-digging," said Pandy, lifting her spoon. "Mountain climbing. Making snowmen."

He laughed, and didn't seem to notice when Aunt Hesta glared at Pandora from across the table, although Pandora certainly noticed Hesta's well-placed kick.

Pandora glared briefly at Hesta, then defiantly stared past her, at the painting above the room's mantel. The portrait was of Michael's late father. He had been quite handsome, and Michael favored him greatly. But while Michael's eyes were a deep, bottomless blue, his father's had been pale, a piercing, icy aqua. Staring down from the portrait, they were quite unsettling. She wondered if they glowed in the dark.

"Dear Pandy," Michael said warmly, blue eyes sparkling, laugh lines winging out in a most attractive way. "I'm sorry I missed out on the snowmen."

Pandora tried not to look at him. Admirable though he was, she didn't believe it would be too wise a thing to get used to admiring him. After all, there still might be a way out of this. She set her mind to thinking about parties and balls and dances and crowds of admiring young men.

"It's a fortunate man who can boast a witty wife, don't you think, Hesta?" Michael was saying.

At least nobody's said anything about the dress, Pandora thought, staring at her reflection in her soup. It was odd to see one's own face amid bits of corn and tomato and barley, which for some reason made her think of all the broken glass and porcelain on her floor. She hoped Constance or someone was sweeping it up.

They all raised their heads at the staccato clanging of a distant bell. Michael smiled. "Mother's ringing for her dinner, I suppose," he explained. "Sorry you haven't been able to meet yet. She's usually quite energetic, but every once in awhile she has these spells. . . ." He shrugged apologetically.

"Of course," said Hesta diplomatically. "We understand, don't we, Pandora?"

Pandora gave a polite but brief smile. She was doing her best not to look at Michael, not to listen to his voice. The dangerous purr of his baritone was what had gotten her into all this trouble in the first place and landed her in the middle of nowhere. She didn't need any more difficulties.

"We *both* look forward to meeting her," Hesta continued. "I do hope she'll be enough recovered to attend the wedding."

Michael leaned back while a servant removed his soup and slid the next course into place. "As do I," he replied.

There was a pause in the conversation, after a few moments of which Pandora, immersed again in her own reflection—this time in the polished back of a soup spoon—suddenly felt her neck go hot and looked up. Michael was staring at her, his face full of some emotion she couldn't identify.

"You're so beautiful," he said softly, his voice thick. "Each time I see you, you're even more . . ." Then he seemed to remember himself, or perhaps that Hesta was present. He cleared his throat and sat up a bit straighter. "I've been thinking that I'd like to get you a dress. A Mexican fiesta dress."

Pandora's brows shot up involuntarily, but Michael evidently misread her twinge of guilt, because he hastily added, "Oh, not that your own dresses aren't beautiful. You're gorgeous in them. You're never anything less than gorgeous. I just thought you might like something, well, something from the region. They're really colorful. I'm told that the needlework in some of them is quite extraordinary."

Pandora wadded her napkin and dropped it on the tablecloth. "I don't think you're very nice to tease me, Michael."

"Tease you?"

"Aunt Hesta, you put him up to this, didn't you?"

Hesta appeared genuinely shocked. "Why, Pandy, I don't understand what you're—"

"About the dress!" Pandora found herself on her feet, and didn't remember having stood up. She was only vaguely aware that she'd just broken one of her own cardinal rules about avoiding public scenes.

Michael stood up, too. "Darling, what *is* the matter?"

"I just couldn't wear it! I know it probably cost a great deal, but— "

He took her by her shoulders. "Pandy, please! If you don't want a new dress, then we won't order one."

Aunt Hesta hurried round the table and gathered Pandora into her arms. "It's the strain," she heard Hesta say to Michael. "Days of travel, a new place. You understand. She's such a spirited thing. . . ."

Pandora allowed Hesta to lead her to the foot of the stairs before she managed to compose herself and pull away.

"Hesta, tell me something honestly."

"Of course." Hesta's thin dark brows were furrowed with concern.

"Tell me about the dress. The dress Michael sent me this morning."

Hesta reached a hand toward her, felt her brow. "Dear, I haven't the slightest idea what you're talking about. You need some rest, that's all. I have some sleeping powders in my room. Would you like me to— ?"

"No." Pandora backed away. "No, I'm all right, really. Please convey my apologies to Michael. I'll go on up to bed. Tell Constance she needn't come up unless she hasn't gotten to the glass yet."

"The glass?"

Pandora clicked her tongue softly. Aunt Hesta was beginning to irritate her. "The broken glass and porcelain on my floor!"

Hesta clasped her hands together, then frowned. "Oh goodness! Pandora, did you break something? I hope it wasn't valuable!"

Hesta started past her, but Pandora stopped her. "No," she said. "It was nothing at all. Forget I mentioned it."

Long after Michael had gone back to the hotel and the other occupants of the hacienda had blown out their lamps and drifted to sleep, Pandora sat upon her bed, the coin resting before her in the center of a pillow.

It worked. Not only had no one noticed the absence of the dress, they'd seemed unaware of its existence. The coin's magic, and not any seamstress, had mended it.

She had made several more wishes since returning to her room: "I wish this mess on the floor would disappear!" had been the first. And the mess had indeed vanished. A few moments later, when she hopped barefoot from the bed, she jumped back quickly, feeling carefully for the thin, invisible shard of porcelain embedded in her toe.

"Drat!" Taking one of her discarded shoes in hand, she leaned over the side of the mattress and scraped the shoe's toe along the floor. The floor looked immaculate, if scratched, but she could still feel and hear the grit beneath the shoe.

Obviously, the coin took wishes quite literally. *I am going to have to be systematic about this,* she thought.

"I wish I hadn't hurt my foot," was the next

wish, and instantly the sting was gone and the blood ceased to flow.

The third was even more carefully thought out. "I wish . . . I wish that the figurines I broke earlier today were back together again, whole and perfect and in their right places."

She almost added, *And visible,* but didn't. She'd wished once that they would disappear, and wishing them visible again might counteract that wish and take away the coin's magic.

She had wished with her eyes clamped shut. When she opened them, nothing seemed changed. But when she carefully felt along the surface of the nearest nightstand, her fingers met the smooth glass figure of a bird. Smugly, she went around the room, feeling for each piece—the shepherd and shepherdess, the glass birds, the small metal inkwell which had only been dented but was now undamaged—and shut them in the bottom drawer of the bureau. Strange to feel the weight in the drawer, to hear the objects rattle dully as she pushed it closed, and yet see nothing there but the drawer's wooden bottom.

Magic. Real magic.

She studied the coin carefully, thinking what to do next. Perhaps the coin couldn't cancel her engagement or get her home, to civilization. Those were definitely "big" things. Perhaps she was doomed to live in this awful town, she thought with a shudder. And there was Michael to consider. There were certainly one or two things about him that she'd change. The question was what to do first.

She admitted that she was extraordinarily attracted to him on some sort of primal, perhaps even ethereal, level. This dismal, depressing place he'd brought her aside, Michael was quite fine. Perhaps she even loved him. But how could one tell when one was in love? Ringing in the ears, sickness in the stomach? Pining away for hours on end when the object of one's desire was not at hand? So far as Pandora was concerned, that was all a load of silly schoolgirl rubbish. If one married the first man who made the back of her neck rise in carnal gooseflesh, one surely was a fool.

Pandora had met many men whose physical presence titillated her in that way, but she'd always been wise enough to let her head take charge. *Well, all right,* she admitted, *sometimes I didn't think about it until it was a little late. . . .*

The Upton boy, along with young Freddy St. John and David Forsythe were just a few of the recent examples of that.

Michael Crane, too, although Michael was different. With him, the physical yearning was something far stronger than a vague itch that longed to be scratched: it was a nearly irresistible, targeted urge. She believed that she could probably marry Michael and live happily ever after (if there truly existed such a thing), if only she could make a few small changes. Get him to move to San Francisco, for instance. But she supposed that was too large a thing to pull off all at once.

And then there was that disturbingly dangerous quality to Michael. It was something she didn't like to think about. It unnerved her. It made the back of her neck prickle. With the boys and young men back home, she had always felt safe and in control. They were too awed by her to be outrageously forward, too blinded by her presence to threaten her in any way, good or bad.

But Michael? Michael had never been intimidated by her. Michael was not a man who could be controlled or cowed by the snap of a fan or a withering look or a flutter of lashes. It wasn't that he was a bully—far from it. It was just that he seemed closer to his instincts than any man she'd known before. He seemed the sort of man who would not only want to do . . . well, to do things married people did—private things—and do them a lot, and never once feel guilty.

Worse, she had the feeling that he'd expect her to do and feel the same way—to actually *enjoy* them—as if she were some sort of . . . well, she didn't know what.

Things like that undoubtedly mussed your hair and made you perspire. Or made you forget just who you were. Such things seemed far too animal, far too base, when one had spent a lifetime concentrating on keeping one's spine stiff and one's emotions precisely controlled and orchestrated for public consumption. Worse, when she was near Michael, she *wanted* to do those things.

Yes, Michael was, in that respect, too dangerous. He threatened her composure. Not to say that he wasn't, in many other ways, quite nice.

But one could make him nicer.

Five

Order: that's the key, Pandora thought as she started down the stairs the next morning.

The coin was tied into a hankie and tucked in her pocket. It wasn't safe to leave it in her room: what if one of the maids accidentally picked it up and just happened to make some silly wish or other? No, best to keep it with her at all times. Order— perfect, harmonious order— had to be established, and she was the one to do it. But where to start?

Last night, she'd made only one more wish after restoring and hiding the brac-a-brac: she wished the fiesta dress away. No point in having a dress that no one remembered her having received. It would only cause trouble. One must keep things tidy, she had decided. No stray ends to complicate matters.

Michael did not join them for breakfast, but at ten o'clock, as she gazed through the shaded parlor window, she saw him striding across the plaza toward the hacienda. Casually dressed, his thick golden hair glinting in the sun, he balanced a large, flat box before him, and he appeared to be whistling. She went to the cavernous foyer and posed herself demurely at the foot of the stairs before she called for a servant, who opened the front door for Michael before he was halfway across the veranda.

"Morning!" he said happily, his long steps eating the distance between them. He dropped the box into a chair and, before Pandora realized it, he swept her into his arms and kissed her.

Oh drat, she thought, even as she melted into him. Why did he have to feel so good, look so good, even *smell* so good, for heaven's sake?

"Michael, please," she managed to whisper against his lips. She wanted to say, *Stop it, stop making me enjoy this, stop making me want you,* but instead she said, "The servants will see!"

Chuckling, he brushed a kiss against her temple, then released her. "I'm betting the servants are tickled pink," he said softly, smiling. "Me, too. I can't wait until Saturday, Pandy. I can't wait to carry you over the threshold." A shock of sun-gilded hair had tumbled down over his brow, and Pandora was irritated with herself for finding it charming.

"What's in the box?" she asked, eager to pursue any subject but that of their impending wedding—and wedding night.

"Thought you might want to go riding," he said good-naturedly, and bent to open it. "I didn't know if you brought a habit, so yesterday I sent one of the boys over to Bisbee to pick this up. . . ."

He pushed away the tissue and brought out a long split skirt of soft doeskin. "I guessed on the size," he said, holding it out before pressing the waistband against her. His hands wrapped round her waist, fingers touching in back.

Unexpectedly, Pandora found herself engulfed in shivers. "M-Michael," she began before he kissed her again, this time pulling her body firmly against his. She felt his fingers spread over her skirted hips. Worse, she found she had lifted her arms and wrapped them round his neck.

She dropped her hands to push against his shoulders, then stepped back, hoping he wouldn't notice how shallow her breathing had become. This wouldn't do, it wouldn't do at all! Order and symmetry, those were the goals. Not panting in the front hall like some Barbary Coast hussy! Michael simply had no sense of decorum. Surely no gentleman, not even one's fiancé, should be so forward! Never had any man had the nerve to be so blatant in his advances toward her. There was a part of her—a growing part, she realized with dismay—that actually *welcomed* it. Well, she would put that in order, too. But first there was Michael to tend to.

He was smiling at her, the skirt still in his hands. Was he going to try to kiss her again?

"I don't know that I'm up to a ride this morning, Michael," she said, pulling her hankie from her pocket. "It's very warm, isn't it? Is it always so warm this time of year?" Deftly, she freed the coin and secreted it in one hand before patting at her temple with the hankie.

"You'll get used to it, sweet," he said, smiling as he folded the split skirt back into its box.

"Sure you wouldn't like a ride? I'd like some time alone with you." His voice grew softer, his tone quite intimate. "We've never really been alone, have we?"

There was something in his eyes that both frightened and exhilarated her. Michael Crane, she realized, was a man with definite plans. Plans for which an innocent horseback ride was only the means to an end. Well, there'd be none of *that!*

She stared at the floor, gripped the coin so tightly that it cut into her palm, and breathed, "I wish Michael were more . . . more courtly."

"Did you say something, my dear?"

"No, I only— " She looked up and gasped. Michael had been transformed. His clothing— trousers and a plain blue, open-collared shirt— had been replaced by an elaborately tailored, rose-colored, velvet suit complete with a pale ivory satin brocade vest stitched with gold, and heavy gold watch chain with diamond-studded fobs. A pale pink rose sprouted from his buttonhole. Gold rings sparkled on his fingers.

"I only . . . I only . . . ," she stammered.

"Oh, my little dearest!" he exclaimed, brows arched. Only then did she notice that his usually untidy hair was elaborately arrayed in ringlets. Golden spit curls surrounded his face. He stepped toward her and limply lifted her hand, patting it softly. "This heat *is* beastly, isn't it? Come, sit on the divan. You look faint."

As he took her arm and led her to the front parlor, she thought, *This isn't what I meant! This isn't what I meant at all! He's turned into a fop, and I only meant . . . oh, I wish—*

She stopped the thought abruptly and, biting her lip, slipped the coin into her pocket. If the wishes one meant to make turned out so disastrously, she shuddered to think what the coin might make of a careless request.

"A sherry, my pet?" Michael asked. He posed before the unlit fireplace, one elbow cocked just so upon the mantel. From his sleeve he pulled a large white handkerchief, frilly with lace trim, and waved it about his neck.

Pandora, seated upon the sofa and not quite certain how she'd come to be there, managed to squeak, "No thank you."

"Of course. How right you are, my blossom! It's much too warm for sherry. I don't know what I *could* have been thinking." Pursing his lips disdainfully, he flicked a bit of dust from his lapel. He tipped his head toward the doorway. "Juanita?" he called, and when a few seconds later one of the maids appeared, Pandora cringed. What would the girl think to see her master so changed?

"Señor?" the girl said with a curtsey, and if she thought there was anything odd about seeing Michael Crane (of whom, Pandora thought, the most accurate description— up until a few moments ago— would have been "rugged") dressed in pink velvet and waving a lace handkerchief and studying the shine on his fingernails, she gave no indication.

Maybe it doesn't just change the person I wish it

on, she thought as Michael ordered a pitcher of limeade. *Maybe it changes everybody else. Or perhaps this girl is just too polite to give any sign that something's out of the ordinary. . . .*

While they waited for refreshments, Michael chattered. She had sometimes been bored by his conversation before, but not because his conversation was boring, exactly. It was just that he often spoke, in company, about things that didn't interest her: politics, business, his plans for the mines, his plans for the town. But at least he'd always sounded intelligent. And like, well, like a *man!* At the moment, he was prattling on about new fabric for the dining room drapes.

"Don't you think so, my dear?" he said, arching a brow.

Pandy jumped. She'd been busy trying to decide how to remedy this little blunder without taking the wish back and losing the magic of the coin. *If you take back a wish, any wish, the coin takes back everything,* the woman had said. . . .

"Certainly," Pandora said, although she had little idea what she was replying to. "Whatever you think, Michael."

"Mauve it is, then," he said with a satisfied tip of his head. Those spit curls really did look ridiculous. She couldn't stop staring at them.

I've got to do something about that, she thought. *And right now.* She thought a moment before she dipped two fingers into her pocket and found the coin. Holding it gently out of sight, she whispered, "I wish Michael's hairstyle were a little less . . . formal."

The change was instantaneous, and shocked her into dropping the coin back into her pocket.

Michael, still leaning against the mantel, still blathering on about color and fabric, lifted one limp-wristed hand and smoothed back hair— wild, matted, filthy hair— from his brow. It hung over his shoulders and trailed nearly to his waist in thick, oily cords. Flies buzzed about it. He flicked his handkerchief at them and went on talking.

This is not good, Pandy thought as she strained to keep from crying. *This is not good at all! I can't wish to take it back. I have to do something, though. Perhaps, perhaps . . .*

She thought of all the young men she had known at home, and finally decided that Bobby Upton, one of the fellows to whom she'd found herself engaged, had probably the handsomest head of hair she had ever seen: thick, fair and wavy, almost lush. Quite similar, in fact, to the hair poor Michael had sported before she wished him out of it.

She made herself smile at Michael and nod as if she cared what he was talking about, and quickly found the coin again. When Michael turned his head for a moment, she whispered, "I wish Michael had Bobby Upton's hair."

And, quite suddenly, Michael had Bobby Upton's hair.

Hanging, a giant tasseled fob, from his watch chain.

Señor?" Juanita stood in the doorway, a tray with a pitcher and two glasses held before her.

As the maid came into the room and placed

the tray on the low table in front of the sofa, Pandora thought, *She really, truly, doesn't see that he's any different from the last time. She doesn't notice the flies or the mop of disgusting hair, she doesn't even notice that horrible, horrible thing hanging from his watch chain. Nobody notices the differences. They all think it's always been that way. No one remembered the dress last night, either. No one remembers Michael the way he was, nobody but me. Not even Michael.*

Despite the monstrosity across the table (who was currently dismissing the maid and pouring limeade into two glasses and chattering about this simply *fabulous* set of imported hand blown glassware he'd seen in a little shop in San Francisco), Pandora felt quite relieved. She might have ruined Michael and changed, for all she knew, the course of human events, but at least nobody knew *she* had done it.

She had made a mistake. Well, several mistakes. And this was not an easy thing for her to admit, even to herself. Where before she'd had only vague curiosity about— and dissatisfaction with— the minor details of life to propel her forward, she now had a mission. Her hatred of the desert— of being anywhere other than her father's house in San Francisco— was forgotten, as was all thought of anything other than repairing what she had done to poor Michael Crane.

She wanted to make him right again. She wanted to wish him into some semblance— some *superior* semblance— of the man he'd been before.

But she also wanted to retain the coin's magic, which meant she'd have wish him into superiority bit-by-bit. She couldn't take back what she'd done and start over.

It did briefly cross her mind that poor Bobby Upton might be at this moment walking around San Francisco bald as a billiard ball, but since Bobby wasn't likely to turn up and point an accusing finger, she pushed him from her mind and concentrated on Michael.

The clock in the main hall began to chime.

"Ah, luncheon!" said Michael. The hank of Bobby Upton's hair (or what, at least, *looked* like Bobby's hair) swayed from Michael's watch chain as he held the watch out to look at it. He tucked the timepiece away and held out his hand. "Allow me the honor?" he asked. A fly landed on his nose, and he flicked the lace tip of his handkerchief at it.

Pandora made herself stand up and take his arm. The coin was safe in her pocket, but she wasn't touching it. She'd think longer and harder about wishes after this.

As Michael (still swatting at flies) escorted her toward the dining room, she said, "Darling, I wonder if you wouldn't like to try a shorter hairstyle? Not that there's anything wrong with the way you're wearing it, you understand," she added when he arched a brow. She used her most practiced persuasive tone, and gave her lashes an artful flutter. "But they're wearing it short this year. And I'd think it would be so much cooler. My maid Constance is an absolute wizard with the scissors. . . ."

* * *

After lunch, as Pandora sat in one of the swings on the hacienda's long front porch and fanned herself, she thought to herself that even with that awful mop of hair and his newly fey ways, Michael was still a good sport.

Inside, Constance was cutting his hair. Pandora had assured him it was the very latest men's style from Paris, and that Constance was highly skilled in the tonsorial arts. It hadn't been a lie, since she had made one more small wish when no one was looking. And this wish, thank goodness, had had neat and tidy results. Constance had been completely unchanged save for a sudden development of barbering expertise.

Through an open window, she could hear the faint but sure *snip, snip, snip* of scissors as well as the monologue of Aunt Hesta who, not ten seconds after Pandy had wished Constance into the consummate hairdresser, had begun to brag about the fine haircuts Constance had given to most of San Francisco's society gentlemen, and how she, herself, would never go out of the house if Constance were not there to arrange her hair each morning.

While she waited for the "new" (and hopefully less insect-attracting) Michael, she tried to decide how to proceed. There were his looks to think of. It might be nice if he were a tad taller, for instance. Six feet was all well and good, but six feet three-inches might be . . . better. She decided she liked his face well enough: she hadn't realized how breathtakingly handsome he was until she'd seen that gorgeous face of his ill-framed by spit curls, and then that horrid matted tangle.

There was his character to consider, too. Hadn't he been more single-minded before? Perhaps that was the wrong word. One had to be very careful about words, it seemed. But she couldn't imagine the original Michael sitting still while somebody's maid fussed over his hair. He'd become too pliable. No, that wasn't the right word either. . . .

For now, she decided, she would concentrate on his mind. She supposed he'd always been intelligent. He'd had a very insightful look about him, as she remembered, and some of the discussions he'd carried on with her father had certainly been over her head. He was probably *still* intelligent under all that brocade and velvet and talk of fashion and glassware. He'd been quite entertaining at lunch. At least, Aunt Hesta had been charmed by his chatter. *Bon mots* fairly gushed out of him.

All right, he was witty. But there wasn't much substance there. That, she decided, was the thing to work on next.

She reached into her pocket and found the coin, paused, then released it. If she was going to make him into much of a thinker, she'd best wait until *after* the haircut.

"How handsome you look!" Pandora exclaimed when Michael, newly shorn and coiffed by Constance, joined her some time later in the hacienda's rear courtyard. He did look quite handsome, actually, if one ignored his clothes and the scalp dangling from his watch chain. Constance had done a brilliant job. He almost looked like his old self, if one didn't look below the neck.

He bowed slightly and swept up her hand to kiss it. "Sorry for the delay in joining you, my dearest, but Mama rang, and I went up to visit with her." Flicking back his pink velvet coattails, he sat down on a wrought iron bench, pulled out that extravagant handkerchief and, with tight little flicks of his wrist, fanned his neck with the tip of it.

"Beastly warm," he said, stifling a yawn.

He always called his mother "Mother" before, Pandora noted. Now it was Ma*ma*. How annoying.

"And how is your mother feeling this afternoon?" Pandy asked, although, truth be told, she didn't much care.

"A trifle improved," he replied, staring at the flower bed. "She hopes to be able to leave her rooms tomorrow. Perhaps join us for supper. And, of course, the day after. For the wedding." He leaned forward and frowned at the rose bed. "Someone really *must* attend to my floribundas."

He leaned back again, as if exhausted by the conversation, and spoke no more until Pandora, who was accustomed to being the honey men buzzed about like worker bees, said, "Michael, is it possible that I'm *boring* you?"

He looked up from his reverie, startled. "My dovelet, it's not you." He lifted one hand and pressed the back of his wrist to his forehead.

"Not you at all. It's just that, generally speaking, I find myself a prisoner of ennui. I can't imagine why."

"I see," she said, forcing a pretty smile as she reached into her pocket for the coin and thought, *A prisoner of ennui, my foot!*

"Michael," she continued, "I wonder if you might ask one of the girls to bring us some more of that limeade we had before lunch? It's thirsty weather."

"What? Oh. Certainly." He made a bit of a show of getting to his feet, gave his neck an extra flick or two with his handkerchief, and left her.

As he disappeared into the hacienda, she brought out the coin and held it before her on her palm.

"All right," she said determinedly, closing her eyes. "I wish . . . I wish Michael were more cultured— educated, I mean!"

She opened her eyes and started to put away the coin, then had second thoughts. Quickly, she added, "I wish he were a little taller, too."

She barely had time to slip the coin back into her pocket before, across the courtyard, the doors swung upon. "They'll be right out with it, my pet," he said before she saw him and gasped.

He was at least eight feet tall.

He stooped low to come out the doorway, and still scraped his head on the top of the frame. His clothing had made the transition to a larger size along with him— all but his trousers. The velvet ended just below his knees, exposing hairy lengths of shin and calf between pantscuffs and the gar-

tered tops of satin stockings. He crossed the courtyard in three strides, and sat himself back down
on the iron bench. He'd looked big before, sitting
there. Now, he looked, well, ludicrous.

Pandora crossed herself.

After he stuck his long, cranelike legs out before him, he said, "What was it we were talking
about? Ah, yes! My poor roses. Here in Arizona,
if we coddle them, we get an extra blooming season. Did you know that?"

Slowly, Pandora shook her head. The sheer size
of him had taken away her power of speech. On
a lark, she'd been to an exhibition of freaks the
spring before, and Ingo the Giant— billed as
"The World's Tallest Man"— had nothing on Michael Crane.

A little taller!, she inwardly wailed. *I asked for
just a little! I can't let this go on. He'll never be able
to ride a horse or fit into a chair at dinner— his knees
would knock the table over! But how do I unwish it
without un-wishing it . . . ?*

"— prefer the evenings," Michael was saying.
He must have noticed an odd expression on her
face, because he added, "I was just remarking,
my dear, that my favorite time of day is the evening. Perhaps Milton said it best in 'Il Penseroso':
*Hie me from day's garish eye, While the bee with hon-
ied thigh, That at her flowery work doth sing— "*

Pandora, feeling ill, managed, "Wh-what?"

*"And the waters murmuring, With such consort as
they keep, Entice the dewy-feathered sleep,"* he went
on, seemingly transfixed by his own recitation.

"Michael?" she heard herself croak. "Michael, what are you talking about?"

"Ah," he said sympathetically. "Perhaps you're not a fan of Milton. The latter works, I can understand. Too much Latinate syntax in those, you're probably thinking, and I'd have to agree with you. But the earlier are quite Spenserian, don't you feel? Wonderfully sensual, if I might use that term. But darling, what's wrong? Are you ill?"

He rose— unfolded, rather, like a gigantic, lace-ruffled, pink preying mantis— and came toward her. Despite all intentions, and despite the kindly look in his eyes, she cringed.

"Why so pale and wan, fond lover?" he recited as he bent to her.

The scalp dangling from his watch chain brushed against her face, and she bit her lips.

"Prithee, why so pale?" continued Michael before he added, as if she cared, "That's Sir John Suckling, from 'Aglaura.' Quite a favorite of mine. You don't look at all well, Pandora. Shall I send for your dear aunt?"

She shook her head.

By then he was down on his knees before her, sitting back on his heels and still having to crouch to be on her eye level. His head was so enormous, Pandy thought macabrely, that he could have worn one of her parasols for a hat and not had much brim left over.

He took her hands. His palms were the size of salad plates. "My light, my beloved, you're trembling!"

The old Michael Crane, she thought as he left her to call for Aunt Hesta, might have taken trembling as a sign of passion. He might have put his arm— his lovely, strong, normal-sized arm— about her and held her close to comfort or kiss her or both. But not this new Michael— this ridiculously dressed, monstrously tall, foppish boor— whom she had made, piece by unfortunate piece.

"Now what?" she whispered, a single hot tear trickling down one cheek, as she watched him crouch to squeeze through the door. She heard him mutter *ouch* before he called for Hesta.

"Oh Lord," she whispered as she watched after him. "What do I do to fix this?"

Six

Pandora spent the rest of the afternoon in her room, alternately staring at the ceiling or out the window. When she stared at the ceiling, she tried, with little result, to think of how to proceed with Michael. When she stared out the window, she searched every window, every shadowed nook and courtyard that faced out onto the plaza, for the old woman who'd given her the wretched coin. There had to be a way— a particular way— of phrasing things so that they didn't turn out so . . . so inauspiciously.

Even the room— his room— had changed. The massive Spanish furniture was gone, replaced by spindly French stuff. At least, she thought it was French. She didn't claim to know much about furniture. It was all white and trimmed with gilt, and there was a flouncy white canopy over the bed, which was amazingly long. At least eight feet. All of *her* things were the same: her clothes were still in the drawers in the same order. It was just that they were in a different bureau now.

On the far wall, where antique dueling swords had once been mounted, there hung a large and rather well-done watercolor of a ballerina.

The coin had such a bizarre way of interpreting things! Constance— that was, giving Constance a real talent for cutting and arranging hair— was really the only wish that hadn't gone completely and utterly wild. *Well, it did do a good job of getting rid of the dress and putting my room to order last night,* she reminded herself.

But poor Michael! She'd wished him just a *little* taller, and *poof!* he was eight feet tall! At least she hadn't wished him *very* tall— she would have had to spend the rest of the afternoon talking to his ankles.

And now she was afraid to wish him shorter. How short would he end up? Two feet tall? Three feet? She'd decided she'd best not try any more height wishes until she developed a little more expertise with the coin.

She'd been staring at the ceiling for quite some time when the distant tinkle of Michael's mother's bell brought her out of her thoughts and to the realization that night had fallen. She sat up and stretched her arms. Was Michael still in the house? She hoped not. She couldn't bear the thought of sitting across the table from him. If he could manage to sit at the table at all.

"Pandora?"

She turned toward the door. Aunt Hesta was just coming in with a supper tray.

"Sorry not to knock, my dear," Hesta said. "I thought you might be napping." She slid the tray atop one of the dressers and lit a lamp. "Here," she said. "Let's have a little light, shall we? I didn't imagine you'd be up to coming down for dinner. How are you feeling?"

"Fine," Pandora said without animation. "Why didn't Constance bring my tray?"

Hesta took the tray to a small table beside the French doors and slid out a chair, then beckoned Pandora toward it. "Constance is no longer in our employ."

Napkin half unfurled, Pandora paused. "What? Constance is gone? She's been with us as long as I can remember!"

Hesta shrugged. "She decided to go back to San Francisco and open a public hair salon. For ladies. It's unheard of, I know," she added as she stooped to pick up Pandora's napkin, which had just slipped from her fingers to the floor, "but her mind was set on it. Michael had one of his men drive her over to Bisbee to catch the stage."

Pandora sat numbly while Aunt Hesta placed the napkin over her lap.

"Pandy," her aunt said softly, "are you certain you're all right? You seem so . . . disheveled. It's not like you."

"Disheveled?" Pandy repeated, the word seeming foreign in her mouth. Constance had run off to be a hair dresser? A *public* hair dresser?

"Your clothes, your hair . . . and your face. You look, well, did you have those little lines around your eyes before? Frankly, dear, you seem a little haggard. Perhaps this climate doesn't agree with you."

Yesterday, or any day before that, any such words directed toward Pandora would have sent her racing for a mirror. But suddenly it didn't seem very important to look perfect. She simply said, "Yes, perhaps it's the climate. Is Michael still here?"

Much to her surprise, Aunt Hesta made a rather disgusted face.

"Hesta?"

Hesta sighed. "Well, you must admit he can be a bore at times, Pandy. Don't take this as criticism, dear. Michael is a lovely man. But if it were me marrying him, I think I'd soon weary of all this literary talk."

"Literary talk," Pandora repeated flatly. He was still at it, then.

"The man eats, breathes and— for all I know— sleeps seventeenth century English literature. Ever since we got here, he's talked of nothing but Butler and Pepys and Locke and Milton and Lord knows how many others I've never heard of."

"What's he doing now?" Pandora asked suddenly.

With a weary sigh, Hesta went to Pandora's door and opened it. Softly, from below, came Michael's voice. It was still a beautiful voice, Pandy thought. How pleased she was that she hadn't managed to mangle that part of him.

"Through sense and nonsense, never out nor in," came the rumbling, melodic recitation. *"Free from all meaning, whether good or bad, And in one word, heroically mad. . . ."*

Aunt Hesta closed the door. "You haven't touched your food," she said.

Pandy picked up a fork and pointed it toward the door. "What was that?"

"Something called Absalom and Achi— Achit— " Aunt Hesta's features twisted with something like disgust. "It's *Absalom and Something-That-Sounds-Like-A-Sneeze,*" she said finally, and put her hand back on the door's latch, as if to leave. "And it's been going on for *hours.* He has half the staff captive in the parlor. I'm told this is a frequent occurrence."

"Aunt Hesta?"

Hesta paused. "Yes, dear?"

"Does Michael seem . . . does he seem bigger to you?"

"Bigger than what?"

"Bigger than, um, usual."

Hesta tipped her head to one side. "Are you sure you're feeling all right?"

She couldn't eat much of her supper. She finally pushed away from the table and began to pace. Something must be done. She couldn't just leave poor Michael in his present condition.

After nearly an hour of shuffling possibilities, she took out the coin again. Slowly and with great determination she intoned, "I wish Michael Crane was six-foot-three. I wish he wore normal clothes for this time and place. I wish he had another interest besides seventeenth century English literature."

And after she tucked the coin safely at the back

of the top bureau drawer, she added, *"Those* wishes ought to be specific enough!"

There had been a small rustling sound behind her, and she turned to find the bed substantially shortened. A tad longer than normal, she decided, but just the right custom-made length for a 6'3" man. She sat upon it, relieved, and looked up to discover that the ballerina watercolor had been replaced by a large, framed chart of the solar system. Curious.

Michael was still downstairs, but as much as she wanted to have just a peek at him and make absolutely certain she'd wished away his giganticism, she couldn't quite convince herself to do it. Instead, she stationed herself beside the window, and it wasn't long before a shaft of light appeared on the deserted plaza's cobbles to let her know the hacienda's front door had opened.

Quickly, she slipped through the French doors, tiptoed to the edge of the balcony, and knelt to secret herself in the shadow of a planter box. Breath held, she peeped over the rail. She heard his boots on the cobbles before he appeared beneath her and strode out onto the plaza, all six feet and three inches of him.

"Oh no . . ." Pandora whimpered.

Michael Crane, dressed not in rose velvet, but in the baggy pants, serape, and broad sombrero of a Mexican peasant—and just as big of girth as he was tall—stopped beside the plaza's central well and gazed up into the sky.

"My lovelies!" he exclaimed, throwing wide his arms and looking straight up. He still had that frilly, foppish handkerchief in one hand, and he waved it at the stars. "Ah, Vega," he proclaimed. "There you are!" Belly wobbling before him, he turned toward the south and pointed out toward the heavens.

"There! The teapot! Sagittarius!" he cried gleefully before he danced in a little circle, and began to sing, *I'm a little teapot, short and stout. Here is my handle—* " Elbow cocked out, he rammed one pudgy fist against a roll of fat at his side. *"— here is my spout!"* But instead of curling the other arm up and out, in the fashion of every child who had ever played the game, he cocked it against the other hip, then exclaimed, "Good heavens, I'm a sugar bowl!" and laughed in a silly staccato.

"Oh, Michael," whimpered Pandora, clinging weepily to the rail. "I tried to fix you, I really did . . ."

Below, Michael, still giggling, began to swivel his immense bulk in a slow, tight circle. "Arcturus!" he exclaimed as he turned, arms raised to the stars again. "Dear old Ursa Major!" When he stopped facing the east, he doffed his sombrero, laid it over his heart, and dramatically intoned, "Greetings, O Great Square of Pegasus!"

In the darkness above the plaza, Pandora slid softly to the balcony floor. Barely aware of the grit grinding into her cheek, she whispered, "Dear Michael, I'm so sorry."

From below came the thuds of Michael's boots marching heavily toward the hotel, and his gleefully muttered, "I *must* break out the telescope!"

And then, just when Pandora thought she

could feel no more abjectly guilty, he stopped in front of the hotel and turned back to look at the hacienda from the other side of the deserted plaza.

"Give me a kiss," he recited to the night, to Pandora's windows, *"and to that kiss a score. . . ."*

"Don't do this to me," breathed Pandora, flat on the balcony, hidden from him. His voice: Oh, his voice. If she didn't look at him, if she remembered the way he'd been. . . . Oh, his voice . . .

"Then to that twenty," he continued, the baritone words clear and rumbling all at once, a beacon of the most seductive sound in the starlit night, *"add a hundred more: A thousand to that hundred: so kiss on, To make that thousand up a million. Treble that million, and when that is done, let's kiss afresh, as when we first begun."*

Pandora rubbed a fist against one teary eye as she heard him add, "Goodnight, beloved," before the scuffs of his boots faded and, distantly, the hotel's doors softly closed behind him.

"I am the most wretched person on the face of the earth."

Pandora sat slouched on the foot of the bed, grimy hands limp in her lap, a frizzed coil of hair hanging down over her forehead and resting on her nose. "I've been playing at being God, and obviously I'm no good at it. I've ruined Michael, just ruined him!"

Stuck in her mind was the image of him as

he'd once been. As he'd been naturally, without her confounded, ill-focused, unnatural tinkering. It seemed so long ago that she'd first seen him— gloriously handsome, proud of carriage— across that crowded San Francisco ballroom. Had it only been two months?

She silently cursed the woman who'd given her the coin. It was all that old hag's fault.

And then, with a small and unexpected jolt, she realized it wasn't the old woman's fault at all. The fault was all in her. How haughty she'd been to think she had the right to "improve" Michael, or anyone else for that matter! The old woman's coin might have been the vehicle, but she'd been the one to climb in and whip the horses. How vain she had been, how self-serving. Had she always been that way?

The revelation that she had, indeed, crushed down upon her with a nearly physical impact, and she collapsed back upon the bed.

Her father was ashamed of her. She'd pushed Hesta's words from her mind, but now they came back to accuse her, to make her feel small and petty and beneath contempt.

But I thought I was supposed *to be that way!* she thought dismally, knowing it for a weak excuse even as she formed the thought. *I thought I was supposed to be perfect. They all expected it! I thought Daddy wanted me that way. I thought everybody wanted me that way.*

She sat up abruptly. "*I* thought I had to be that way," she whispered.

Slowly, she got to her feet and went to the bureau's mirror. The image that greeted her was not one that would have been recognized by any of San Francisco's high society. Disheveled hair, wrinkled dress, dirty, tear-streaked face, tiny worry lines winging out from her eyes and etching their way into her forehead. . . .

"If I met you on the street," she muttered to her reflection, "I'd cross to the other side."

Wearily, she went to the door. She opened her mouth to call for Constance before she remembered that Constance was gone: off to the city to cut people's hair for money, like a common barber.

She washed her face and changed into a nightgown, then sat herself down and began to brush the tangles from her hair. She didn't ever remember feeling so tired or so forlorn.

Poor Michael.

Poor me.

She had just finished braiding her hair when she heard Michael's mother's bell jingling.

"Maybe that's what I should do," she muttered as she climbed into bed. "I should just shut myself up in here and get a blasted bell."

Sleep did not come easily to Pandora. She couldn't keep her thoughts from Michael, from what she'd done to him, and from what he'd been before the coin.

He'd been the pick of the lot. She'd always known it, really, although she'd never before been able to admit it. She'd managed, somehow, to keep herself from acknowledging how wonderful he truly was. Did she love parties and glamour and public adulation so much that she'd trade a lifetime's happiness for a youth in the superficial glare of the social spotlight?

Perhaps Michael *was* a little dangerous. Perhaps that was the way things were supposed to be between grown men and women. Maybe it was all right to feel those primal feelings Michael used to bring out in her, right to want him in that way, right to forget convention and welcome the animal part of her nature instead of always pushing it aside and denying its existence.

She hadn't thought about it in quite that way before. She hadn't thought of anything but the here and now for quite some time. She had become, she realized, a creature of the moment—the trivial moment at that—with little thought of consequences in the long run.

Have I been so very shallow? she asked herself, and had to answer truthfully that she had been. What was it Hesta had said the other day?

That the prettiest girl in San Francisco was just about all I was, Pandora remembered sadly. *And she was right. I've been shallow and vain and—*

"No!" she said, pounding a fist into her pillow. "I'm not! I'm a *nice* person!"

Would a nice person have done to a cur dog what I've done to Michael?

She rolled over and pulled the covers above her head. It hurt too much to think about. What was worse was that she felt more sorry for herself than she did for Michael, which only served to make her feel that much sorrier. The guilt was like a monster feeding on itself, growing and growing and growing.

"Daddy's right," she whispered in the darkness, and then she cried.

After an hour of self-recrimination and self-loathing and feeling more pitiful than anyone else, she thought, had probably ever felt, she threw back the covers and padded through the darkness to the bureau. She found the coin easily, and clutched it tightly in her hand.

"I wish that Michael Crane . . . ," she paused. It had to be exactly right. "I wish that Michael was the normal weight for a healthy man of his current height."

The moment she said the last word, she dropped the coin back into the drawer, slammed it, then rubbed her hands on her nightgown. One wish, just one very careful wish. *There*, she thought hopefully. *I don't think anything can go wrong with that one.*

She groped her way back to bed and climbed in. She fully realized that, considering the coin's rather wobbly interpretation of previous wishes, Michael might not get back anything so magnificent as his original body— and she had only just realized how beautifully imposing he had been— but at least he'd be something close to *normal*.

It did cross her mind to simply take back her wishes. But if she did that, there'd be no more magic in the coin. No way to slowly wheedle her way back to San Francisco. There'd be no magic to control any little emergencies that might arise after she had her life the way she wanted it.

But how *did* she want her life to be? The day's events had certainly opened her eyes to more than a few of her own foibles. In the beginning, she had wanted simply to go back home and continue her life as before. No entanglements, no ties, nothing to keep her from the adulation of the crowd.

But she couldn't deny that she did feel something for Michael, something almost supernatural. She'd held her deeper emotions back, forced them from her mind and her heart. Oh, they escaped every now and then, those feelings, but she'd always pushed them away. They frightened her. She was accustomed to passions less powerful, to a life more fragile and dainty and far more easily manipulated than anything she might expect to find in Michael's arms, at Michael's side.

But the sound of his voice, reciting love poetry from across the plaza, had touched not only her heart, but a part of her she didn't understand. A part she feared: what one didn't understand, one couldn't control.

No. She would keep the coin. She would keep its magic intact. She'd try her very best to bring Michael back to what he once had been. Perhaps, with enough practice, she could even improve him. That had been the original plan, hadn't it, before everything had gone so horribly wrong?

Maybe going back to San Francisco right away isn't so important, she thought. *Maybe going back isn't necessary.*

It was the first time she'd imagined such a possibility with anything less than dismay, and she was a little shocked by the revelation. Had she changed so much that home no longer beckoned?

"It's Michael, after all, isn't it?" she whispered in the dark. Admitting it made it real, made her feel suddenly warm and oddly powerful. "Michael is the one. I'm supposed to be with him. Maybe it doesn't matter at all about going home. We could go someplace else. New York, perhaps . . ."

She thought of him, the way he'd been, of how it had felt to be held by him as they danced; how his eyes—that direct, unwavering gaze—had intoxicated her senses. She remembered walking through a park with him, her arm through his, and how strong and safe he'd seemed. And, at the same time, how dangerous.

She remembered, her cheeks growing warm, of the night he'd proposed. They'd stood on a broad balcony. The windows behind them glowed bright and filtered the laughter and music from the party within.

"I love you, Pandy," he'd said, holding both her hands gently within his. "I never knew I could love anybody like this."

"Michael," she had breathed, for that moment embraced by a happiness and a rightness that she'd never known possible.

"I know it's sudden, darling," he'd said, lowering his head to brush a kiss against her temple. "But I want us to be married. Right away."

"Yes, Michael, yes," she'd whispered, and he had kissed her: warmly, deeply, a sort of unimaginable, madly intimate kiss. It had been like becoming a part of him for those few seconds. Her arms had risen, of their own accord, to fold about his neck. His hands, which had ringed her waist, rose slowly until one arm held her against him, and the other was between their bodies, stroking her breast, his thumb gently gliding over the fabric that covered her.

Never had any man been so bold as to touch her in this way, but her shock at the impropriety had been almost instantly replaced by a strange internal fire that had melted her insides and turned her knees to jelly.

And then her father had appeared, clearing his throat and harrumphing, and Michael had said, "Mr. Drummond, I believe you and I should speak privately."

"Indeed we should," her father had replied with an arched brow.

Aside from one more, rather public, meeting, it was the last time she'd seen Michael. He'd gone back to Arizona, and a month later Pandy's father had shipped her to the same destination.

And how she'd fought against it! That month had been the breathing space in which her chilly logic negated the heat of Michael's kiss. No matter how much she'd enjoyed it, no matter how handsome and kind and wonderful Michael Crane was, she'd arrived in Arizona determined to escape her destiny. For that was what she believed on this cool fall evening, as she lay at last tucked into a silly, frilly bed after a busy day of wreaking havoc upon her fiancé: that Michael was, after all, her inescapable destiny.

As she at last dozed off, it occurred to her that, to be perfectly honest, she couldn't remember exactly what details of Michael had needed improving in the first place, and she pined for his original condition. But that was something she couldn't have, not if she wanted to keep the coin's magic intact.

And she was not ready to throw that magic away.

Seven

Pandora woke earlier than usual. The sun had not yet cleared the horizon, and her room was deep in shadow.

She rubbed her eyes and sat up smiling, for her dreams had been full of Michael: memories of that exquisite kiss, of the feel of his arms about her, the scent of him, and the solid feel of his body against hers.

"Really," she whispered happily into the charcoal light of pre-dawn, "I don't know what's come over me."

It occurred to her, as she lazed there, fiddling idly with the coverlet, that she'd made Michael into such a sissy that he might never wish to kiss her again. Well, any part of her other than her hand. He seemed a great one for hand-kissing of late.

If only she hadn't made that first wish yesterday morning, when he kissed her in the hall! *I was worried he'd muss my hair, wasn't I?* she accused herself disgustedly. *I was worried he'd take liberties.*

But today, Michael's "taking liberties" with her seemed a commendable thing— quite a welcome thing, actually. *I didn't want him to touch me because*

*I knew that if he did, I'd want him. Well, I got him
to stop touching me, but I want him anyway.*

She imagined him, across the plaza in his hotel
room, lying naked and tangled in white sheets,
the first shafts of morning light painting dim
golden stripes across his body. And then she
flushed hotly. It wasn't like her at all, but it
felt . . . delicious.

And then she realized that the picture she'd
just blushed over was likely far from correct. Michael was probably clutching that stupid lace
hankie in one hand and a telescope in the other,
and he was probably dreaming about the early
verse of John Milton.

But then again, he might be dreaming about
her. The only things she hadn't changed about
him, with all her inept fiddling, had been that
chiseled face, the music of his voice, and his feelings for her. Through it all—brocaded, matted,
gigantically tall, obscenely fat; spouting poetry or
ostentatious frippery or astronomical sightings—
he had cared for her.

The old woman had told her that the coin
could not do "big" things. Was it possible that
his love for her was so great that the coin could
not affect it?

Again, she flushed warmly. Never had she
known such a wonderful tribute, and it made her
yearn for him all the more.

Her father would arrive today. Tonight there
would be a small private banquet in the hacienda's dining hall, and tomorrow the wedding
would take place.

But what about after the wedding? Michael still loved her— his poetic "serenade" last night proved that. But she'd made such a mess of him. Would he still want her physically? She had a horrid suspicion that even though he still cared for her, those feelings had been channeled into a chaste expression.

It was just the thing she'd yearned for, once upon a time. But after a night full of scandalous dreams of the old Michael, a "chaste expression" of his love was not what she had in mind.

She very nearly made another wish on the coin to insure that he would want her in the old way, but then thought better of it. "I've made too many wishes in haste," she said to herself as she struggled into her clothes, fighting with the tiny buttons that climbed up her bodice. "I'll bide my time on this. I'll see what he's like today. And I'll see about training a new personal maid, too!"

"Daddy!" Pandora cried a few hours later when her father arrived on the doorstep, dusty and a little out of sorts.

"It's a godawful trip," Hector Drummond replied crankily as he hugged her in a perfunctory way. "Where's your Aunt Hesta?"

"Right here," came the reply, as Hesta joined them in the foyer. "How good to see you!"

Pandora took her father's arm and led him into the main parlor which, as she had discovered when she came down from breakfast, was newly festooned with star charts and large drawings of wheels meant to indicate the universe.

It seemed the new passion she'd wished on Michael was astrology, not astronomy, and wherever she looked there were dusty volumes with titles like *The Effects of Transiting Jupiter on the Native Sagittarian,* or *Thoughts on the Quincunx: Associations with Destiny,* nestled side by side with volumes written by long-dead English poets and essayists. Scattered everywhere were stacks of paper, scribbled with mathematical equations and occult symbols.

Neither her father nor her aunt appeared to find any of this clutter unusual. They brushed aside papers and piles of rolled charts to sit on the couches. They made no remark on the ornate bronze zodiac over the fireplace. Her father took a match from a holder shaped like the twins of Gemini, struck in on the base of a small bust of Samuel Pepys (which Pandora only identified because his name was inscribed upon it), and made no remark other than to ask, "And where might your fiancé be, Pandora?"

"He'll be joining us shortly, Hector," Aunt Hesta volunteered cheerily. "I understand he's up on the roof, working on his telescope."

Michael arrived in time for the midday meal and, to Pandora's relief, he was no longer obese. He was hardly a striking specimen, being much thinner and more commonly proportioned than he'd been in his original condition, but at least he fit the furniture. His face and voice, she was pleased to note, were still pure unadulterated Michael Crane. The rest, however, left quite a bit to be desired.

"Ah, Mr. Drummond," he said, doffing his ball-fringed sombrero with a sweeping bow. "Father."

"Son," said Hector Drummond, and offered his hand.

Michael shook it (somewhat limply, Pandora noted) and replied, "Venus and Mars conjunct tonight. A good omen for a marriage, don't you think?" And then, turning to Pandora, chirped, "My pet! And how was your morning?"

"Introspective," she replied, and fingered the coin in her pocket.

Michael handed his sombrero to a servant, then removed his serape. Beneath it he still wore the gold brocade vest.

"Interesting fob you've got there, son," Pandora's father remarked, pointing to the hank of hair dangling from Michael's watch chain.

Why didn't that go away when I wished him into different clothes? Pandora wondered. But then, he always retained something, didn't he, whenever she wished him different?

"Thank you, sir," Michael replied. "Might I be so bold as to call you Hector?"

They gathered in the dining room, Michael at the head of the banquet table, Hector Drummond at the foot, the ladies centered on either side. From the portrait above the mantel, Michael's ghostly-eyed father seemed to preside over the gathering.

Michael perched on the edge of his chair while

he quoted poetry and made astrological predictions and played with his cutlet, slicing it into tinier and tinier pieces which he pushed about on his plate. Pinky finger extended, he sipped his wine and made amusing comments which had Pandora's father and aunt nearly weeping with mirth.

Pandora, however, found none of it amusing. She was the only one who remembered the real Michael. She was the only one who could mourn the man he'd been. She'd given long thought to the steps she might take to remedy the situation, and as Michael launched into yet another long passage of Milton, she reached into her pocket and took a firm grip on the coin.

"I wish," she whispered, closing her eyes for an instant, "that Michael was more rugged."

"Goddamnit!"

Her eyes popped open.

"Damn it, Maria," Michael continued when one of the maids scurried forward, "there's no pepper plate on this table! How many times do I have to tell you people that I want a side of jalapeños with my steak!"

Steak?

As the maid sped toward the kitchen, Pandora looked down at her plate, and then at her father's and Aunt Hesta's. A half second before they'd all been eating veal cutlets and escalloped potatoes and three-bean salad off exquisite gold-rimmed china. Now, in various states of pillage, there rested before each of them a huge slab of beef, half-drowned in soupy beans and fried onions that drizzled juicily over the edge of chipped enameled plates. Even the table itself had changed. The linen cloth was gone, revealing a rough, splintery top formed by uneven wooden planks.

"Yes, peppers *would* be nice," said Pandora's father quite matter-of-factly.

"Delicious," remarked Hesta, happily popping a bite of bloody beef into her mouth.

Michael, his jaw now shaded with stubble, his brocade vest smeared with dirt and sporting a few new rips, leaned back in his chair and swung one leg up on the table. The boot landed with a thud.

"Hurry up, damn it!" he yelled toward the kitchen, then burped loudly. "You'll have to give me the particulars of your birth place and time, Pop," he said to Hector. "I'll do you up a chart. Be good for your business."

"A fine idea," Hector replied around a mouthful of onions.

Michael reached down and produced the largest, nastiest-looking knife Pandora had ever seen, and began to pick his teeth with the tip of it.

"Read much Thomas Fuller, Pop?" Michael asked a moment later. He stabbed the knife downward, sinking the tip of the blade into the tabletop.

"Can't say that I have."

"Thomas Fuller? You know, 1608-1661?"

Hector shook his head and kept eating. Pandora tried not to cry.

"Deceive not thyself by overexpecting happiness in the married estate," Michael quoted loftily, the knife

still swaying before him. He scraped his boot off the table, then leaned forward to prop his elbows. "I want you to know, Pop," he added conspiratorially, "that our little ol' Pandy, here, is safe with me. She's a lady, and I aim to keep her in that condition. That *other* kind of happiness," he added with a wink, "I can get down the road for two bits. I think you know what I mean, Pop."

Hesta flushed and even Hector stopped chewing, but Michael went on, "This little gal means too much to me to sully in that way. Yessirree."

"But what about children?" Hector, cutlery poised, asked with mild curiosity.

"I can't believe we're discussing this!" Pandora cried, standing so quickly that she toppled her chair. "I can't believe we're discussing this at the *table!*"

She ran from the room and out into the foyer, where she fell flat over a bale of pronghorn hides that hadn't been there before.

Weeping as she got up and straightened her skirts, she heard Michael's voice from the dining hall. "Gemini with Leo rising," he said with a shrug in his voice. "Flighty. Say, Pop, I've got a first edition of *The Pilgrim's Progress* you might be interested to see, if we ever get our jalapeños. Maria, hurry up! And bring s'more beer, too!"

Pandora stormed up the stairs, pausing momentarily when she heard the far-off tinkle of Michael's mother's bell. "Oh, shut up!" she hissed, and fled to her room, slamming the door behind her.

She began to pace frantically, repeating "What'll I do, what'll I do, what'll I do?" like a mantra. The bedroom had changed again, too. Now the bed frame was rough-hewn and heavy and draped with animal skins. A gun rack, stocked with glinting shotguns and rifles, hung next to the door. As she paced back and forth, she occasionally tripped over the enormous, glass-eyed head of a grizzly bear, whose hide spread over a good part of the floor.

Before she'd come here, she'd convinced herself that she didn't want Michael or any part of him. She'd too late come to realize that she loved him, and that loving him was more important than any artificial pretense— and they had been legion— she had constructed about herself. That being with him and being loved by him for one day was more important, more necessary, than a lifetime of adoration by scores of nameless boys and men, more important than a thousand photographs reproduced in society pages. How tragic that she had to learn this by destroying Michael and thereby destroying her only real chance at true happiness.

Desperation clutched at her, took away her reason. *The coin,* she thought, *only the coin can save him, and only if I can hit upon the right combination of wishes. . . .*

She brought it out again. She could barely look at it, and only half-realized that she had grown to hate it. "I wish— "

The door opened with no preface of a knock, and Michael, knife strapped to his leg, strode into the room. "Pops and Aunt Hesta want to take a ride out to the mine. You coming?"

"I wish you'd be more polite," she said without thinking.

He bowed low, the dangling scalp swaying below his ripped brocade vest. "Dear future wife," he intoned, "I wonder if you might do me the great honor of accompanying us on a jaunt through the desert?"

"Not that polite," she said, taking a step back and clutching the coin tightly.

Forlorn, he dropped to one knee. "Forgive me if I've offended you, dearest. If I thought I had insulted you in any manner, I should perish. In the words of—"

"I wish you'd stop quoting people!"

"— the lowly desert sparrow, *twit-twit, cheep-cheek-cheep—*"

"Or animals!"

His mouth snapped shut, and he stared at her in curious silence.

"Michael," she said slowly, "I think we should talk about our marriage."

"Yes, love?" he said, assuming an air of boredom.

"Do you love me?"

A light came into his eyes. "More than my life."

"Will you ever . . . will you ever, um . . ." She searched for a polite term. "Will you ever husband me?"

Beneath his chin stubble, he blushed brightly.

"Oh darling," he said earnestly, "I respect you far to much for that. You needn't worry."

She felt suddenly drained and empty. Never? Never would he touch her? Despite what she'd done to his body and his mannerisms and everything else, she knew Michael was still in there somewhere: the Michael she had tried not to love but found she needed, the Michael who still loved and had once wanted her.

"Michael," she said softly, "if only you could be more, well, I wish you were more . . . forceful."

Abruptly he lunged at her, lifting her as he came forward, flinging them both upon the hidecovered bed. She dropped the coin as Michael landed on her, heard its impact upon the floor as he began to tear at her bodice.

"Michael!" she cried as his stubbly whiskers scraped against her cheek, her neck. "Michael, stop it! Not like this!"

Fabric ripped with a sick sound as he tore another layer of her clothing away. "Now," he grunted, his eyes wild. "I need you now, Pandy." With another tear, he had bared her to the waist.

He eased his weight from her momentarily to reach between them to lift her skirts, and in that instant, she slithered out from beneath him. He caught her almost immediately, roughly clamping his mouth to her nipple and sliding one hand up her thigh, but her head and shoulders were off the edge of the bed.

Twisting beneath him, she reached toward the floor and began, blindly, to grope for the coin.

"Yes, honey-girl, yes—this is Venus and Mars conjunct," he breathed, and began to rip away her skirts.

Please, please, she thought wildly, *please let me find—*

One finger touched metal. She couldn't get a grip on the coin, couldn't pick it up, but she pressed her fingertip down upon it. As Michael shoved her skirts out of the way and wrenched her knees apart, she cried out, "I take them all back! I wish I'd never changed Michael!"

She found herself at once in the midst of a sparkling shimmer, as if the light, the air itself, were clouded with golden dust motes. And then, as suddenly as the effect had come, it was gone.

She lay upon the bed, her bodice partly undone but not ripped, and she lay in the crook of Michael's arm. He was kissing her neck. His hand rested upon her, his fingers delving beneath her chemise to lightly pet the upper swell of her breast.

"Michael?" she whispered.

The room was back to its original condition, although the figurines she'd broken were no longer there. Michael was dressed like . . . well, like Michael. His shirt was open, and she was surprised to find her hand on his chest, her fingers combing through wavy, wheaten hair.

"Yes, darling?" His breath wafted warm against her neck.

"Michael, tell me everything you know about the poetry of John Milton."

Chuckling, he raised his head. "Who?" He kissed the tip of her nose. His fingers trailed a long line up, then down, the side of her neck, then deftly freed another of her bodice buttons. A shiver sped through her and her breath caught in her throat.

"Michael, where are Aunt Hesta and Father?"

"Honey, you know where they are." He was smiling, and tiny lines crinkled out from the corners of his eyes. Oh, what beautiful eyes he had. And he had that *look* again— that look that made her feel as if the two of them were the only people in the world.

"Tell me anyway," she breathed as his head dipped and he kissed her, just below her ear, then again, above the hollow of her collarbone.

"I sent them out to look at the mine," he said softly, and without taking his eyes from hers, freed another button on her bodice, then another. "They won't be back for at least an hour."

"Then, Michael . . ."

He kissed her, a soft brush of his lips upon hers. Another button. "Yes, Pandy?"

"Love me."

He drew in a long breath, then gently kissed the top swell of the breast he had just revealed. "I thought you were set on waiting until after the wedding."

She eased back the sides of his shirt and slid her hands up his chest and neck to hold his beautiful face between her palms. "I changed my mind," she whispered just before he kissed her again.

* * *

"Daughter, I don't believe I've ever seen you look so, well, so fresh!" Hector Drummond remarked as he escorted his daughter toward the dining room, from which the scent of roasting chicken beckoned.

"It's just the excitement, Daddy," Pandora replied, and almost giggled when she felt another blush bloom hotly over her cheeks. She felt absolutely radiant, and as if she possessed great secrets. Although she no longer possessed the coin. After Michael had at last— and reluctantly— taken his leave of her, she had looked and looked for it, but to no avail. It was as if it had simply evaporated.

"Your father's right, Pandy," Aunt Hesta said. "You look so . . . dewy. And flushed. Are you feeling well?"

"Perfectly well, Aunt Hesta. It's just . . . after all, I *am* getting married tomorrow."

"I suppose," Aunt Hesta said. "Is this the dress Michael sent you the other evening? I'll admit I thought it was a little bright for your complexion, dear, but it's quite lovely. Very exotic."

Pandora brushed her fingers over a bit of her bodice's exquisite needlework. "It is beautiful, isn't it?"

"And speaking of Michael, just where is that bridegroom of yours?"

"He'll be along, Aunt Hesta."

"You didn't do— you haven't thrown something at him, have you? Pandora, please don't— "

Pandy patted her aunt's hand. "Everything's

fine. His mother is well enough to join us for supper, and he's gone to fetch her."

"Finally. I've been anxious to meet her." Hesta gave a little tug to Pandora's bodice. Head tilted and brows softly furrowed, she leaned forward and whispered, "Are you certain you're all right? There was a bit of lining showing at your neck." She glanced toward Pandy's hem, and both her eyebrows shot up. "And your shoes don't match! Pandora, this isn't like you. It's not like you at all! Didn't you let Constance help you dress? I'll have to speak to her. . . ."

"Constance is back?" Pandora chirped brightly.

"Back? Whatever has gotten into you?"

Pandora hugged her father's arm closer and, standing on tiptoes, whispered into his ear, "I'm going to make you proud of me, Daddy, I promise."

"What?" Hector said, coloring slightly. He tugged, with one finger, at his collar. "Pandora, I haven't the slightest idea . . ."

"Good evening!" Michael appeared at the top of the stairs. On his arm was a small, elderly woman, frail but elegant. "May I present my mother: Madelaine Crane," Michael said as, slowly, he accompanied her down the stairs.

Pandy found she couldn't stop staring at the woman. There was something about her eyes. It was only when Michael and his mother reached the foot of the stair that Pandora realized something of significance.

"Oh, what a lovely necklace, Mrs. Crane,"

Hesta exclaimed once Michael had made introductions all around.

"Yes, thank you, it is, isn't it?" the old woman said softly, in a strange accent Pandora couldn't identify. With lined but still-slim fingers, the old woman lifted the pendant coin and let it rest in her palm.

"Spanish?" Pandora asked hesitantly. Her entire body tingled. "Roman, perhaps?"

"Persian," the woman answered, eyes twinkling. Pandora knew those eyes: eyes which had once twinkled mysteriously from beneath a pale blue cloak on the moonlit plaza.

"A family heirloom," Michael's mother continued as she took Pandora's arm and they began to walk toward the dining room. "It has been in the Crane family for generations, and someday it will be Pandora's. To keep. Although she may find, one day, that she will wish to loan it to a future daughter-in-law."

"How nice," said Hesta.

"It is a magic coin, you know," Michael's mother added. "You may loan it out once, and when its work is done, it comes back."

Pandora's father laughed as if the old woman had just told a very witty joke.

Michael smiled quite endearingly. "All my life she's been telling me that coin's magic. I keep telling her I'll believe it when I see her do a trick with it."

His mother returned the smile. "And I keep on telling you, my darling: the kind of magic this coin works is the kind you would be the last to notice."

"My mother," Michael said fondly, "is a woman of mystery."

"Your father agreed with you," she replied, and everyone chuckled. Except Pandora, who found herself speechless.

Noisily, the others filed in ahead. The table was set in the household's finest silver. Candles flickered softly on polished surfaces and washed gold light over platters of food and low vases stuffed with flowers.

Pandora stopped in the doorway and drew in a breath. It was so beautiful! Why hadn't she noticed before how beautiful this room was? Today everything seemed strange or beautiful or both.

Beside her, Michael's mother said softly, "When I fell in love with Michael's father, I was a very spoiled and silly young girl. I did not want to leave my home and my parties in Budapest and go to a strange new country. And then my future husband's mother gave me this coin."

"And the magic," Pandora whispered.

"I never knew," the old woman said as they moved slowly forward to join the others, "if it truly changed Michael's father so dramatically, or if it merely changed my perception of him. But either way, it taught me very much." She paused and smiled at Pandora. "As, I believe, it has taught you."

In the dining room, they stopped to stand beside their chairs. "One thing I don't understand," Pandora said softly, her lips close to her future mother-in-law's ear. "You said the coin would take back everything, and it did. Except . . ." She touched the rich brocade of her bodice.

"This dress—I mended it with the coin's magic. Why is it still mended?"

The old woman shrugged slightly. "For me, it left behind one small wish, also." She lifted her eyes to the portrait of Michael's father. Even in the hazy, golden candlelight, the cool aqua of his eyes glowed from the canvas.

"What wish did it leave you?" Pandora whispered.

The other woman's eyes never left the portrait. "Before I used the coin," she said, a soft smile floating upon her lips, "Michael's father's eyes were brown."

"My dears?" Michael was beside them. He seated his mother and kissed her cheek, then turned to Pandora. "I love you very much, you know," he whispered as he bent to slide her chair beneath her. His fingers trailed over her shoulder, hesitated at the nape of her neck. "We're going to be wonderfully happy."

Had she ever felt so right, so effortlessly perfect? In the beginning, she had wanted to make him as coldly impeccable as was she herself: icy, chiseled in fine detail, too flawless to be real. But now she knew the perfection in imperfection, the warmth in humanity, in making mistakes, in loving the man for what he was and not for what he might have been.

She touched his fingers, resting at her shoulder. "Yes," she said softly. "Perfectly, spectacularly, magically happy."

About the Author

Along the path to becoming a full-time writer, Ellen Archer made her living at a number of odd and interesting occupations, including dog groomer, market research interviewer, tree planter, ticket-taker, and tarot card reader.

Her debut novel, *Taboo*, a contemporary love story, was released in early 1995 to rave reviews. Her next novel, a historical romance, titled *Darling*, is due from Zebra in February, 1996.

Ellen currently lives in Arizona, where three dogs and several cats mill about her office. She enjoys swimming, gardening, and books, and although she no longer reads tarot professionally, she still collects unusual decks.

Smoke and Mirrors

by

Stephanie Bartlett

One

Stepping from the cable car at Geary Street, Josephine LeClair shivered, as much from nerves as from the chill of the encompassing gray fog. As she pulled the Persian lamb collar up around her ears, she caught a faint whiff of the attar of roses favored by the coat's owner and smiled, grateful now for the warmth, if not the weight, of her borrowed costume.

An hour before, as she set out through the warm spring sunshine, she had silently cursed the high neck, the huge leg-o-mutton sleeves, and the yards and yards of black velvet draping the heavy bustle. But that was San Francisco weather for you— summer one minute, winter the next.

She hesitated for a moment in the welcoming glow of the gaslights in front of the St. Francis Hotel, then crossed Powell street behind the departing cable car, the disembodied clanging of its bell muffled by the enveloping mist as it rolled down the hill toward Market Street.

Much as she longed to hurry across Union

Square through the deepening gloom, she was forced to check her pace in deference to the stiff, tight corset that kept her lungs from expanding to their normal capacity. Nor could Josie afford to stain Mrs. Elder's best mourning gown with perspiration.

She had never understood why some women went around trussed up like this every day. What she wouldn't give to be wearing her usual looser, lightweight Gibson-girl stays beneath a simple skirt and waist, with a straw boater over her red hair.

She grimaced at the thought of the delicate black chapeau now perched on her head, its soft felt base entirely hidden by a stuffed raven, complete with the taxidermist's best glass eyes. That was one good thing about the fog— it would keep people from staring.

And she could count herself lucky that this monstrous hat was in the new mode, with a back veil. She'd have been in a pretty pickle if it had been the old style mourning veil covering her face. She squinted into the mist, making out faint patches of ghostly light hovering in the distance, all that could be seen of the gas streetlights. It would be difficult enough finding Mr. Jordan's seance room in this weather without being blinded by yards of black silk tulle.

She sighed and instantly regretted it when the stays dug into her ribs. At least her benefactress had let her keep her own drawers and chemise. And thank the *Bon Dieu* that her feet wouldn't fit in Mrs. Elder's pointy-toed, high-heeled "Trilby" shoes.

Hearing nothing but the eery echo of her own muffled footfalls, she crossed Stockton Street in the middle of the block and stopped to pull the reporter's notebook from her handbag. She'd have to be careful no one saw her taking notes, but she planned to sit in the back and be as unobtrusive as possible. After checking the address she'd written down against the number of the building in front of her, she turned north, stepping wide around an alleyway piled with stinking refuse.

A high wailing cry paralyzed her, making the hair at the nape of her neck rise. Following a metallic clamor, a coal black cat emerged from the mouth of the alley, its fur on end and its back arched. This apparition stopped long enough to hiss at her, then darted away into the gloom.

One hand cupped at the base of her throat, she breathed as deeply as the corset would allow as she struggled to calm her racing heart. Only a cat, but a black one at that. It had crossed her path, and today was Friday the thirteenth!

It was a good thing she was too educated and modern to be superstitious. Or at least not *very* superstitious. Whatever had possessed her to allow her editor and his wife to talk her into this scheme, and tonight of all nights?

The scene at the Elders' home in the fashionable Mission District came rushing back to her.

"Why, you look every inch the fashionable

young widow, doesn't she, Felix? I just knew we'd wear the same size." Mrs. Elder had clasped her hands in front of her padded bosom and glowed. Josie knew that this woman, like so many of her set, bought a complete new suit of mourning each spring and fall, just in case of need. The editor's wife appeared delighted with the opportunity to costume one of her husband's cub reporters.

Mr. Elder grunted. "A bit young if you ask me. How old are you, LeClair?"

"Twenty-one next Thursday, sir."

"Eh? Happy birthday." He stroked his drooping salt-and-pepper mustache. "Well, it can't be helped. You know I wouldn't ask you, except that you've got the best chance of getting the inside scoop. Nobody would suspect you're a newspaperman, being a woman and all."

And that was the reason, of course. She'd do almost anything to get a crack at a real story. Excitement simmered in her veins at the thought. An exposé of the city's spiritualists and how they preyed upon the grief of the newly bereaved. Let the Doubting Thomases in the newsroom chew on that for a while.

In control of herself once more, Josie crossed the alley and approached the nearest doorway. In the fog she could see little of the building's brick front other than a sign bearing the house number and the words, "Andrew Jordon, Clairvoyant and Medium. Group Readings 7 PM Fri. Eves. Individual Readings By Appt."

She checked the time on the small pocketwatch.

Six fifty-two. With one last calming breath, she drew herself up to her full five feet and four inches and mounted the three shallow steps. The door swung open at her touch, and she found herself alone in a dingy foyer.

Following the murmur of voices, she emerged into a spacious area vaguely reminiscent of a chapel, even to the rows of pews and the smell of stale incense. Except that where the altar should be, two empty armchairs, upholstered in plain horsehair, stood in a circle of light thrown by a coal-oil piano lamp. Taking advantage of the dimly lit "congregation" area to avoid drawing attention to herself, she sidled into the last row and sat, the large bustle forcing her to perch on the edge of the hard wooden seat.

She peered at those around her, noting the looks of fearful anticipation on their faces. Most of them, like herself, wore mourning, or half-mourning. She found that she relished the idea of spoiling Mr. Jordan's lucrative swindles. And if she succeeded in unmasking this impostor to-night, she might be able to get statements from some of the audience, complaining of the hoax perpetrated upon them, with which to spice up her article.

The sibilant murmurings of her neighbors hushed suddenly, and all eyes turned toward the altar platform. Standing in front of the righthand chair was, without doubt, the most handsome man Josie had ever seen.

While the female part of her could do nothing but stare in breathless sensual response, the trained reporter noted first that he was above six feet tall and of medium build, his wide shoulders and narrow hips accentuated by a severe but expensive-looking cutaway jacket of the inkiest black.

His hair was dark as well, the same shiny black of the raven upon her hat, but crisp and unfashionably free of brilliantine, and combed smoothly back from his long oval face. His features were smooth and regular—a broad forehead, high cheekbones, and straight nose—and kept from prettiness by slightly heavy brows and a bushy and unwaxed mustache partly concealing his sensuous mouth.

But it was his eyes that drew and held attention. Almond shaped and dark lashed, they shone an arresting cobalt blue. "Ladies and gentlemen, I bid you good evening, and welcome." His voice was deep, but soft and smooth, with a faint huskiness. "My name is Andrew Jordan."

Josie let out a breath she hadn't known she was holding, squelching a surge of disappointment. It was silly, but she had been hoping that somehow he would prove to be someone else, someone not directly involved in preying on the vulnerable. Her hands, in their black kid gloves, tightened into fists. *Why, oh, why did she have to find him here, and why must he be a charlatan she had sworn to expose to the world?*

She unclenched her fists. She was being ridiculous! Becoming besotted with a handsome stranger at first glimpse. The boys in the newsroom would hoot if they ever guessed. Well, she'd just have to make sure they had no cause. She was a reporter, and it was high time she acted like one.

She forced herself to listen, to try to pick up the thread of his speech.

". . . beyond the veil. I do my poor best to interpret their symbols and convey their messages to you." Eyes the color of lapis lazuli swept the crowd. "And now we will begin." He seated himself, moving with grace and economy, leaning back and resting his forearms on the chair's pillowy arms.

His features took on a softened, dreamy look, and his eyes unfocused, turning to the softest delphinium. "I see an empress, standing beside clear water. The letter J hovers over her head." His mouth twitched up at the corners. "And now I see Napoleon. Is there someone here named Josephine?"

Josie's mouth dried, but she knew she was being silly again. It was a common enough name. She glanced about in case some other woman responded, but saw only rapt attention on the faces around her.

The spiritualist's eyebrows raised. "A loaf of Frenchbread in the clear water." He frowned. "French for clear. LeClair. Yes!"

Suddenly his eyes sharpened and he stood, pointing his finger directly at her. "Josephine Le-Clair, come forward. I have a message for you from one who has passed on."

Andrew Jordan watched the young woman's progress up the aisle, wondering why she had seemed reluctant for the reading. Most who sought him out were eager for the communion, especially those dressed, as she was, in deep, albeit stylish, mourning.

As she stepped into the circle of light and lifted her face to his, something in her winsome features and cloud of dark red hair made Drew long to take her in his arms and comfort her. She wasn't beautiful, but there was a vibrancy, a love of life that poured out of her. It was a shameful waste for one such as this to be consigned to widow's weeds for months or years. Looking at her, he felt unaccountably frightened, not of her, but of his own response. He'd gone down that road once, to his detriment, and he'd sworn never to return. But—

A sardonic look from the spirit reminded him where he was and what he was doing— He was a channel, nothing more. He gestured the young widow to the chair and let his eyes unfocus again, allowing the image of the spirit to strengthen.

Now this woman, when she lived, had been a great beauty, with her soft blue eyes and the long, pale blonde curls cascading over the shoulders of her lavender robes. The spirit moved to stand beside the young widow's chair. A cloud of black formed over the subject's head. Drew noticed for the first time the absurd black bird perched on her hat. The spirit stomped her foot and frowned, and he shifted his focus back to the symbol. A large red X appeared over the cloud, then a bachelor's button appeared in its place.

Drew smiled, pleased by this revelation. "The

spirit says you are not a widow. That you have never been married."

Miss Josephine LeClair gasped and blanched, her milk-white skin growing even paler, and the sprinkling of pale freckles standing out on her delicate nose. Bull's eye. He didn't bother to wonder at the reason for her masquerade. It wasn't the first time someone had posed as a bereaved relative to try to prove he was a fraud. If only he *didn't* really possess the power to see the dead. Life would be so much easier.

He turned back to the spirit. *Now a hand holding a pen hovered over the false widow, and a wooden case full of moveable type.* "You write for a newspaper."

At this, an angry murmur arose from the audience. He refocused his eyes and stood, holding up his hands for silence. "Ladies and gentlemen, this is not the message. The spirits see no need to unmask the many who come to try to discredit me. Please be patient. The spirit assures me the true message is of vital importance."

He seated himself and let the image of the spirit clarify once more. *The symbols were coming faster now— a dog, a caduceus, Charon on the River Styx, a horse.* "You have a friend, a doctor, who works at the coroner's office. You must take me to meet this friend— " He didn't scruple to include himself, nor did he wait for a response. *An earthworm floating in a puddle with a red X over it.* "— and we must convince him that the cause of death was not drowning." *The spirit stood before him now, smiling and holding a bottle with a skull-and-crossed-bones on the label.*

He let his eyes focus again and looked down into the terrified face of Miss Josephine LeClair. "The spirit commands us to prove to the world that she was murdered."

Two

Saturday, March 14

Josie rubbed her hands up and down her arms as she paced the hallway in front of the city morgue, trying not to think about the reason for the chill seeping from the dank walls lined in dreary green marble veined with white.

Down here below street level, with the flickering gaslights doing little to dispel the gloom, it was hard to remember that it was a beautiful spring day outside. Somehow the idea of flowers blooming and birds singing made the faint tinge of decay and carbolic acid in the damp air even more oppressive. She couldn't imagine working in a place like this six days a week.

She gritted her teeth, asking herself for the hundredth time why she had agreed to Mr. Jordan's demands. The night before, after he ordered her to prove someone was murdered, he'd insisted she meet him here this morning to talk with her friend, the doctor.

She allowed herself a tiny triumphant smile as she contemplated the surprise awaiting the heretofore imperturbable spiritualist. Her smile faded, replaced by a frown. Unless he knew a great deal more about her than he let on.

That thought, among others, had whirled round her head for hours last night. And this morning she'd realized she had no choice but to accede to his request. Otherwise, she'd never find out how he learned her name and occupation.

She knew she would've remembered such a striking-looking man if he'd ever come to the city room, and he couldn't have read her byline, because so far she hadn't been granted one, although this story promised to change all that.

No, it was obvious he'd gotten wind of her plan somehow, but how? No one but Mr. Elder and his wife had known. Perhaps that good lady had let something drop to a friend. In any event, beyond mere personal curiosity, she was on assignment, and her job was to expose him for the fraud he was.

Nothing she'd seen the night before had been of any help. After her "reading," he'd called on some half-dozen other people from the audience, giving them all seemingly inconsequential messages from their "dear departed." Most of them seemed comforted by what he said.

It was obvious he paid someone to find out about those who came to him. Then when the bereaved returned, he'd give them a special "message." The best way to prove that was to find out everything she could about Mr. Jordan, and that meant going along with him on this murder investigation.

If it *was* murder. For all she knew, he'd made

up the whole story. Or if there really was a corpse, and the woman had been murdered, he could very well be the murderer himself. But then why would he want to lead a reporter to the evidence? Or maybe he truly did possess the power to communicate with the dead. She shivered, not sure which thought unnerved her more.

Or perhaps he merely witnessed the crime and had chosen this way to gain notoriety, free advertising for his unholy business. Yes, that made a twisted sort of sense. And all the more reason to expose him.

She stopped to peer at her watch. He was already a little late. She'd give him another five minutes, and then she'd go in alone. Of course, she didn't have a description of the supposed murder victim, but just how many people could have drowned in the last few days? She grimaced at the thought, then stopped pacing and turned toward the echoing sound of footsteps coming toward her down the connecting hallway. An unreasonable fear gripped her, and it was all she could do not to bolt for the stairs.

But just then, he rounded the corner and nodded to her in greeting. Equally unreasonably, her heart lifted at the sight of him.

He was even more handsome than she remembered, still dressed in somber black, but with the corners of his mouth lifted in the hint of a smile. "Miss LeClair, I almost didn't recognize you for a moment, now that you've shed your widow's weeds."

Her mouth twisted in a rueful grin. "Well,

there was certainly no point in continuing my masquerade after you penetrated my facade last evening. I'm sorry if you're disappointed by my work-a-day attire."

His smile widened. "Far from it. I am enchanted to see you in a costume even more flattering, and I daresay more *comfortable* than the one you wore last night."

Her cheeks burned. Not only did he think she'd been fishing for a compliment, which she had been, but he understood far too much about her after only one encounter. She could think of no appropriate reply, so she turned toward the dark wooden door, with the words "San Francisco City Morgue" emblazoned in gold leaf on its frosted glass window. "Yes, well, shall we?"

He leaned around her, extending one long arm to turn the brass knob and hold the door open for her.

Marveling at how she could look so fresh and crisp in such surroundings, Drew followed Miss LeClair's trim form into a shabby anteroom, even more chill, damp, and smelly than the hallway outside, if that were possible.

As he closed the door behind him, a woman bustled through an inner doorway, wiping her hands on a bloody rag, her long, once-white apron stained with fluids he didn't care to identify. She glanced at them. "May I help— Josie!" Her face alight, she hurried toward them. "But what are you doing here? I thought you would be at work today!"

Josie. It suited her. He savored the sound of

the name as its owner turned toward him, her eyes glittering. "But I *am* working. Mr. Jordan, may I present my good friend, Cecile Balfour? *Doctor* Cecile Balfour."

Drew tried to mask his surprise, but he could tell by Josie's triumphant expression that she had seen it, and that she relished his discomfiture. But instead of minding, he found he liked her better for this show of spirit. However, if she expected him to retire into the background and let her run the show, she had a surprise coming herself. He tipped his hat. "Dr. Balfour, I am delighted to make your acquaintance. Forgive me for coming directly to the point. I asked Miss LeClair to introduce you to me so that I—that is, we—might request your assistance in a matter of utmost urgency."

The doctor's face sobered. "But of course. How may I help?"

Josie took a step forward and began to explain their mission.

As she spoke, Drew took advantage of the opportunity to compare the two friends. Cecile Balfour and Josie must be close in age and height, but any similarity stopped there.

His companion's hair was a rich red-brown and swept up to halo her face in the Gibson-girl style, with a top-knot undoubtedly hidden beneath a fetching straw boater. The doctor's honey-blond hair was pulled tightly back from her face and clubbed at the nape of her neck, and her blue eyes hid behind wire-framed spectacles, giving her regular features an owlish aspect. Where Josie wore a fashionable blue-and-white striped blouse and dark blue skirt, what showed of Dr. Balfour's gown beneath her apron appeared old-fashioned and dimmed with many washings.

As Josie began to describe the events of the night before in detail, Drew decided it was time to intervene before she convinced the good doctor that he was insane. "Dr. Balfour, have you a drowning victim brought in recently?" *He sensed the spirit's presence beside him.* "She was about this tall—" He held up his hand to indicate her height. "—slender but well-rounded, with pale blond curls and light blue eyes."

Dr. Balfour's eyes widened behind her glasses. "But yes. How did you know? We have only just identified her. Her family hasn't even been contacted yet."

Again, Josie took control of the conversation. "Mr. Jordan is a spiritualist—a clairvoyant and medium, to be exact. He claims the dead woman's spirit came to him and told him she didn't accidentally drown, and that she was, in fact, murdered."

The doctor's color rose. "Oh, I see. Well, yes, I suppose she could have been murdered. Only an autopsy would tell for sure, but none has been ordered. The coroner has already determined the cause of death and signed the death certificate."

Josie turned to him. "Mr. Jordan, would you mind very much waiting for me outside in the hall? I'd like to talk with my friend alone for a moment."

Drew shrugged, then gave the only possible answer. "Certainly." *The spirit smiled, then floated ahead, beckoning him to follow her as she passed through the closed door.* Gritting his teeth, Drew turned the knob and stepped into the hall. Miss LeClair may have put him to the rout, but the battle was far from over.

Josie waited until the door shut behind Andrew Jordan, then turned to her friend. "Well, what do you think?"

Cecile grinned. "He's magnificent! But a spiritualist? I've never known you to be interested in such a colorful character before."

Josie's face heated. What a time for her usually serious friend to turn playful! "Not *him!* The corpse, the murder—do you think it's true?"

Cecile plucked at her lower lip and shrugged. "It's possible, but how should I know?"

Josie clenched her fists in determination. "Well, I've got to find out. This may be the proof I need to expose him as a fraud. Can't you do an autopsy?"

Cecile shook her head. "No, Josie. I could get into big trouble if I don't have the family's consent."

Josie frowned. "But what if it's true, and she *was* murdered? Wouldn't the coroner want to know so the police could find the murderer?"

Cecile gave a bitter laugh. "And admit he made a mistake? I don't think he'd thank me. Besides, what if she *wasn't* murdered? How do I explain it to her family? I can hear myself now: *'So sorry about cutting up your loved one.'*"

Josie sighed. "I guess you couldn't just say it

was an honest mistake? No, I didn't think so. But couldn't you do it so it didn't show, or sew her back up afterwards or something?"

Cecile's eyes narrowed. "It's really that important to you?"

Josie nodded and held her breath.

The corners of Cecile's mouth quirked up. "Oh, all right, I'll do it! I'll tell you all about my findings tonight at church."

"Thank you!" Josie clasped her friend's shoulders and bussed her on either cheek.

Grinning, Cecile shook a finger in Josie's face. "But if I lose my position here, I plan to stay with you until I get another job, and you know how long it took me to find this one."

"It's a deal!" Laughing, Josie danced her around the little anteroom.

Just then the door opened, and Mr. Jordan peered inside. "Sorry to interrupt, but I just thought perhaps you might like to ride the train out to Seal Rocks with me this evening, Miss Le-Clair."

Part of her wanted to leap at the chance of being alone with this man in such a romantic setting, but she knew she had to refuse. Not only would it be unprofessional, but for all she knew he might be a murderer, or at best a crazy man. "No, thank you very kindly. I have to go to confession."

One heavy eyebrow raised. "I see. Perhaps tomorrow after mass instead?"

She opened her mouth to speak, but Cecile cut

her off. "I think you should go, Josie. It'll be good for you."

Startled, she stared at her friend, but when Cecile's only answer was an impish grin, Josie turned back to Mr. Jordan, ready to decline his offer once and for all, and to put him in his place while she was at it.

He smiled down at her. "I just thought you might want to see where the body was found." Without waiting for a reply, he tipped his hat and closed the door again.

When she glanced around to see her friend's reaction to this revelation, she wasn't disappointed.

Cecile's smile had disappeared, to be replaced by a worried frown. "But how did he know?"

After leaving the confessional, Josie genuflected and crossed herself, then slid into the last pew beside Cecile. The afternoon had dragged by with the usual busywork for the late edition. Now she couldn't wait any longer. Without turning her head, she breathed out a whisper for her friend's ears only. "What did you find?"

The beads of her friend's rosary clicked together in the quiet church. "It was murder, all right. A slow-acting poison that affected her brain and nervous system."

A catch in Cecile's voice made Josie risk a quick glance at her friend. Something had shaken the doctor's usual unflappable calm. "Was it dreadful?"

Cecile's whisper came back with studied clinical dispassion. "Alkaloids turn living tissue to jelly. It wasn't pretty. But that's not the worst of it. Her stomach was full of undigested food, probably a dinner she ate at the Cliff House—it looked like one of their specialties." She paused, then continued, her whisper strained. "And she'd had—*relations* with a man shortly before she died."

Josie frowned. She supposed these were valuable clues. "Is that unusual?"

Cecile cleared her throat. "It is if the victim was a widow—a very young, very beautiful, very rich widow."

Josie settled back to think, lulled by the glow of the candles and the lingering smell of incense. So the woman *was* murdered, and in a very nasty way, probably by her lover.

She didn't want to believe that Andrew Jordan was capable of making love to a woman shortly before poisoning her. But how else could he know so much about it? Still, if he was the murderer, wouldn't he want to cover it up instead of insisting she expose it, especially since the coroner and everyone else thought the woman drowned by accident? She shook her head to clear it, then glanced at Cecile again. "Did you tell your boss?"

A ghost of a smile played over the doctor's delicate mouth. "And get sacked? No, I thought I'd wait until you figure out who did it first."

Josie coughed into her hand to hide a sudden

smile. "And just how do you expect me to do that?"

"I thought you'd never ask." Cecile's hand slipped into the pocket of her wool coat and held out a crumpled piece of paper. "Copy this down."

Josie complied, squinting at the water-stained paper and scribbling the name and street number in her notebook.

As she wrote, Cecile continued. "I found it in the victim's pocket. It's the woman who identified the body. Peggy Quinn. She told me she'd be at home Sunday after church. I think you should go see her."

Josie nodded. "By the way, who did she say the victim was?"

Cecile slid the scrap of paper back into her pocket. "Her girlhood friend, Frannie, better known to the world as Mary Frances Kelly."

"Kelly? Widow of Seamus Kelly? No wonder you were shocked." Not just some anonymous murder victim any longer, but the widow of one of the lesser Comstock Silver Kings. She allowed herself a tiny smile. This was big! If she could solve this murder, not only would she get a byline out of it, but the story would probably land on the front page as well! Provided Mr. Elder didn't get wind of it and assign the story to a more seasoned reporter. "I'll go see her after mass. I told Mr. Jordan I'd meet him at the Cliff House at two."

Cecile's hand reached out and gripped hers, hard. "Do you still think it's a good idea?"

Surprised as much by her friend's intensity as by the question, Josie squeezed back. "Of course it's a good idea. Maybe I can find somebody who saw Mrs. Kelly the night she died—a waiter or someone. I might get a clue about who was with her." She released her hold on Cecile's hand.

But her friend's grip tightened. "Fine. Go by yourself. Tell Mr. Jordan you've changed your mind."

Josie turned to stare at her companion. "But why? You're the one who told me to go with him."

Cecile's eyes were dark with fear. "But Josie, he knows too much. What if he's the murderer?"

Josie forced herself to smile, trying not to let her friend's worry infect her. "Then he's a fool to go there, and the waiter will recognize him, and the case will be solved." She retrieved her hand, then used it to pat her friend's. "Don't worry. We'll be in public, and in broad daylight. It's not as if I'll be alone with him. What could happen?"

Three

Squinting into the noonday sun, Josie checked the address in her notebook against the number on the nearest house. The right block, at last! She glanced at her watch. If she wanted to reach the Cliff House by two, she only had a few minutes to talk to the victim's old school chum before catching the train.

As she hurried along the quiet street of modest homes, she frowned, trying to remember all the tips the other reporters had given her about conducting interviews. She wished she had more time to draw the woman out and win her sympathy. Not that she expected much from the interview, but maybe the woman could give her a lead on the lover.

Josie hesitated on the sidewalk in front of a one-story cottage. It reminded her of a doll's house, with its pastel yellow walls and white gingerbread trim. Bright yellow jonquils lined a white picket fence, and at the far end of the front porch, a wide swing hung in the shade of a burgeoning vine. Almost hidden from view by its shiny leaves, a woman knelt on the ground, digging in a flowerbed.

Putting on her best smile, Josie rested one hand on the top of the gate. "Mrs. Quinn?"

The woman started, then set aside her trowel and rose, wiping her hands on her apron before clasping them in front of her. "It's 'miss.' Can I help you?"

"I surely hope you will agree to, Miss Quinn. My name is Josephine LeClair. I'm a reporter with the *Examiner,* and I've been assigned to write a tribute to your friend, Mrs. Kelly." She couldn't risk getting Cecile in trouble by telling the truth. "Might I talk with you for a few minutes?"

"About Frannie?" The woman hesitated, then crossed the yard. "Well, I guess that would be all right." Slender and of medium height, she wore a coronet of braids of the dullest brown and a gown of the same color, far from flattering in its severity, its only decoration a black armband. Her face was young but quite plain, and the hand she held out to open the gate was red and work-roughened.

As she followed her hostess up the walk and across the porch, it struck Josie that Miss Quinn looked more like a servant than the mistress of this charming domicile. Not the type of friend she would have expected the widow Kelly to choose.

The woman gestured toward the swing. "Won't you have a seat?" Settling herself on the opposite end, Miss Quinn turned to Josie and attempted a timid smile, but tears welled up in her soft brown eyes. "Forgive me. My grief is so new. What was it you wanted to know about Frannie?"

Josie gave a silent prayer that the woman wouldn't break down completely. "Were you friends a long time?"

Miss Quinn nodded, pulling a plain white handkerchief from her skirt pocket and dabbing at her eyes. "We went to convent school together, and then we shared a small flat until Frannie got married. Then she and her husband bought me this little house."

"And did you continue to see each other after that?" Josie strove to keep her tone soothing.

The crown of braids bobbed up and down as she nodded. "Oh, yes. She was such a faithful friend, even though our situations were so different."

Mentally comparing this woman's life to that of a Comstock King's wife, she thought this quite an understatement. "And when did you last see Mrs. Kelly?"

Miss Quinn pressed the handkerchief to her lips for a moment. "Thursday evening." Her voice was husky with tears. "They told me she was found the next morning— dead— " She broke off on a sob.

Although she knew a good reporter didn't give way to emotion, Josie couldn't help but sympathize with the woman's pain. After all, how would she feel if anything happened to Cecile? She reached out, giving the stricken woman's hand a comforting pat. "I know this is difficult. I only have a few more questions. Do you know if Mrs. Kelly had given any thought to marrying again?"

The teary eyes widened, and Miss Quinn shook her head.

Josie strove to keep her voice neutral, even though she found she cared very much about the answer to the next question. "Did she ever mention a spiritualist named Andrew Jordan?"

Again, the woman shook her head. "Frannie was a good Catholic. She didn't go in for that sort of thing."

Relief eased the muscles in Josie's neck and shoulders. She still couldn't rule him out as a suspect, but there was nothing here to condemn him, either. "Miss Quinn, the last time you saw Mrs. Kelly, did she seem upset about anything?"

Thin lips formed an O, then pressed together in a thin line. "You don't think that—are you saying it wasn't an accident, that Frannie *meant* to drown?" Peggy Quinn's back stiffened and her soft eyes blazed with a glittering topaz light. "I told you, Frannie was a good Catholic. Suicide's a mortal sin—"

Josie held up both hands in denial. "No, no, of course I don't think that! I'm just trying to reconstruct her last few hours, for the article."

Mollified, Miss Quinn drooped once more. "I'm sorry." She covered her eyes with the hand-kerchief for a moment.

Josie hated to press the woman in her grief, but time was running out. She didn't want to be late meeting Mr. Jordan. She used her most coaxing voice. "So, she *was* upset?"

Pressing the cloth to her eyes, Miss Quinn nodded. "It was something to do with her late husband's estate and her lawyer, Liam O'Sullivan. They never got along for some reason." She peeped over the hanky's rolled hem. "But you won't print that, will you?"

Josie gave what she hoped was a reassuring smile. "Just one more thing, Miss Quinn. Do you have a likeness of Mrs. Kelly I might borrow?"

Nodding, the woman rose. "I'm sure I must. Let me just go take a look." She strode away into the house.

Josie looked at her watch. She still had time to catch the train, but waiting always made her restless. Schooling herself to patience, she leaned back, enjoying the spring sunshine and the sweet scent of the small yellow trumpet flowers clinging to the vine behind her.

Perhaps this man, O'Sullivan, was the murderer, and instead of being Mrs. Kelly's lover, he'd raped her, then murdered her to keep her from talking. Tomorrow she'd pay a visit to his office and see what she could learn.

Her hostess returned, carrying a small photo. "I remember the day this was taken. A few of us had gone to Seal Rocks for a picnic. Frannie always loved the beach there." She ran a finger along the ragged edge where the dark line of a man's sleeve remained. "I had to cut it to get it into the frame." She held it out with a tremulous smile. "You must forgive me for not being a better hostess. Can I get you a glass of cold tea?"

Slipping the photo into her handbag, Josie

rose. "Oh, no thank you. I have another appoint-
ment." She offered the woman her hand. "You've
been a big help."

Miss Quinn's work-worn hand gave Josie's a
perfunctory shake. "I'll look for your tribute. Do
you know when it will run?"

"Soon." The deception tasted bitter on Josie's
tongue. "I hope you won't be disappointed."

Miss Quinn gave her another watery smile.
"Oh, no, I'm sure it will be just lovely."

"Yes, well— " She patted her handbag. "— I'll
return the photograph in a few day's time. Goodbye." Her conscience smiting her, she nodded
and left the porch, letting herself out the gate
and turning to wave in response when the woman
called goodbye to her. She hoped Peggy Quinn
would forgive her lies once the murderer was
brought to justice.

As she hurried toward the train, her thoughts
turned to Mr. Jordan, and she couldn't help but
smile. One way or another she was determined
to find out tonight whether or not she'd let herself become enamored of a *real* lady-killer.

Drew sipped at his wine, his eyes never leaving
Josie's face as he rolled the rich *Chambertin*
around his tongue, savoring the luscious, full-
bodied flavor. The afternoon had been perfect,
from the moment he saw her alight from the
open railway car on Point Lobo. The time had
passed swiftly as they rode the Firth Wheel and
Haunted Swing, toured the museum, even renting

bathing costumes to take a dip in the warm salt-water pool at the Sutro Baths.

And now she sat across from him, sipping wine and looking at the moonlight on the waters of the Pacific from the window of their private dining room at the Cliff House. An ease, a camaraderie, had grown between them, making the strong physical attraction even more piquant. It had been a very long time since he had enjoyed himself this much, and he was sorry it would have to end so soon.

He could almost regret the depth of his feeling for her because it would make the pain of her imminent rejection so much greater. Perhaps he should have heeded the warning Brutus gave Caesar to beware the Ides of March. But no, he could not regret the joy, even though he would undoubtedly have to pay its high price.

Drew sighed as a young man in shirtsleeves entered the private dining room, bearing the photograph of the departed Mrs. Kelly. Josie had given the likeness to their waiter, with directions to show it around and see if any of the staff recognized her.

The spirit hovered near the young man, her face wreathed in smiles.

This second waiter was young, perhaps Josie's age, taller than average, and with a very earnest face. He wore a dark waistcoat over his white shirt, with a long white apron tied around his waist. "Excuse me, miss. My name is Daniel. My friend George said you were asking after this lady. I waited on her here late Thursday night, in this very room."

Drew sighed again. So that was why the spirit had insisted on coming here.

Josie leaned forward in her chair, her aquamarine eyes sparkling. "And the man she was with—what did he look like?"

The ends of his waxed mustache turned down as Daniel frowned, then shrugged. "He was an Irish fella, with a kind of medium build and reddish hair. I didn't pay much attention." He gave a sheepish grin. "With a woman like that in the room, a man has a hard time noticing anything else."

The spirit clasped her hands at her bosom and smiled fondly at her admirer.

Josie's color heightened, but her voice remained calm and businesslike. "Could anyone else have seen them?"

The young man shook his head. "George asked everybody. See, I met them at the door and escorted them here, and I was the only one to wait on them."

Josie nodded. "And after they ate?"

"After dinner—," color rose in Daniel's clean-shaven cheeks, "—they, ah, *lingered* for a few hours, if you know what I mean."

Josie blush darkened. "I see. And after that?"

The waiter swallowed, his Adam's apple bobbing beneath his high celluloid collar. "I just left the mess for the breakfast crew to clean up like I usually do."

Josie cleared her throat. "So you didn't actually see them leave?"

The waiter shook his head.

Drew stood and walked to stand beside her, careful to turn his face into the light thrown by the gas wall-sconce. "And me, Daniel. Have you ever seen me before?"

The young man's gaze traveled up to Drew's face, and then he grinned. "No, sir. I would've remembered you." He set the photo on the white tablecloth. "Sorry I couldn't be of more help. I'd better get back to work now."

Josie handed the young man a silver half-dollar. "Thank you, Daniel. You've been most obliging."

Murmuring his thanks, the young man gave a short bow and departed, closing the door softly behind him.

Drew paced the length of the table and seated himself across from her once more. "So, do you still think I might be the murderer?"

Josie looked up from the photograph, her eyes wide. "No, that is— " Her frown made her pixie face even more endearing. "But how do you know so much? Did you witness the murder?"

Suddenly weary, he shook his head. "I never saw her until she crossed over to the other side."

Skepticism lifted the smooth arch of one of Josie's dark eyebrows.

The last ounce of joy drained out of his evening. "I know you don't believe that her spirit came to me, that she's here in the room with us now."

Josie gazed around the room, then gave a deli-

cate shudder and crossed her arms over her
bosom. "No, I'm afraid I don't."

Drew held out his hands, palms up in a gesture
of submission. "And why should you believe me?
If I were you, I wouldn't believe me either. But
I see that I shall have to give you proof. Would
you like that?"

Josie hesitated, fear and doubt written on her
lovely face. "Yes, please." It was the voice of a
young girl accepting another helping of liver and
spinach.

Filled with deep sorrow, Drew bade his lovely
companion a silent *adieu* before he leaned back
and let his eyes unfocus. *After a moment, the spirit
of a handsome red-haired woman appeared before him,
some years older than Josie, but very like her. She held
out a small purple flower to him.* "Your mother's
name was Violette."

Josie gasped. "But you could have found that
out any number of ways."

He didn't answer, but concentrated on the
spirit's message instead. *A calendar appeared with
a date circled in heavy black.* "She passed over on
April 3, 1895." *The spirit levitated to horizontal, pil-
lowing her head on her hands.* "On her deathbed—"
*A strong sensation of father energy came to him, fol-
lowed by a floating question mark, and then the familiar face of a famous author, once a habitué of San
Francisco, and a set of initials.*

Shocked, Drew sat forward, focusing his eyes
on Josie's blanched face. "Is it true— he was your
father? No wonder you want to be a writer!"

Josie's eyes widened and her mouth dropped

open. "My God! The dead really do speak to you! It can't be so, but it must be! My mother swore to me on her deathbed that she never told another soul, not even—my father!" She leaned across the table, grasping his hand. "What else does she say?"

Well, she wasn't too frightened yet, at any rate. He relaxed his gaze. *The famous writer now stood beside Violette, holding up their hands to show matching wedding rings.* "Your father and mother are together on the other side." *A white rose and a quill pen appeared on the table in front of Josie.* "He says he is proud of your writing." *As his vision dimmed to red and the spirits dissolved before him, he heard a choked sob.*

Surprised by the warning from the spirits to stop the reading, and filled with compassion for Josie's pain, he let his eyes refocus and hurried to her side.

She had risen and moved to the window, staring out at the moonlight as tears slid down her cheeks.

His heart pounding with dread but unable to resist trying to comfort her, Drew rested his hands on her quaking shoulders. But instead of shaking off his hateful touch, she turned toward him, stepping into the circle of his arms and pressing her face against his chest.

Unwilling yet to believe, or even to hope, he ignored the scintillating sensation of her body pressing against his as he smoothed the palm of his hand up and down the middle of her back as if she were a frightened child.

After a few moments, she sniffed, then wiped her eyes on her handkerchief and tipped her lovely face up to his. "Oh, Mr. Jordan—"

"Drew, please."

A ghost of a smile played over her lips. "Drew, then, and you must call me Josie."

He nodded, unable to speak for the gratitude that welled up, threatening to overwhelm him. She knew, she *believed* in his unasked-for power, but she didn't seem the least bit repelled, or even frightened.

She dropped her gaze. "I apologize for going off like that. I'm really not much given to tears." Once again, she lifted eyes of purest robin's-egg blue for a moment, then hid them by leaning her forehead against his black brocade waistcoat. "It's just—oh, Drew, to know his love, now, after he's gone. I never thought to have that. Thank you."

He lifted his hands to wipe the tears from her cheeks, awed by the silken magic of her skin beneath his thumbs. "You're more than welcome, Josie." He breathed out her name on a whisper.

She tipped her face up to his, and her dark lashes fluttered down.

What could he do but kiss her? Schooling himself to restraint, he bent and tasted her lips.

With a sigh, she leaned into his embrace. Her hands slid up to twine about his neck, pressing her soft bosom against his chest.

He longed to plunder her mouth, bruise its delicacy with all the ardor in his being. But he knew from the innocent willingness of her response that she had never been kissed before, and he would not betray her newfound trust for anything.

With gentle hands he set her away from him and smiled down into her tear-stained face. "And now, young lady, I think it's time I saw you home."

Four

Josie didn't like Mr. Liam O'Sullivan, but she was trying her hardest not to show it. "It's so good of you to make time in your busy schedule to see me." First, she couldn't get away from the city room until late afternoon, and then the victim's lawyer had kept her waiting for more than an hour in his outer office. She hadn't even been able to enjoy indulging in pleasant thoughts of Drew because of the intimidating presence of the man's secretary.

Now, if one was to judge from the near-empty bottle on his monolithic oak desk and the reek in the air, the lawyer had been sitting here quite alone the whole time, drinking a good deal of Irish whiskey and smoking a particularly disgusting cigar.

The man half-rose and gestured toward an armchair across from him before sinking back down onto his cane-backed oak swivel chair. She noted with satisfaction that this "Irish fella" was of medium height and build, with thinning hair and a drooping mustache the color of rust. He cleared his throat and spoke with drunken precision. "What can I do for you, missy?"

Josie controlled her desire to bash the man over the head for his pompous rudeness. "I'm a reporter from the *Examiner*, Mr. O'Sullivan, and I'm writing an article about the late Mrs. Seamus Kelly. I believe she was one of your clients?"

Eyes the color of granite surveyed her. "Not exactly. Her husband, God rest his soul, kept me on retainer before his death."

Josie forced herself to smile. "Of course, but I understood that Mr. Kelly named you executor of his will?"

The man rubbed his red-tipped nose and gave a ponderous nod. "That is true."

After a few more leading questions, she decided there was no point pussy-footing around with this one. He didn't seem about to volunteer any information, drunk or not. "Is it true that the two of you never got along?

The man's cold eyes narrowed. "What is this about? What kind of article are you writing, anyhow?"

"I have it on good authority, Mr. O'Sullivan, that Mrs. Kelly was upset the day of her death, and that it had something to do with you and the estate."

Color drained from the man's face. "I don't have to answer that, you know. Client-lawyer privilege. But off the record, I'll tell you it wasn't me that upset her. It was her son."

Josie frowned. Mrs. Kelly had been very young, and Miss Quinn hadn't mentioned any children.

Come to think of it, neither had Cecile. She wished she'd had time to do a background check. "What son?"

The man's face relaxed into a smug grin. "Didn't know about that, did you? Not her son, really. Stepson, old Seamus's boy by his first wife. Tim. Same age as his stepmama. Kept complaining about her spending too much of his dead papa's money. Of course, he inherits it all, now."

Another Irishman, and one who benefitted greatly by the widow's death. She wondered if he fit the waiter's description as well. "And how might I locate this young Mr. Kelly?"

The gray eyes narrowed. "If I don't tell you, you'll just find out some other way, I suppose?"

Josie nodded. "More than likely, sir."

"Hmmph. Well, you didn't get it from me, understand?" He scratched a few words on a slip of paper. "Here you go, and good luck. You'll need it. The fellow's a hothead."

Josie rose and bade him farewell, eager to get away, but stopped at the door and turned back. "Just one more thing, Mr. O'Sullivan. Is it possible that you and Mrs. Kelly were something more to one another than business associates?"

The lawyer gave a sudden bark of laughter. "Me, with Mary Francis Kelly? You saw the dragon at the desk outside? Well, that's my wife, and she keeps me on a very short leash. Besides, I wasn't the young widow's type. Not enough of a challenge, if you know what I mean."

She didn't, but neither did she care to listen to O'Sullivan's drunken, and quite probably tasteless, explanation. "I see. Well, good day to you." She didn't wait for an answer, but hurried out, shutting the door. The man's bitter laughter followed her.

Without a word to the secretary-wife, Josie fled down the stairs and out into the street. She stopped to catch her breath. It had grown quite dark, and the neighborhood south of Market wasn't the safest place for a woman to walk alone even in broad daylight. But as there was no help for it, she set off at a determined pace, hoping young Mr. Kelly would be at home this evening.

The area "south of the slot" was nearly deserted as she headed north toward the cable car turn-around at Market and Powell. Light and noise spilled from the front of a tavern, and a drooping horse hauled a rickety wagon over the cobbled streets.

The first time she heard footsteps behind her, she thought Mr. O'Sullivan had changed his mind about giving her his client's address, but dismissed it as an overactive imagination when she looked and no one was there. The second time she put it down to water dripping from a rain gutter. But the third time, she shivered and the hair on the back of her neck rose. Certain she was being pursued, she increased her pace until she was almost running when she reached Market Street.

Josie burst from the side street only to find herself in the midst of a procession of fashionably dressed women parading up and down the sidewalks. The city's demi-monde nightly trod the so-called Ambrosial Path, displaying their wares to the businessmen who made their way along the Cocktail Route each evening.

Eager to get away from the women of easy virtue, she fought the tide until she reached the corner, hesitating for a moment under a gas streetlamp. Across the way, the conductor and brakeman released the mechanism that held the wooden turntable in place and began to push the empty car in a circle so it would point up the hill again. Josie glanced to the right and left, then seeing a break in the traffic, lifted her skirts and darted into the street.

The sound of nearby hoofbeats startled her, and she turned and looked up as the carriage bore down on her, its driver's face swathed with a dark scarf as he applied the whip to the horses' backs. She stopped, frozen with fear.

At the last moment, strong hands grabbed her upper arms and pulled her out of the horses' path. The carriage swept by, the wind of its passage stealing her breath as the vehicle careened around the corner and disappeared from sight.

"Are you all right?" The voice, like the hands, was strong and warm.

"I think so." Quaking, Josie turned to thank her rescuer and found herself staring up into a handsome and familiar face. "Drew, what are you doing here?"

Heavy eyebrows rose, and his sensuous mouth twitched into a grin. "You're quite welcome."

Josie's face heated as she realized how ungrateful and unwelcoming her words had sounded, especially since she was very glad to see him. "I'm sorry. I was just so surprised. Thank you. I believe you've saved my life."

Another carriage sped by, its driver cursing in Italian and shaking his fist. A vertical line appeared over the bridge of his straight nose. "Perhaps we should continue our conversation somewhere less busy."

He led her across the wide street, then stopped under another streetlamp. "I'm here because the spirit kept showing me this intersection and a broken carriage wheel. She wouldn't let me alone until I came down here. I've been standing here for fifteen minutes."

The oddity of his answer made Josie smile, despite the circumstances. "I guess I owe her my thanks as well." Her face sobered. "So you weren't the one following me?"

Drew's handsome face hardened into a mask. "Now let me get this straight. First you heard someone following you, and then you were almost run down by a carriage. Has it occurred to you that maybe someone doesn't want you asking questions about this murder?"

The idea had crossed her mind, but his authoritative tone goaded her into disagreeing. "Nonsense. No one even knows it *was* a murder."

"Except the murderer." His tone was deadly serious.

Fueled by fear, anger flared through her. "You're just trying to scare me!"

"No, I just couldn't bear it if anything happened to you." This time his words were a tender caress.

Her heart was pounding in her chest again, but not from fear. "Don't worry, nothing bad will happen to me." She tried for a nonchalant shrug. "It's just a coincidence. The driver didn't see me, and I probably just imagined I was being followed. After all, that isn't the safest place to walk after dark." She gestured toward the south.

Drew paused, his eyes narrowing. "Just what *were* you doing down there?"

"Interviewing the victim's lawyer." She glanced at her watch. "And now, if you'll excuse me, I have to go see her stepson."

"Fine. I'll go with you." It was a statement, not a question.

She should be angry at his presumption, but what she really felt was pleasure at his concern. Still, she didn't wish to appear too easily persuaded. "Thank you, but that's not necessary."

His expression softened again. "I don't intend to accept no for an answer. I'm not taking any more chances with your safety tonight." He held up his hand to silence her protest. "Don't worry, I'll wait for you outside. Now where does this stepson live?"

Relieved and excited, she read him the address O'Sullivan had given her.

Drew whistled. "Pacific Heights. Very fashionable."

"Very expensive, you mean." She smiled up at him.

"Same thing." Offering her his right arm, he gestured with the other toward the cable car. "Shall we?"

Joy flooded through her as her fingers touched the solid warmth of his forearm. She knew he would keep her from physical harm tonight, but who would protect her poor vulnerable heart?

Josie followed the Chinese houseboy up the final flight of stairs and paused in the foyer to catch her breath. She wondered why anyone would choose to live in the top two floors of a five-story townhouse complex. The silent houseboy led her through an archway into the front parlor, then bowed and hurried away again.

As her heartbeat returned to normal, Josie wandered into the crowded sitting room, admiring the rich upholstery, the jewel-colored Oriental rugs, and the ornate gilt frame surrounding a good copy of Rosa Bonheur's *Horse Fair*. Drawn by the lushness of the velvet drapes, she approached the bay window and stood spellbound by the panorama spread before her.

The light of a full moon drenched the houses stair-stepping down the hillside to the waters of the bay. Far to her left, Fort Point brooded over the Golden Gate, while on the right lay the harbor, where schooners bobbed at anchor, their masts and rigging silvered by moonlight. She had never seen San Francisco more beautiful.

Now she understood. It was worth climbing all those stairs be able to look out and see this every day. With a sudden pang of envy, she wondered how the view would appear on a sunny morning or in the fog.

Tipping her face down, she caught a dizzying glimpse of the street, and Drew standing at his ease on the corner beneath a streetlamp. Her lips trembled into a smile as she recalled his offer to wait below so she could conduct the interview alone. She felt safer knowing he was there, but grateful that he wouldn't intimidate her subject with his inexplicable presence, and especially pleased that she hadn't needed to ask.

Just then he looked up and lifted his hand in greeting. She waved in return, anticipation warming her. If she made short work of this interview, she could spend the rest of the evening with Drew.

A step sounded behind her on the wooden parquet floor, and she dropped her hand, turning to face her host.

"Lovely view, isn't it?" Mr. Timothy Kelly gave her a correct half-bow.

She nodded, noting the brick-red hair framing his handsome face, and the way his expensive but tasteful evening wear showed off his medium height and build to advantage.

"Forgive me, but as you can see I was just on my way out. My houseboy gave me your card. What can I do for you, Miss LeClair?"

She knew reporters needed to grow thick hides, but the man's tone was almost rude. Clenching her fists, Josie kept her face and voice businesslike. "Then I'll come right to the point, Mr. Kelly. It's about your stepmother, Mr. Kelly."

His handsome young face hardened. "Please, go on."

"I'm writing an article about her life. Her lawyer told me you were unhappy lately with her spending habits."

He blinked. "It's true that I was intending to speak with her about her recent extravagant donations to the Catholic Church. But she died before I could say anything to her."

Josie nodded. "I see. Mr. O'Sullivan also seemed to think there was bad blood between you and Mrs. Kelly, and he did point out that you inherit your father's entire estate now that she's gone."

His lips twisted into a bitter smile. "He said that, did he?"

She nodded again, suddenly almost sorry for his unhappiness.

"It's true. I do inherit. But I never wished her any harm. That's what this is all about, isn't it? You don't think her death was an accident, do you?"

Josie swallowed her surprise at becoming the questioned rather than the questioner. Mr. Kelly was nothing if not acute. But she didn't hesitate to turn the tables on him once more. "What do *you* think, Mr. Kelly?"

He looked her in the face, his face and voice earnest. "I think you should go talk to Father Brian Riordan at St. Andrews. He's not only the recipient of those donations I mentioned. He was also her Father Confessor." He paused, then cleared his throat. "And now, if you'll excuse me?"

Five

Humming the tune to "I'll Take You Home Again, Kathleen," Josie strode through the hallway leading to the city room, her spirits still bouyed by the previous evening. After her brief interview with Tim Kelly, Drew had seen her home, and they had lingered together on the stoop in the warm spring air, talking of everything and nothing until quite late.

Small wonder if today all seemed right with the world. She didn't even mind working on St. Paddy's Day, when the rest of the city was either home preparing for a picnic dinner at one of the parks, watching a parade, or marching in one. In San Francisco, everyone was Irish on March 17. She was a reporter, with a paper to put out. Besides, Drew was coming by at five to drive her to St. Andrew's Church.

Her humming was drowned out by the rattling of typewriter keys as she stopped inside the doorway of the city room to let her eyes adjust to the negligible illumination coming from the dusty skylights. The air in the long windowless room was stale with old tobacco smoke, sweat, and ink, but she didn't mind. Kicking through the drifts of discarded copy paper, she made her way down one side of the room, past a line of desks facing the grimy walls, as she looked for an empty seat to commandeer for the day.

Dropping her handbag onto a scarred desktop, Josie reached up to pull the pin from her straw boater. As she set the hat beside her bag, a boyish voice called her name. She turned and smiled at Bob, the other cub reporter.

"The old man's looking for you, Josie." Bob's beaming smile did nothing to ease her anxiety.

"Thanks." She straightened her shirtwaist and brushed at her skirt, then strode toward the editor's closed door, trying to compose her thoughts.

But Bob made it impossible for her to think by trailing along. "Now when you get inside, don't volunteer anything. Wait for him to ask, then give the shortest answer possible. And whatever you do, don't lie. If you made a mistake, 'fess up and take your lumps like a man."

Facing him, she allowed herself a sour smile. "Gee, thanks, Bob."

He grinned happily after her as she knocked and was summoned inside.

After closing the door behind her, Josie stood straight, her chin lifted and her hands clasped in front of her, hoping she looked more serene than she felt. Her mind was churning, wondering what she could have done— misspelled some society matron's name, mixed up the time of a charity ball, forgotten to mention a key member of some committee?

Mr. Elder gestured her to a seat and stared at her from beneath shaggy brows until she squirmed inside. At last he spoke. "LeClair, this morning I got a telephone call from someone complaining that you've been nosing around, asking questions about Mary Frances Kelly's death. Is it true?"

She bit her tongue to keep from asking the caller's name. "Yessir."

"Hhrmph. And you have reason to believe her death is worth investigating?" His gaze never left her face.

She struggled to keep her voice calm. "Yessir."

"I don't suppose you'd care to share that reason with me, would you?"

Josie swallowed. "No sir."

Mr. Elder's drooping mustache twitched, and she was startled to realize that he was smiling at her, something she couldn't remember ever seeing him do before. "Good for you. If they're squawking, you must be onto something. And don't let me ever catch you revealing your sources or letting somebody scare you off a story, even if that somebody is me. Got that?"

Her relief was so intense she wondered if she might faint. "Yessir. Thank you, sir."

He smoothed his mustache with thumb and forefinger. "Now, how's the spiritualist exposé coming?"

She thought of Drew, of how exposing his colleagues as charlatans might hurt him, even

though his powers were real. And if she wrote
the truth about him, that could serve as a challenge to others to try to expose him. Either way,
he could be hurt. She chose her words carefully.
"I'm not sure, sir. It may not pan out."

Mr. Elder shrugged. "Happens to everybody
sometimes. Don't worry about it. Now get back
out there and get to work on this woman's death.
Is that clear?"

Josie rose, relief lifting her spirits once more.
"Yes, sir!"

Josie turned on the curb in front of the rectory
and smiled up at Drew. "Are you sure you don't
want to come in with me?"

Returning her smile, he shook his head. "No,
thank you. I'd just make the poor priest uncomfortable."

Although she knew it was true, and that Drew
would also be more comfortable waiting in the
rented carriage, she persisted. "But you might be
able to help. The spirit might tell you something
useful."

His blue eyes twinkled down at her. "I haven't
seen her yet today."

Josie was intrigued. "Can't you call her or
something?" She was sure that's what other spiritualists claimed to do.

His smile broadened into a grin. "It doesn't
work that way. I'm a channel for them. *They* come
to *me*."

"Oh." She'd never thought what it might be

like for him before, seeing ghosts all the time. "But can't you shut them out?"

He shook his head.

Heat rose in her cheeks. "Not even when we—when you— I mean— "

"When I kissed you the other night?" He went on, not waiting for her embarrassed nod. "Most of the time they're sensitive to my need for privacy unless it's very, very important."

"I see." She gave herself a mental shake. Why should it embarrass her to have the ghosts of her parents present when she was being kissed, especially since she couldn't see them? "Well, then, if you're sure you won't join me— "

Reaching down, he clasped her hand and lifted it to his mouth. His lips brushed across her tender skin, sending shockwaves of pleasure up her arm and through her body. His gaze sought hers, piercing to the very core of her being. "I'm sure. Take your time. I'll be waiting."

Unable to think of a response, Josie turned and headed up the walk, her cheeks on fire and her thoughts whirling. She only hoped she'd be able to keep her mind on the interview.

She knocked at the door of the small stone cottage attached to the church and waited, wondering if the good father might not be out celebrating with his countrymen and the rest of San Francisco.

At last, footsteps approached from inside, and the door opened. A man wearing a black suit and shirt with a white clerical collar stood in the open doorway. Graying auburn curls topped his rugged face. "Yes?"

"Father Riordan?" She tried to mask her surprise. Somehow she'd expected a housekeeper to answer the door.

"That I am." The skin at the corners of his warm hazel eyes wrinkled as he smiled at her. "And you are?"

An answering smile tugged at her mouth. "Josephine LeClair, a reporter from the *Examiner.*"

"Ah, well. Can't keep the press waiting on the stoop." He stood aside and gestured for her to enter. "Come along, then." He shut the door behind her, then preceded her down a narrow hallway and ushered her into a cozy parlor. "Won't you have a chair? I must apologize for not being able to offer you any refreshment, but I gave my housekeeper the day off to enjoy the festivities."

Josie settled on a worn armchair and murmured a polite response.

He sat across from her and rested his hands on his knees. "Now, how may I help you, my child?"

Josie hesitated. It would be hard enough for her to lie to any priest, but especially one as nice as this. "Father, I'm working on a story that's of a confidential nature. Even though this is not the confessional, may I count on you to keep that confidence?"

He lifted a wiry eyebrow, but he nodded. "Of course, if you wish it."

"I do. Thank you." Relieved, Josie leaned back.

"I'm investigating the death of Mrs. Mary Frances Kelly. I understand you were her father confessor."

Pain flitted across his rugged features. "And her close friend, yes."

Josie silently cursed her blunt tongue, hoping it wouldn't spoil the interview. She never had learned to build up to something gradually. "I'm sorry for your grief, Father, but it's really very important that I ask you some questions."

He nodded, suddenly looking much older than he had at first glance. "I'll be happy to help if I can, but you understand that I can't tell you anything she may have said to me during confession?"

Josie had been expecting that. "I understand. Father, can you tell me if Mrs. Kelly was romantically involved with anyone?"

His ruddy face paled, but he shook his head. "I'm sorry, I can't."

She wasn't surprised by this answer either. "Do you know of any reason why someone would want to harm her?"

He shook his head again. "Not that I can think of."

She ignored a stab of disappointment. It had been a long shot. "Did you happen to see her last Thursday?"

He tilted his head to one side. "Why, yes. She came to the rectory that afternoon. She'd just been to see her lawyer, and she seemed upset about something."

At last. Paydirt! "Was it about her husband's estate?"

His brow furrowed, then he gave a short nod. "Yes, I believe she did say something about that, now that you mention it."

She leaned forward, striving to keep the excitement from her voice. "Father, did you know that her stepson didn't approve of the donations she gave the church?"

His eyebrows shot up. "Tim? But the Kelly family has paid the same tithe to this church since it was consecrated. They helped build it. Why would he object now?"

Josie frowned. "Tithe? No, Father, I was talking about the large donations Mrs. Kelly made recently. *Extravagant* was the word her stepson used, I believe."

The priest shook his head, then shrugged, lifting his hands and turning them palm up. "I'm sorry, Miss LeClair. I really don't know what you're talking about."

"But Mr. Kelly said—" She bit her lip to keep from saying any more.

The priest turned his warm, sympathetic gaze on her. "Perhaps he was misinformed?"

"Yes, perhaps." *Or he had lied to her. But why?* Josie rose and offered her hand. "Thank you, Father. I won't take up any more of your time."

He stood and clasped her hand in a firm, warm handshake, then turned to lead her through the hallway. He opened the door and turned to her, smiling. "I'm sorry I wasn't able to tell you more."

Josie stopped on the stoop and turned, tipping her head to one side. "On the contrary, Father. You've been most helpful." It was true, even if he had raised more questions than he answered.

She strode with purposeful steps toward the waiting carriage and Drew. One thing was very clear to her now: Someone was lying. And Josie intended to find out who.

Six

After the long climb from Union Street, Josie stopped to catch her breath at the corner of Laguna and Pacific, turning to stare at Tim Kelly's fashionable townhouse. If anything, it was even more impressive in the late afternoon sunlight.

As Josie crossed to the uphill side of Pacific, she couldn't help but wonder what her reception might be. After all, the man had been far from cordial the first time, and he could be the person who called to complain to her editor. He could even be the murderer.

But before she could be sure who killed Mrs. Kelly, she had to get to the bottom of these lies about the donations to the church. She only hoped Mr. Kelly was still at home at this hour. Her plan was to arrive much earlier, but Mr. Elder had kept her busy proofing stories all day about the many fires and fistfights the day before.

She reached the corner and turned toward Mr. Kelly's building just as a hired carriage passed her and pulled up in front of the townhouse. She quickened her pace, reaching the front gate just as the man himself stepped through and onto the sidewalk.

He frowned down at her. "Miss LeClair, I wasn't expecting you." Nor did he sound pleased to see her.

Josie forced herself to smile. "I know. I'm sorry to just drop by this way, but I hope you'll forgive me when you hear what I have to say."

Mr. Kelly's frown deepened as he glanced from her to the carriage. "In that case, would you care to come inside?"

The thought of climbing all those stairs so soon after trudging up the hill overwhelmed her. "No, thank you. That's very kind, but I can't stay that long."

He glanced again at the carriage driver, then touched her elbow to steer her a few feet down the walk, out of earshot. He looked down at her, a hint of a smile hovering around his mouth. "Then, Miss LeClair, I beg you— speak!"

Josie took a deep calming breath. "Very well. I took your advice and went to see Father Riordan. I asked him about the donations. He said Mrs. Kelly never donated anything beyond the usual tithing."

His green eyes widened, then narrowed. "But if she didn't give the money to the church, what happened to it?" Either the man was an accomplished liar, or he was truly surprised.

Josie hoped it was the latter. She rather liked young Mr. Kelly. She gave him a conspiratorial smile. "That's the question I plan to ask Mr. O'Sullivan."

Mr. Kelly's young face hardened. "I'd be interested to hear his answer myself. I was just on my way to supper, but I think the young lady will understand if I'm late."

Josie wondered briefly who the lucky girl might be.

"I believe I'll just stop by Mr. O'Sullivan's office on my way." He gave her a grim smile that boded ill for his lawyer. "Would you care to accompany me?"

"I'd be delighted." Gratitude surged through her as he handed her into the waiting carriage and she settled back on the worn leather seat. She'd been dreading another solitary walk through Mr. O'Sullivan's neighborhood.

As he gave the address to the driver, she studied Tim Kelly's profile, wondering why he had offered to take her along. He could've been and gone by the time she got there, and she'd never know what transpired between them. He certainly didn't act like a man with something to hide.

No, despite his strong motive, the more she thought about it, the less Mr. Tim Kelly looked like a murderer to her. But then, who did that leave?

Drew glanced up at the sign over his head once more. "Liam O'Sullivan, Attorney at Law." A group of dockworkers passed, open suspicion written on the hard faces. He'd never liked the area south of Market Street, and he felt even less comfortable in his good suit, just standing around.

As a hired carriage pulled up to the curb, Drew looked around for the spirit to see if those arriving had anything to do with their reason for this trip. When he realized she was gone, he stifled a twinge of resentment. The spirits always seemed capricious, but this one more than most. In fact, he wasn't at all sure he would've cared for Mrs. Kelly when she was alive.

With a sigh, Drew stepped away from the side of the dingy building as a handsome and expensively dressed red-haired man alit from the vehicle and turned to help a young woman to the sidewalk. At the sight of her nutmeg-colored hair, jealousy stabbed through him. He knew his reaction was absurd. He had no claim on her. But it was all he could do not to wrest her from the young man's hands. "Josie!"

He felt somewhat mollified when she turned toward him and her face lit with pleasure as she hurried toward him. "Drew! What are you doing here?"

"*Our friend* kept showing me this address and scenes of a battle until I came down here. Why are you here?" He tried, and failed, to keep the accusation from his voice.

She didn't seem to notice anything amiss as she explained her mission. She turned to her companion and introduced him.

Drew couldn't bring himself to offer the man his hand, so he gave him a curt nod. "Kelly."

The young man returned his greeting in kind. "Jordan." He turned to Josie. "Miss LeClair, shall we?" He gestured toward the stairway.

Drew's hackles rose at Kelly's proprietary air.

But Josie quickly set the younger man straight. "Mr. Jordan is my colleague. I must insist that he accompany me." She linked arms with Drew.

One of Kelly's fine arched brows lifted. "Very well." He turned and led the way up the narrow stairs.

Josie clung to the solid warmth of Drew's arm, surprised as much by her own reaction as by his unexpected presence. But she was even more surprised to reach the top of the stairs and see Tim Kelly kissing the cheek of the now smiling Mrs. O'Sullivan.

"You're looking well, Nora." Mr. Kelly's voice held a warmth and charm Josie hadn't expected to hear.

The lawyer's wife giggled. "Ah, go on with you, Tim."

Josie noted that these two were on a first-name basis as Mr. Kelly turned. "Nora, these are my friends. You remember Miss LeClair?"

Doubt flickered in the depths of the woman's blue eyes, but she nodded.

"And her colleague, Mr. Jordan." Mr. Kelly's smile seemed a bit forced, but she didn't have time to figure out why right now.

The woman looked up at Drew, blinked in confusion, then turned back to a more familiar face. "Now, Tim, just what brings you here today, you young scalawag?"

Mr. Kelly's eyes danced as he tipped his head in the direction of the inner office. "Is he in?" At her smiling nod, he went on. "Think he can spare a minute to see us?"

"Of course!" She opened the door and stuck her head inside, her voice echoing out behind her. "Liam, it's Tim Kelly and some of his friends." Without waiting for a reply, she held the door open. "Go on in."

Eyes fixed on the man who was now undoubtedly his most wealthy client, Liam O'Sullivan stood behind his desk, smiling and pumping Mr. Kelly's hand up and down. "Tim!"

Josie hardly recognized the hearty voice.

Then Mr. O'Sullivan caught sight of her and sank back down onto his chair. "You! Say, what's this all about, anyway?"

Mr. Kelly gestured for Josie to take a seat across from the lawyer. "Miss LeClair has a question for you."

Palms sweating, Josie cleared her throat. "Mr. Kelly told me his stepmother had made extravagant donations to St. Andrew's Church, but Father Riordan never received them." She leaned forward. "So what happened to that money, Mr. O'Sullivan?"

The man's smoke-gray eyes shifted from side to side, his expression reminding Josie of a trapped animal. At last he sagged in his chair, a look of resignation on his face. "All right, I took it! Mrs. Kelly found out somehow. She came by last Thursday and told me off, then said she'd be back the next day to settle my hash. Those were her very words." He slumped forward, leaning his forearms against the wide desktop. "I waited all day Friday and Saturday for her. And then I saw in the newspaper that she drowned, and I thought maybe I'd be all right after all. I just needed a little time to pay back what I'd borrowed. I— I'm sorry, Tim, really I am."

Mr. Kelly's ruddy cheeks darkened as he rested the heels of his hands on the desktop, towering over the lawyer. "Just how much of a fool do you think I am, O'Sullivan?" His voice shook with rage. "If I know my stepmother, she threatened to fire you, expose you to the world as an embezzler, and send you to prison, and you expect me to believe you were content to do nothing but *wait?*" He swung his head back and forth in menacing negation. "I don't think so. I think you killed her."

Josie held her breath.

Mr. O'Sullivan's eyes bulged out. "Killed her? But I heard— the papers said she drowned!"

Mr. Kelly gave an ugly laugh. "It wasn't common knowledge, but my stepmother was a very strong swimmer. I don't know how you made it look like an accident, but I do know you had every reason to want her dead."

Mr. O'Sullivan's chin came up, and a vicious gleam lit his gray eyes. "Me? What about your reason for wanting her dead?" He turned to Josie. "He was in love with her. Took her home to introduce her to his father. It didn't take her long to give him the mitten. She had a bigger fish to fry— his father! She broke his heart and drove a wedge between him and his father that lasted until the day Seamus died." He turned back to his client. "If I had reason to want her dead, you had more. Revenge, and complete control of your father's estate."

The two men glared at one another.

Josie cleared her throat. "Mr. Kelly, is what he says true?"

The young heir straightened and turned to her, his face a mask of pain, then gave a little shrug. "Some of it. But I never wanted revenge. I could never hurt her. No matter what she did, I still loved her."

Drew stepped forward and took Josie's hand, tugging her to her feet. "Thank you, gentlemen. This has been most enlightening. And now Miss LeClair and I will leave you two alone. Obviously, you have things to work out between you."

Mr. Kelly favored Drew with a dim smile. "Thanks, Jordan." The two shook hands, and then the younger man turned to Josie. "Miss Le-Clair, I know I have no right, but I'd like to ask you to keep what you heard out of the newspapers. This kind of scandal won't help anyone, and I'd rather not get the law involved." He sent a chilling look at the lawyer, who seemed to crumple in on himself a bit more. "I'll take care of Mr. O'Sullivan in my own way."

For a long moment, Josie's news-sense warred with her sense of decency, but decency won. "Yes, all right, unless I uncover more evidence that points to one of you as a murderer, and then I'll tell everything to the police."

"Thank you." Mr. Kelly smiled at her and held open the door to let them pass. As Josie followed Drew down the dark stairs, she heard Mr. Kelly's voice raised once more. "Nora, would you come in here, please?"

Josie shuddered. She wouldn't want to be in O'Sullivan's shoes right now, although he richly deserved whatever he got. When she stepped onto the sidewalk, Drew captured her hand and tucked it between his arm and his side as he turned and led her north through the falling gloom, toward Market Street.

After a few moments of silence, she stopped him, gazing up into his shadowed eyes. "So what do you think?"

Drew shook his head. "The spirit says both men are telling the truth."

Josie frowned. "But if neither of them killed her, I have no idea who did. What do I do now?"

In the dim light, she thought he smiled. "I suggest you agree to have supper with me tomorrow night in honor of your twenty-first birthday."

Josie gasped. "But how did you know?"

He chuckled—a dark, rich, seductive sound. "A little bird told me." He turned and began walking again.

Josie couldn't help but smile as she matched his stride. "And did this little bird suggest a good restaurant as well?"

"I thought we might go back to the Cliff House."

She hoped the darkness would hide the color burning her cheeks as she remembered the last supper they shared at the Cliff House, and the kiss that followed. She tried to keep her voice cool and businesslike. "That's a good idea. There's always the chance we'll learn something more."

He chuckled again. "One can only hope."

Somehow, she didn't think he was referring to the murder.

Seven

Thursday, March 19

Leaning back in the comfortable chair, Drew schooled himself to patience as Josie questioned the waiter once more. It wasn't exactly his idea of a romantic interlude, at least not yet. But he could afford to wait. And if interviewing Daniel gave her an excuse to be alone with him here, so much the better.

Besides, she might get a new lead, and Drew wanted this murder solved for his own selfish reasons. Most important, of course, was his desire to keep Josie safe. He feared that even if she dropped her investigation now, her life might still be in danger. The only true protection would come from seeing the murderer behind bars. And for his own peace of mind, he couldn't wait to be shed of this particular spirit's almost constant presence.

The spirit wrinkled her nose at him and floated across the room to hover near Daniel.

Oblivious to the ghostly presence, the waiter furrowed his brow. "I wish I could be more help, miss. But I wait on so many people here."

Josie leaned forward, her piquant face shining with a vibrant sincerity. "I understand. But think, Daniel, did he remind you of anyone?"

The waiter stroked his chin with thumb and forefinger as if smoothing an invisible beard. "Maybe." He shook his head and shrugged. "I can't think who, though."

Josie's sigh carried across the room, making Drew long to wring the skinny kid's neck until he *did* remember. She handed the waiter her card. "If you do think of anything—anything at all—will you come see me at once?"

With a grin and another shrug, Daniel slipped the card in the pocket of his waistcoat. "Sure thing, Miss LeClair. I'll be back soon with your supper." He left, closing the door behind him.

Josie sighed again, then stood and stretched her bare arms over her head.

At the sight of her breasts pressing against the low neckline of her pink silk taffeta evening gown, something tightened in Drew's groin.

She turned to face him, letting her fists rest on either side of her narrow waist. "Well, there's only one more person to question."

He stretched his legs out and laced his fingers together over his flat belly. "Really, who's that?"

She strode toward him, her skirt swaying from side to side with each step. "The victim." She settled into a chair opposite him. "Is she here?"

He nodded, wondering if the dead woman would cooperate.

The spirit moved to hover between his chair and Josie's, her smile beatific.

Josie's blue-green eyes shifted around the room. "Where?"

He gestured to the spirit's current location.

She turned toward the area he indicated. "Will you answer my questions?" She spoke to a spot above the spirit's head.

Giggling, the spirit moved to intercept Josie's gaze and nodded.

Less than comfortable in the role of translator, Drew sought to keep his voice colorless. "She agrees." If this experiment didn't go well, he wouldn't want the failure to taint Josie's feelings for him as a man. Assuming she had any.

Josie smiled. "Thank you. Do you know who poisoned you?"

The spirit shook her head, her pale blonde curls swinging.

"She says she doesn't."

"I'm not sure what else to ask." Josie's brows drew together in thought. "Are you sure neither your stepson or your lawyer could have done it?"

A smile wreathed the lovely ethereal face as she nodded.

Drew fought to keep from groaning in frustration and anxiety. They were getting nowhere. "She's sure."

Josie tipped her head to one side. "What about the man you had dinner with?"

The spirit held out her delicate hand, a clerical collar dangling from her fingers.

Drew sighed. "She says to ask the priest.

Josie's small hands closed into fists. "I already did. He won't tell me, and if he did, I'm not sure it would prove anything." Her eyes unfocused, and she tapped her forefinger against her lower lip, in deep thought. "Did you have *relations* with your dinner partner here that night?"

The spirit giggled and tilted her head to one side with calculated coyness, then nodded.

Drew cleared his throat, surprised but not scandalized, either by the question or the answer. "She says she did."

Josie gave a sharp nod. "And could he have poisoned you?"

With a look of great sadness, the spirit shrugged and faded from sight.

Drew placed his hand on Josie's, drawing her attention from the now empty air where the spirit had been. "She's gone, but before she left, she said she didn't know."

Just then, a quiet knock announced the arrival of their supper. Daniel entered, carrying two white china plates heaped with the most delicious-smelling food. He set their suppers before them and turned toward Drew, one eyebrow raised in question. "Will there be anything else, sir?"

Josie's lips quivered into a nervous smile as Drew's negative reply sent Daniel on his way. She knew what the waiter must be thinking, and why not? After all, they were in a private dining room at the Cliff House, the most notorious spot in the city for assignations.

Her heart fluttered in her bosom from a mixture of fear and anticipation. Would he kiss her again tonight in that way that made her bones seem to melt? She lifted a forkful of small fried oysters to her mouth and chewed, savoring the faint coppery taste of the local delicacy.

Still, much as she longed to feel his arms around her and his lips against her own, she didn't want to cheapen herself by appearing too eager. Besides, there was so much she wanted to learn about him. "You know, you haven't told me how old you are. It hardly seems fair, since you know so much about me."

He wiped his heavy mustache with a linen napkin and smiled at her, leaning his forearms against the edge of the table. "I turned thirty last Halloween. What else would you like me to tell you?"

Her cheeks warmed. How did he always seem to sense what she was thinking? Still, she wanted to know, and he didn't seem averse to answering her questions. "What's your family like?"

He chuckled. "I wish I could tell you my father was a Medici prince and my mother a Spanish Gypsy, but I can't. They were just normal people, good Catholics, especially my mother. I was born in a little seaport called Mystic, in Connecticut. My parents still live there."

She tilted her head to one side. "You must have been a wonderful little boy." Her cheeks blazed as she realized how ingenuous her words sounded.

This time he laughed out loud. "My mother always said so.

She took a deep breath and crumpled the napkin in her lap. "Have you always had the power to see spirits? I mean, were you born with it?"

His expression became thoughtful. "No. I had a high fever when I was six and almost died. I was ill for weeks. Then one morning I woke up and I was fine, except that I started talking about things that were going to happen. I didn't understand why everyone got so upset when my predictions came true, but I decided pretty quickly to keep my visions to myself."

Josie's heart ached for the confused little boy he'd been. She reached across the table and covered his hand with her own. "It must have been frightening."

He gave her an unreadable look. "Not really. I didn't realize for quite a while that I was different." His mouth twisted into a bitter smile. "Once I figured it out, I was afraid to make friends with the other children. When I grew older, my parents and teachers decided I was insane. I barely escaped being put into an asylum."

"But that's terrible!" The anger in her own voice surprised her. Studying his closed face, she squeezed his hand. "Didn't you have anyone to help you?"

He nodded, his expression guarded. "Before my parents could commit me, I met a woman who called herself a clairvoyant. She persuaded me to run away from home and travel around doing seances. But once she realized my powers were genuine, she called me a freak and sent me away."

He stood and circled the table, drawing Josie

up to stand before him. "She was just as frightened as everyone else. But you're different. You're not frightened of me, are you?" His deep blue eyes peered down at her, as if he could see into her soul.

Josie's mouth dried. "Yes, yes I am afraid of you."

His mouth twisted and he dropped her hand.

But she grabbed his wrist and clasped his hand to her bosom. "Hear me out, please. It's not your power to see spirits that scares me." She swallowed, searching his face for understanding.

Was that a glimmer of confusion or hope she saw in his eyes?

Her cheeks flamed, and she couldn't believe she was baring her soul to a near-stranger. But there was no way to stop now without hurting him, and that she couldn't bear to do. "It's you, yourself that scares me, as a man."

A vertical line appeared above the bridge of his nose, but she blundered on. "And it's me, the way I feel when you kiss me. . . ." Heart pounding, she let her voice trail off as she stared up into the handsome face that had become so unaccountably dear to her in a few short days.

One forefinger stroked the curve of her cheek, echoing the caress in his voice. "Don't you know that I could never do anything to hurt you?"

She closed her eyes as his lips came down on hers, gently at first— tentative, tasting— then hungrily demanding. Standing on tiptoe, she slid her arms up his silken waistcoat and around his neck, pressing her aching bosom to his hard-muscled chest.

As she leaned into him, his hands caught her shoulders, then slid down the planes of her back to her waist, pulling her against the hard heat of his desire and kindling an answering throb in her most secret female core.

After a moment of eternal pleasure, aching for something beyond her experience, she was startled when Drew released her lips and set her away from him. But when he scooped her up into his arms, she buried her face against his neck, savoring the tinges of bay rum, boiled cotton, and wool that overlay the faint musky man-scent that was his own.

As if she were a child, he lowered her to recline against the raised arm of a velvet lounge and knelt beside her, gathering her hands in his and kissing her fingertips. "Will you trust me a little?"

Unable to speak, she nodded.

He released her fingers and bent over her, plundering her mouth until she thought she would swoon with desire.

Her hands came to rest at the back of his head, smoothing his silky hair with her fingers.

At last he released her lips to trail kisses down her throat all the way to her low neckline, bringing little moans of longing to her lips. Sliding his fingertips between her neckline and the tender flesh of her bosom, he blew a tantalizing stream of warm breath beneath the delicate armor of her strapless corset.

The peaks of her breasts rose to aching taut-
ness in response. It was all she could do to keep
from moaning aloud and squirming beneath his
ministrations.

With gentle fingers, he tugged her bodice down
and revealed one erect bud, then bent to tease
this treasure with whisper-soft kisses.

Arching her back, Josie pulled his head down,
encouraging him to ravage her delicate flesh with
tongue and teeth and lips as she closed her eyes
and gave herself up to pleasure so intense that
it bordered on pain. A faint pounding throbbed
through her.

And then he was gone, leaving cold, empty air
in his place.

The pounding sounded again, and she realized
it was coming from the door. Dizzy, she tugged
her bodice into place and sat up, swinging her
legs to the floor.

Across the room, Drew's eyes blazed as his
hands gripped, white-knuckled, the tall upholstered back of the chair he stood behind. He
looked a question at her.

Rising, she twitched her skirt into place and
gave him a tiny nod.

He turned toward the door. "Yes, what is it?"

An abashed Daniel opened the door and
peered inside. "I'm so sorry to interrupt, but this
envelope was just delivered for Miss LeClair, and
the messenger told me it was urgent." He
glanced at Drew's taut face, then set the silver
salver on the table and hurriedly withdrew, pulling the door shut behind him.

Josie stood for a minute, too stunned to move. An urgent message for her? But no one knew she was here, except— dear God, please don't let anything have happened to Cecile.

She lurched toward the table, grabbing up the envelope and ripping it open. It held a plain piece of lined paper, with a handful of words printed in simple block letters. *MIND YOUR OWN BUSINESS OR DIE.*

Eight

Josie was tired. She flagged down a copy boy and handed him her final article for the day. At least the flood of rewrites had kept her too busy to think about the threatening note. Of course, every time she stopped working for even a minute, the worry crept back in. As it was doing again.

Although it hardly mattered. She'd come to the end of her investigation. Unless something new emerged, she'd have to drop the story anyway. It rankled that the killer would think his threat had scared her off, but it couldn't be helped. There was nowhere else to turn, and she knew it was time to call it quits.

With a sigh, she rose and reached for her straw boater, ignoring the sound of footsteps coming toward her. The city room was full of reporters scurrying around to put the late edition to bed so they could go home to their families.

The feet stopped behind her. "Miss LeClair?" The male voice sounded young and somehow familiar.

Dropping her hat, Josie whirled and stared at the young man. It took her a moment to recognize him with his jacket on. It was the waiter from the Cliff House. "Daniel!" She pulled up a chair from a neighboring desk. "Won't you sit down?"

He waited until she was seated before he settled on the edge of the chair, balancing his black derby on his knees with nervous fingers, turning his head this way and that.

Josie smiled, remembering how intimidated she felt the first time she stepped into this very room and sensed the raw power of the printed word. "Thank you so much for coming, Daniel. Did you think of something else to tell me?"

Daniel's gaze locked on hers and he nodded, his Adam's apple shifting his celluloid collar as he swallowed. "I've been thinking about what you said last night, about the Irishman maybe looking like somebody."

Josie nodded encouragement. "Yes?"

Daniel wiped his palms on his dark trousers. "Well, I remember thinking at the time—" He ran a finger under his collar, then leaned toward her and lowered his voice. "I hate to say it, but he reminded me of the parish priest at St. Andrew's."

Josie struggled to hide both her shock and her growing sense of excitement. "Thank you, Daniel." The spirit had told her to go ask the priest because *he* was the man she ate dinner with that night. She rose and held out her hand. "I'm sure your description will prove very helpful."

The young waiter scrambled to his feet and shook her hand, a pleased grin pushing up the waxed ends of his mustache. "Glad to help, miss. Goodbye." He turned and strutted back down the row of desks and out the door.

Josie reached for her own hat again, her thoughts churning. If Father Riordan was Mrs. Kelly's lover, he could also be her killer. She pulled out the long hatpin and set the boater on her head. It made some kind of twisted sense that a priest who would break his vow of chastity might kill to keep his lapse quiet. She stabbed the long pin through the straw crown, anchoring the hat to her Gibson girl topknot. Well, there was only one way to find out for sure. She had to go ask him. Her heart pounded as she recalled the carriage bearing down on her, the telephone call to her editor, and the threatening message last night.

She glanced at her watch. It was almost seven. Drew would be starting his readings now. After last night, he'd made her promise not to take any chances. He'd be angry if she went to the rectory alone. Maybe she should wait until he could go with her.

She gave herself a mental shake. She was a reporter, working on a story. Risks were part of the job. Besides, there was nothing to worry about. If she hurried, she could get there before the priest's housekeeper left. Not that she thought he'd try to kill her anyway. The first murder had been a crime of passion, but once his secret was known, there would be no point in killing again.

But just to be on the safe side, she'd send a message to Drew, telling him what she suspected and where she would be. Satisfied with her plan, she sat back down and threaded a fresh piece of copy paper into the typewriting machine.

Josie settled on the worn armchair and glanced around the priest's parlor. The warm glow of lamplight reflecting off the dark windows mirrored the scene, making the room even cozier than it had seemed on her first visit.

The priest settled across from her and smiled. "You mustn't think I make a habit of answering my own door. But Mary Margaret sent me to let you in while she made you a pot of her jasmine tea." He pointed to the small table beside her. "It's there, but you want to let it steep a minute."

Glancing at the small Japanese pot and the delicate cup and saucer, Josie smiled in relief and gratitude for the unknown housekeeper. Her safety assured, she clasped her hands in her lap. "Father, I've come to ask you some more questions about Mrs. Kelly."

He nodded, his rugged features grave. "I suspected as much when I saw you. I'm not sure what else I can tell you, but please feel free to ask."

Josie paused, searching for just the right words. "I understand that you can't reveal anything told you under the seal of confession. But if you happen to have firsthand knowledge outside the confessional, you would tell me, wouldn't you?"

His ruddy cheeks paled, and his smile seemed forced. "I would do my best. But first, try a sip of tea."

Not wishing to appear rude, Josie turned and poured out a cup of the dark, fragrant liquid. The scent seemed somehow familiar, but she couldn't place it. She lifted the cup to her lips, then paused. "But aren't you having any, Father?"

He leaned back and gave a hollow chuckle. "Never touch the stuff myself. Give me a bottle of Irish stout any time."

Josie brought the gold rim to her mouth once more, but the heat seared her lip. "I'll just wait until it cools a bit." She set the tea down again untasted. "Father, where were you on the evening of March twelfth?"

He cleared his throat and smiled, rubbing his palms together. "Why, where do you suppose I should've been but right here working on my sermon for Sunday?"

Josie cocked her head. "Yes, I suppose you should've been here. But how then do you explain that a waiter saw you at the Cliff House that night, alone in a private dining room with Mary Frances Kelly, only hours before she was found dead?"

The priest's pallor deepened, turning his face a faint gray color. His smile ebbed, replaced by a look of deep sorrow. "I wondered how long it would be before you found out."

He rubbed both hands over his face. "I told myself all the way out there, all during supper that it was perfectly innocent, that we were just two lonely people dining together, two friends enjoying a meal and each other's company."

Josie waited, barely breathing for fear he would stop.

He sighed, his mouth twisting into a wry smile for a moment. "I was lying to myself. I knew perfectly well why she asked me to join her there. That's why I left off my priest's clothing." He reached up behind his head, and the smooth white clerical collar came free from his neck. He tossed it onto the table beside him. "I don't have the right to wear it any more."

Josie swallowed, waiting for him to continue. When he remained silent, she cleared her throat. Her cheeks warmed at the thought of what she was about to say to a man of the cloth, but she had to know. "So you— you made love to her?"

Eyes closed, he nodded. "Afterward, she started acting very strange, complaining that her head hurt and she felt dizzy. She'd had a lot of wine, so I thought she was drunk. When she got up and staggered out of the room, I felt so guilty I just let her go. But then I started to worry that she might hurt herself, so I went after her. I finally found her on the beach, stripped down to her undergarments."

Josie struggled to hide her own embarrassment.

The priest's cheeks darkened, and he averted his eyes. "She pulled me out into the water with her. She was trembling, and her hands felt like ice, and she was mumbling things that didn't make sense. She started shaking all over, and then she just went limp in my arms. I checked her pulse, but she was already gone. So I carried her to the shore and gave her extreme unction. And then I left her there and came home."

Josie reached for the cup of tea beside her, eager for the warmth it offered, but her hands shook so badly that it spilled into the saucer, and she set it down again. She took a deep breath and strove to keep her voice gentle. "So you didn't give her the poison?"

Confusion narrowed the priest's eyes and slackened his mouth. "Poison? Good God, no. Is that how she died? And you think I—to keep her quiet?" He gave his head a violent shake. "No, I may be weak and unworthy of my calling, but I'm not a monster." He sighed. "Not that it makes much difference. Once the bishop finds out, I'll have to leave the order. And if I can't be a priest, I'd rather be dead myself."

"Brian, how can you say that?" A woman stepped from the shadows, her eyes glittering. "You have me, don't you?"

"Miss Quinn!" Josie gasped the words as the woman took another step into the lamplight.

The priest turned to stare at this apparition. "Mary Margaret, I didn't know you were there. How much did you hear?"

Josie held her breath as the woman smiled down at him. "All of it. But don't worry. Everything will be all right. Just leave it to me."

She turned to Josie, her smile fading. "And now, Miss LeClair, I think it's time you were leaving. I'll show you to the door." Lamplight reflected off something she held in her left hand, partly hidden by the folds of her skirt.

It was a butcher knife.

Josie pointed a shaking finger at the woman. "You! You killed Mrs. Kelly."

Miss Quinn gritted her teeth. "And you should've drunk the tea."

Josie suddenly recalled where she'd smelled that sweet scent before. "Those little yellow flowers on the vine by your porch." She turned to the priest, praying that he wasn't the woman's accomplice. "They're deadly poison. She put them in the tea."

Miss Quinn gave a high giggle. "Evening trumpet flower. Better known as yellow jasmine. Frannie always did like jasmine tea." She frowned. "It was supposed to work fast, but she didn't drink enough. Said it tasted too bitter."

Josie sat paralyzed as the priest rose and gently touched the woman's shoulder, turning her to face him. "But Mary Margaret, why? You told me she was your best friend."

Miss Quinn cocked her head and smiled. "To save you, of course. I miscalculated, but don't worry. I'll fix it." She reached up her free hand to stroke his cheek. "You men, you're just like children. I tried to tell Tim what she was, but he wouldn't listen. It just made him hate me, and she broke his heart anyway."

Josie's thoughts whirled. "The man in the photo you gave me, the one you cut off— it was Tim Kelly, wasn't it?"

The woman turned eyes like glittering topaz to-

ward her. "I met him first. I made the mistake
of introducing him to her. She took him, and
then she threw him away. She tried to destroy
every man I ever loved." Her face softened as
she turned back to the priest. "Frannie came to
see me that day, you know, to tell me how she
planned to seduce you, Brian." She pointed to
Josie. "She sat right there, smiling, and drinking
tea, and then she got up and walked out the
door." She gritted her teeth. "She was supposed
to be dead before she got to the Cliff House,
before she could tempt you with her wantonness."

Miss Quinn lifted the priest's hand to her
mouth and kissed it. "But it's all right. I know
you couldn't help it. I forgive you. Now be a
good boy and sit down while I take care of Miss
LeClair."

The woman's face hardened into a mask of hatred as she turned to Josie and lifted the tip of
the knife in her direction. "You busybody! Three
times I tried to warn you to mind your own business. Now it's too late. Get up."

Before Josie could comply, a dark figure darted
from the shadows, wrapping a strong arm around
Miss Quinn's throat and grabbing her wrist and
squeezing until the knife clattered to the floor.

"Drew!" Dizzy with relief, Josie collapsed
against the back of the chair.

Miss Quinn's face crumpled and she turned beseeching eyes toward the priest. "Brian, help
me!"

Father Riordan stood, frozen, his face contorted with anguish.

Drew's voice held the ring of authority. "Father, use your telephone to call the police."

As if awakening from a bad dream, the priest started. "Oh. Oh, yes." He turned and hurried from the room.

"See, people occasionally do what I tell them." Drew's face and voice were dark with irony as he led the softly weeping woman to a chair and stood gripping one of her shoulders.

Josie smiled up at him. "You can scold me all you want to. I'm just glad you got my message."

His heavy brows lowered. "Message? What message?"

Josie couldn't stop the laughter bubbling up inside. "You mean—? Is she here?"

Drew's mustache twitched into a faint smile. "Right in front of you."

Breathless, Josie forced herself to stand and make a circle with her arms. "Thank you, Mrs. Kelly." *A chill tickled Josie's cheek, and a faint voice sounded inside her head. "It's Frannie, and you're welcome."*

Josie tiptoed into the private dining room and stopped behind Drew, spreading the newspaper on the table in front of him with a flourish. "Front page center." She leaned over his shoulder, breathing in the intoxicating man-scent of him, and touched her forefinger to the bottom of the long article. "By Josephine LeClair of the *Examiner.*"

Drew rose and held out her chair for her before taking his own seat again. "I know. I read every word. Congratulations, Josie." His handsome face sobered. "But what's going to happen to everyone now?"

Josie waited to answer until Daniel had filled her champagne glass and retired. "Well, Mary Margaret Quinn, or Peggy as her friend Frannie called her, pleaded guilty to premeditated murder and was committed to an asylum for the criminally insane." She ticked them off on her fingers. "And instead of defrocking him, the bishop sent Father Riordan to a retreat to seek guidance through prayer and meditation." She touched the tip of another finger. "And Tim Kelly told me he worked out a plan for Liam O'Sullivan to pay off the money he embezzled."

Drew gestured across the table with one graceful, long-fingered hand toward the two extra place settings. "And what's this all about?"

Josie reached across the table and squeezed his hand. "I asked Cecile to join us and bring a friend. After the last two suppers we ate in this room, I thought it might be a good idea to have a chaperone."

His eyes blazed, but his voice was gentle. "Oh, you did, did you? And what makes you think I would care to repeat those last two interludes?"

She gave a breathless laugh as a warm glow started from where his hand cradled hers and traveled up her arm and throughout her body. "Didn't I tell you, I can read your mind?"

He lifted one heavy eyebrow. "Oh? Then what am I thinking now?"

She leaned close to him, tilting up her chin. "You're thinking you want to kiss me, right here and right now."

He gave a lazy smile and leaned toward her.

"Excuse us." Laughter suffused Cecile's voice. Josie jumped up, and Drew rose with her.

Cecile's eyes sparkled with mischief as she turned to draw her companion forward. "Josie, I'd like to introduce you—"

"We've met." Josie looked up into a familiar handsome face. "Mr. Kelly, I didn't realize you knew Dr. Balfour."

"Cecile and I met when I claimed my stepmother's body." He gave her his most charming smile. "And please call me Tim."

Her initial shock gave way to pleased surprise. She glanced at her friend, approving her unusually stylish gown and hairstyle. That, coupled with the glow of happiness on Cecile's face was all the reassurance she needed. And as for Mr. Kelly, well, she supposed a girl could do a lot worse. "All right, Tim, but only if you'll call me Josie." She turned toward her own partner. "You both remember Drew."

He smiled and nodded, then gestured toward the waiting chairs. "Shall we sit?"

Once settled on her chair, Cecile reached across and gathered up the newspaper. "Oh, Josie, is this your article?"

Tim rested his forearms on the edge of the table, steepling his hands. "I read it. I thought it was very well written. I can't thank you enough for everything."

Josie slid her hand through the crook of Drew's arm, savoring the warm strength beneath the black cloth. "I couldn't have done it without help."

Drew grinned down at her. "And that's something I don't intend to let her forget."

A faint tinkling laugh sounded inside her head.

Josie smiled. "Don't worry. I don't think there's any danger of that, ever."

About the Author

Stephanie Bartlett lives with her family in southern Oregon. The author of four historical romances, including *Golden Rapture* (available from Zebra Books), Stephanie's newest historical romance, *Dearest Enemy,* will be published in November 1995. Stephanie loves hearing from readers and you may write to her at P.O. Box 1111, Ashland, OR 97520. Please include a self-addressed stamped envelope if you wish a response.

Déjà Vu

by

Christine Dorsey

YOU ARE CORDIALLY INVITED TO GET SWEPT AWAY INTO NEW WORLDS OF PASSION AND ADVENTURE.

AND IT WON'T COST YOU A PENNY!

One

Death hovered, just out of reach, like a lover. A lover I longed to embrace. I waited, impatient as the hours and humid-laden days of autumn droned by.

Age had brittled my bones and grayed my hair. But it was disappointment that hardened my heart. A life wasted that made me give up the fight with nary a complaint.

"Ye didn't eat any of that soup? Is I gonna have to take up feedin' ye again like ye was a babe in arms?"

I closed my eyes but couldn't escape the sound of Mammy, her hickory wood cane clomping on the polished oak floorboards as she entered the bedroom. And countless years had taught me the old Negro woman was impossible to ignore.

"I had Cook make it up special for ye, 'cause I knowed how you liked it," Mammy muttered as she yanked open the heavy brocade drapes.

"Don't open the window." I was Eugenie de Valliers, sole owner of Belle Maison, and my

words should be obeyed. But they seemed to fall
on deaf ears as the subtle scent of rose gentians
wafted across the sash. I turned my face away
from the light invading my sanctuary. Nothing
had changed. I had no desire to see the world
outside this room. The moss-drenched oaks and
the black-watered bayous beyond the sugar fields
held no appeal.

My lips firmly shut, I resisted the heavily
scrolled silver spoon lifted by the frail, dark
hand. Mammy's hand trembled and drops of fragrant chicken broth splattered on the shawl
wrapped around my shoulders. I came close to
relenting as my faded blue eyes met the black
ones staring at me hopefully above the spoon. A
bite wouldn't hurt, would it? But I only shook
my head slowly and watched disappointment
shadow the wrinkled face of my servant.

Nay, friend. Mammy had been my companion
for more years than I could remember. My only
friend and companion since my father, the last
of the de Valliers family other than myself,
passed away some twenty years ago.

Had it been that long? The dreary days had
melded, one with another into years and decades.
My sigh made Mammy glance around as she
lifted the silver tray that seemed to stoop her
aged body even more.

"Starvin' yourself to death ain't gonna accom-
plish nothin', ye know." Mammy set the tray on
the chest of drawers. The mellowed silver service,
a gift from Louis XIV to the de Valliers, shone

in the dying rays of the sun slanting through the floor-to-ceiling windows.

"I told you I'm not hungry."

"And ye haven't been for weeks now."

I settled into the cushions of a chair Mammy forced me to sit in, feeling every ache in every joint of my body. "I'm an old woman and want nothing more than to be left in peace. I think I deserve that at least."

Mammy turned to face me, her gnarled fingers balled around the cane's head, and I felt a pang of guilt. I was old, there was no doubt of that, old in body and spirit. But there was also no denying that Mammy was at least fifteen years my senior.

My earliest recollections were of Mammy, making me dolls, spinning her stories. Stories of the ghosts and spirits that dwelled in the misty bayous. Oddly enough, her tales had never frightened me. I remember those as happy times. Times when anything seemed possible, and life was worth living.

Times before I made the wrong choice.

Swallowing, I turned my face away from the dark eyes that seemed to see too much. "I want to go to bed."

" 'Tis early still and you've hardly been up more than a bit."

"I don't recall asking your opinion," I snapped. Immediately I regretted my words, but they seemed to have little effect on Mammy. Her stare continued to bore into me. "Won't you simply allow me to do as I wish this once?"

"Seems to me ye done as ye wished too much."

My head twisted back and for an instant life sparked through me. A touch of the spirit that had made me at one time the belle of New Orleans society flared. Then sadness veiled my features. "Put me to bed," I whispered in a voice grown weak and listless.

With no more than a thinning of her lips, Mammy hobbled to the bellrope. The maids she summoned were less than gentle as they lifted me into the large four-postered bed. It was the bed where I was born; where I'd slept alone most of my life. The process of being moved tired me even more. I wanted only to drift off into the netherlands of sleep and oblivion.

"Guess ye know what today is?"

I lifted parchment-thin lids.

" 'Tis All Hallow's Eve."

How could the mention of this day cause such pain after all these years? I shut my eyes before Mammy could see the welling tears. "Go away," I murmured. "Go away and leave me in peace."

But there was no peace to be had. Silently I cursed the old woman who reminded me of things better left forgotten. Of my wasted life . . . of my lost love. But in actuality thoughts of him were never far from my mind . . . or heart.

Zachary Hamilton.

I met him on All Hallow's Eve.

All Hallow's Eve when fate first offered me a taste of what life might be. I remembered the night as if it were yesterday rather than over fifty years ago. It was there in my memory, sealed and cherished. The smell of roses, heady and sensual, the excited laughter of those assembled in the ballroom, the awareness in his dark green eyes when I glanced around and saw him.

I was smiling, laughing at some comment my partner for the quadrille made, when I felt a need to look toward the arched doorway. A need so strong that even now as I lay in the bed that would cradle my body in death, I could feel the tug of his presence. Nothing had ever felt so surreal yet genuine before or since, like a paradox that life thrusts your way.

He stood there, staring at me, tall and so sinfully handsome in his uniform my mouth went suddenly dry.

"No, please." The words escaped me now on a sob as I tried to push the memory of the man I would always love . . . the mistake I would always regret from my mind. But it did no good. It never did. As I drifted in and out of a restless sleep his presence followed me. As dreams. As memories. As regrets.

And as it always did the question came, "What if?" What if I would have chosen love over pride, love over selfishness, love over darkness. If I had kept our rendezvous. If I had gone with Zachary? Would my life have meant something? Would I reflect back over the years with emotions other than regret?

But I would never know. For my life was over. And so was his. He'd died in 1816, over a decade after I acquiesced to my parent's wishes and rejected him. And with word of his death, I lost all hope that someday, somehow, we might find each other in this life.

So now there was nothing. Nothing. *Nothing.* The words beat inside my head like the pounding of drums. Pounding. Pounding.

The sound gave me no rest. I took a shallow breath and smoke tickled my nostrils, forming a heavy fog like the mist drifting over the cypress trees in the swamps. Slowly my eyes opened; my sight, weakened by age, focused.

Countless candles flickered, sending grotesque shadows dancing on the walls. It was night now. At least I thought as much, though I couldn't grasp how I knew. And there were people in my room. People I didn't recognize.

Fear pounded through me as incessant as the rhythmic beat of drums. What was happening to me? Turning my head required near all the strength I possessed. My body seemed leaden, weighted down, as if the bayous closed in about me. The air, sweet with a scent I didn't recognize, was too thick to breathe.

"Help me." Was that my voice so far away, so disembodied? I opened my mouth to call out again when a hand settled on my cheek.

Mammy. Relief flowed through me like a balm. Mammy would let no harm come to me. Even if she was dressed strangely in a flowing white gown with a red scarf binding her hair, Mammy would keep me safe. It was the one constant of my life.

"What are you doing?" I wasn't certain if I spoke the question aloud, or if anyone in the

room heard me. Certainly there was no response
from the men and women dancing about my bed.
Or from Mammy. She continued to chant something in a language I couldn't comprehend. And
as her voice droned on, as the hypnotic syllables
lulled, I felt myself drifting off the soft down
mattress to float above my bed. Above my own
form.

Strange.

I wanted to ask Mammy what the words meant.
What she was doing with the feathers. Why they
were brushed across my forehead, over my eye-
lids. But my lips could no longer form questions.

I couldn't even protest when the ornate mantel
clock chimed the last of twelve resonant notes
and Mammy announced my death. How could I
be dead when I could see it all? Hear it all? Yet
Mammy made it sound true enough.

"Dead. Eugenie de Valliers is dead. Gone from
this world."

The words quickened the dancers' frenzied
pace. Sweat glistened on their ebony bodies as
they swirled about the bed, bare feet pounding
the floor.

My body lay cocooned in auderdown and lace,
pale and lifeless, an empty shell like my life.
There was no more to be done. With a sigh and
a last thought of him, I, Eugenie de Valliers, gave
up the ghost.

Two

"Is ye plannin' to sleep the day away?"

I moaned, squinting my eyes against the sudden brightness. Outside I heard a cock crow. What was happening? Moments ago all had been peace and welcome dark oblivion. Now a sense of bustling urgency jarred my senses.

I did my best to ignore it.

"Now, Miss Eugenie, there's no sense pretendin' ye ain't under that pile of blankets. I sees that dark hair of yours spillin' out under the coverlet."

What was Mammy talking about? My hair had lost its dark color years ago, first turning dull gray, then nearly white before I died.

Died.

My eyes popped open as memories assailed me. I was dead. Finally freed from the unhappy tedium of my life. I remembered the event clearly.

So what was happening now?

Why was my bedroom filled with sunshine? And why could I see Mammy, a much younger-looking Mammy, through the gossamer veil of mosquito netting as she bustled her large frame about the bedroom?

"Go away and let me rest in peace."

"Now, Miss Eugenie, I'd do that if I could. Ye know that. But Miz Bernadette says for me to get ye up and ready to go to town."

Was Mammy daft? I hadn't been to town in over thirty years. I'd fled to Belle Maison when word reached New Orleans of a British fleet heading toward the city . . . and stayed after learning of Zachary's death.

A near physical pain shot through me at the memory. The only man I ever loved was dead, had been for decades, and I wished the same oblivion for myself.

My anger began to simmer, forcing aside unhappy memories. Mammy flit about the room, ignoring my order to leave, supervising the filling of a brass tub, laying out my clothing. As if she actually thought I would rise from my deathbed and ready myself for a trip to town.

And all the while she babbled on about parties and masked balls and which gowns did I wish to take with me. The old woman acted as if time stood still. She even looked as if it had with her body fuller and her voice firm.

It was infuriating.

"Go away, I say. Stop this awful charade." A sob escaped, a silly, childish sob and I yanked aside the coverlet, throwing my legs over the side of the bed. I slid to the floor, marched toward Mammy and began crying in earnest.

It wasn't until I was nearly beside her that I stopped. I stared down to where several pink toes peeked from beneath my long cotton gown.

I was standing, nay walking! And my feet had lost the wrinkled rages of age. The shock made me lurch toward Mammy.

"Is ye all right child?" Strong arms wrapped around me.

"What's wrong with Eugenie?"

Glancing around, scarcely able to believe my eyes, I watched my mother walk into the room. Was she an apparition, a ghostly being sent to haunt me? But no, she appeared real enough. Her usually serene expression was only slightly marred by a thinning of her lips. "She is all right, isn't she, Mammy?"

"I ain't sure. She ain't actin' herself and that's for—"

"Stop it!" I pushed away from the encircling arms. "Stop it, both of you. I don't know what you're trying to do to me, but I won't allow it. I won't." Twisting away from the two faces that stared at me wide-eyed and open mouthed, I stumbled back toward the bed.

I would climb in, cover myself up and shut out this nightmare.

And I would have, if not for the glimpse I caught as I passed the gilded mirror hanging above the chest of drawers.

I stopped, my heart pounding like the drums I heard. Was it last night? They seemed still to echo through my head. Slowly I turned, approaching the looking glass as if I faced the guillotine. My fingers gripped the mahogany chest till they hurt.

"What . . . ?" Unable to even formulate the

question my mouth clamped shut as I stared at my reflected image. It was the image of a woman in the first bloom of beauty: eyes blue, long lashed and clear; mouth and jaw firm; skin unwrinkled and pale.

I swallowed, watching the motion of my smooth throat before grabbing a handful of the thick, dark hair curling about my shoulders. I yanked, savoring the pain. It was the only real thing in a world suddenly gone mad.

Tears welled as I realized something else. My legs did not ache, nor my joints. Only my head where I pulled on the thick lock of hair. Slowly I loosened my fingers and took a deep breath.

"What's happening to me? Why do I look this way?" I turned toward my mother when I spoke.

"I have no idea what you are trying to do, Eugenie, but I insist that you stop this instant. Your father is waiting below stairs for us." That said she turned gracefully and left the room.

"It ain't nothin' to worry yourself 'bout, Miss Eugenie. We'll have ye lookin' right fine before ye leave. See?" Mammy's long fingered hands twisted in my hair, pulling it up in some semblance of style. "Ye just need a bit of fixin' up. Come on over to your bath 'for it cools and we need to heat more water."

I wanted to scream and stamp my feet, to insist that I wished to wake from this horror, to plead with Mammy to stop it. Instead I followed meekly as Mammy led me to the tub. It was as if my mind suddenly went numb.

The warm water slipped over my body, a body

both young and supple; a body that should have pleased me, but I could not stand to look at myself. I sat motionless, my eyes closed as Mammy washed, then dried me. A chemise of finest silk slid over my body before I sat on the bench in front of the dressing table for Mammy to arrange my hair.

The routine was as familiar as breathing. I turned, my mind now racing, and my eyes met Mammy's. For a moment, despite the young appearance of her face, I caught a glimpse of infinite age in those dark orbs. Age and wisdom and knowledge.

She knew!

Of course she knew what happened to me. She did it. The drums. The dancing and chants. Mammy had cast a spell upon me.

I opened my mouth to question her, sure that this time she would tell the truth. But before I could speak the moment was gone. Mammy bustled away and my thoughts were in such a turmoil I wondered if it wasn't best to be quiet. At least until I had a moment to myself to think. A moment to decide what was happening.

It wasn't until I descended the wide spiral staircase that I had an inkling. Dressed in a traveling gown of a style popular when I was young, with high waist and no crinolines, I met my mother in the center hallway. I smiled. Despite everything it was wonderful to see her again.

Her expression didn't change. "I'm pleased to see you are yourself again. We will, of course, act as if the scene in your bedroom didn't happen. Naturally we shall say nothing to your father." She paused, her serious eyes looking toward me for confirmation.

"Naturally," I agreed, partly because I didn't know what else to say, and partly because agreeing with my mother came so easily to me, even after all these years.

"I suppose it only natural that you should be a bit . . . unnerved. It is not every day that a young woman's betrothal is announced."

"Betrothal?" I tried controlling the anxiety in my voice, but with little success.

"Eugenie, do not start this again. I will not have it. And see." A door opened and shut toward the back of the hallway. "Here is your father."

As instructed I remained quiet, though not for the reason my mother wished. I stood dumbstruck as my father, full of vitality and life, approached. He was a slight man, barely taller than I, and my last recollection of him was with sunken eyes and skin stretched taut over a wasted skull. Mother died young so the transformation didn't seem so extreme. But Father. I had watched him waste away. And now he was back.

He greeted me as he'd always done, with a slight bow of his aristocratic head and a murmuring of my name. Then we were climbing in the well-sprung coach that would take us the few miles from Belle Maison to our town house in New Orleans and to the ball where my betrothal was to be announced.

I rested my bonneted head against the soft

leather squab as the coach rolled through the alley of moss-drenched oaks. There was no need for anyone to tell me what day this was, or what year. My memory, though dulled by age, was still sharp enough to recall this day.

This All Hallow's Eve.

I even remembered now the journey to town with my parents. The excitement I'd felt as the evening grew near. There was to be ball, a grand ball, for my family was aristocratic and wealthy. They were emigres, true, forced to leave France or lose their heads. But Edmund de Valliers was ingenious and managed to emigrate his small family *and* his fortune.

And tonight, amid the jewels and glittering gowns of New Orleans society, Edmund de Valliers would announce that his only child, the charming and beautiful Eugenie would marry equally rich and aristocratic Phillipe Riene.

Fxcept that I never would.

For tonight I would meet for the first time the American, Captain Zachary Hamilton.

My sharp intake of breath was met with an equally sharp look from my mother. But my father didn't appear to notice. He spoke, in the pontificating style I remembered so well, of the recent purchase of all the land drained by the Mississippi by the upstart country of the United States.

"It is inconceivable to me," he said to no one in particular. "What was in Bonaparte's mind to do such a thing?"

"Perhaps time will show the sale is for the best." As soon as the words were out of my mouth I knew I'd made a mistake. My father, along with many others of French descent, never accepted the fact that Louisiana belonged to the United Sates. Furthermore, it was only when he was very old that he allowed anyone, especially me, to contradict him. He was a man whose every word was obeyed. Over the years I had grown comfortable with blaming him and his dominance for the disaster of my life. It was less painful than blaming myself.

We arrived at the graceful town house on Royal Street without an argument starting. I kept my council, using the time to stare out the window at the impenetrable pine forests. The ride was familiar, of that there was no doubt, but I didn't know if I was remembering this very day or the countless times I'd taken the same route.

No matter, I could not wait to speak again with Mammy, who rode with the other servants, in the carriage behind ours. But there was no time for talk. When we arrived I was immediately bundled off above stairs to rest.

The day was warm and the doors to the gallery overlooking the garden open. As I lay on the cool sheets listening to the birds singing, breathing in the fragrant scents of late flowering roses, I couldn't help wondering when this dream would end.

That's when I heard the cock crowing.

The ball was exactly as I remembered.
Crystal chandeliers gleamed, prisming the light

from hundreds of candles. Urns filled with flowers sat between gleaming white columns. The orchestra sat on the raised dais and a soft breeze off the gulf cooled the room.

A night to match no other. Despite my trepidation, I felt caught up in the excitement. Perhaps this jest of God's was not too high a price to pay for one more glimpse of my beloved Zachary.

My eyes kept straying toward the arched entrance, even as Phillipe bowed over my hand. I stood between Mother and Father, accepting compliments from a man who soon would become my betrothed.

"You shine brighter than all the stars tonight." I could feel the warmth of his moist lips through my glove. "But that is as it should be."

I made some inane reply, probably similar to the one I made fifty years before, and surveyed this man my father had chosen for me to wed.

Like Father, he was slight of build, and very near the same in age. But he was not unhandsome. His plantation, Bon Sejour, bordered Belle Maison. Phillipe was a widower, known in New Orleans for his love of beautiful women, and I remembered being quite happy when originally told of the planned union. I was pleased that all the young women of my acquaintance were quite jealous.

I could feel everyone's eyes on me as I accompanied Phillipe to the head of the line for the first quadrille. My feet remembered the steps as if it were yesterday rather than decades ago that

I last danced. The music swirled about us and sweet compliments oozed from my partner's tongue like honey from a hive.

My skin, my lips, the fresh flowers twisted in my dark curls, this man found everything about me to his liking. It was easy to allow myself to be caught up in the splendor of the moment. Easy to forget that my life was truly over. Easy to forget all but the music and dancing.

Yet I knew the moment he entered the ballroom.

Of its own accord my head turned. Our eyes met. And all the ensuing years evaporated into nothingness. Everything, the music, Phillipe, all the gaily-dressed guests seemed to disappear.

There was only the man I loved.

Three

"Eugenie?"

Though I barely heard him call my name, Phillipe's hand on my arm drew my attention back to him. Like me, he'd been staring at the arched doorway, as was most everyone else, I realized. Why hadn't I noticed the first time the hush that fell over the ballroom when Zachary walked in?

"De Carre has his nerve bringing him here," Phillipe said, then bowed and apologized for his words.

At first I assumed Phillipe knew, knew that the man standing in the doorway so tall and handsome was to be the reason I would never marry him. But then I realized it wasn't Zachary he spoke of.

"Please forgive me," he continued, "but Simone de Carre will not let well enough alone. He continues to insist that we should entertain a dialogue with the American consul, and now he brings him into your father's house. It is an outrage."

My father apparently thought so too. After I was returned to mother's side, I noticed Phillipe and my father approach de Carre and his two guests, the American consul and the young captain by his side. I watched the five leave the ballroom, then without so much as a "by your leave" offered to my mother, followed.

Silver sconces lit the hallway and stairs. The beginning strains of Mozart filled the air as I hurried after the men. Fifty years earlier, I'd danced with Monsieur LaBarre to that melody, wondering the entire time what had become of the handsome officer. Now I knew.

He stood, by himself, in the hallway outside my father's library.

Without thought to the consequences, only knowing that this might be my only chance through the rest of eternity, I rushed toward him. As he glanced my way his expression turned from pleasure to surprise, then shock as I reached for his hands.

"Mademoiselle?" he said, taking a step backward as I threw myself into his arms.

"I know you are angry with me, and I cannot blame you. What I did to you was unforgivable." My voice cracked. "I was cruel and heartless, and you must believe that I have suffered every day for the last fifty years."

I pressed my face to his chest, relishing the strong beat of his heart, the feel of his arms about me . . . except his arms weren't around me. They hung stiffly at his side. And his expression when I pulled away enough to look up, was unreadable.

"You can't find it in your heart to forgive me." Reluctantly, I stepped away— away from his scent, from his warmth. "I don't blame you." Tears welled in my eyes. "You *should* hate me. I understand now. *This* is my hell."

"Mademoiselle, please." His strong fingers encircled my arm. "I don't hate you. How could I?" He smiled.

How could he? I had lied. Abandoned him. Possibly ruined his life as surely as I ruined my own. And now he acted as if he didn't know me.

"I seem to have made a mistake." I looked pointedly to where his gloved hand held me. I had to leave. Being near him, loving him beyond life itself and having him not even know me was too much to bear.

"Please, the mistake is mine. You simply took me by surprise. I saw you in the ballroom and—"

"You saw me?" Warmth spread through me when he smiled.

"Of course. How could I not notice you?"

He said these words to me before, though admittedly they were said in different circumstances. It was when he danced with me. It was history repeating itself. Everything was happening exactly as it had before . . . except when I changed something.

And throwing myself into his arms was definitely changing things. Fifty years ago I had waited demurely for him to approach me. Anticipating and dreading the moment with equal intensity. For even then I knew my life would never be the same again.

I should leave. I knew how forward my actions

were. But though I wondered what he must think
of me, I couldn't bear to go.

"What do you suppose they are talking about?"
I inclined my head toward the door to my father's
library.

"I imagine we are being asked to leave." Again
he grinned, showing the dimples I'd grown very
fond of.

"Because you are an American?"

He shrugged. "Or because we weren't invited."
His laughter joined mine.

"I could invite you." Our eyes met and I realized I was overstepping bounds again. Not that
he seemed to mind. His expression nearly de-
voured me, reminding me of the times I'd lain
with him. But it was too soon. "I must go now."
Turning, I started back toward the ballroom.

"Wait." His smile was self-deprecating when I
glanced back. "If we are allowed to stay, may I
have a dance?"

Our first dance. The one that in reality was
the first time we met. How could I refuse?

"Of course."

I prayed that history would repeat itself . . .
that I would recall enough to do my part.

I hurried back to the ballroom searching my
memory for what I was doing at this very moment fifty years earlier. When I saw my mother
approaching I knew it was no shadow from the
past.

"Where did you go? I can't tell you how common you looked running from the ballroom. I've had Mammy looking everywhere for you."

"I'm sorry. I—"

"We've put up with quite enough of your histrionics Eugenie. This morning . . . well, we simply cannot— will not— condone behavior like yours. Ah, here comes your father now. See if you can't . . ."

I didn't hear the rest of my mother's admonition. I turned hoping to catch a glimpse of Zachary with my father and the American consul. He wasn't there.

I stood, clutching my fan as Edmund de Valliers joined us. "Eugenie, I expected to see you on the dance floor."

"Did you allow them to stay?"

"Them?" My father raised a thin aristocratic brow, looking first at me then my mother.

"Oui." I swallowed, trying to remember that my father and mother seemed to know nothing of my past this night. And I was supposed to know nothing as well. "Phillipe told me the American consul was not invited. He said—"

"I shall have a talk with your betrothed, Eugenie. He should not be filling your mind with all manner of unpleasantness, especially on the night of your engagement ball."

"I'm certain he meant no harm. And I do have an interest in the world about me. You mentioned yourself on the way from Belle Maison—"

"What your father says in the privacy of his own coach is for him to decide, Eugenie."

"I only meant . . ." I sucked in my breath for

in that moment I'd spotted the American consul
and his tall, handsome *affaire de charge*. They *had*
remained at the ball. I could barely suppress the
urge to rush toward Zachary, arms outstretched
and beg him to take me away.

So far away that the past, the wasted years and
my own death could not find us.

But that was impossible.

As impossible as the fact that I was here, now.
Whatever had happened to give me this night,
I would not waste it.

"I apologize, Mother. It was not my intent to
question anything that Father said."

"Do not concern yourself, Eugenie. This is a
night for you to savor. And here is your betrothed coming to request another dance, I pre-
sume."

Whether Phillipe actually wished to dance with
me I didn't know. But he did. And he hadn't
before. Fifty years earlier I hadn't been standing
with my parents when the next quaidrille was announced. I had been with my friend Celeste, momentarily unchaperoned, and it was Zachary
who'd approached.

And Zachary I'd danced with just before he
left. For neither he nor Daniel Clark, the American consul, had stayed for the dinner or Father's
announcement of my engagement.

He would be leaving soon and I was stuck
dancing with Phillipe. I could hardly contain my
tears. Nor could I stop myself from moving toward the glass doors that led to the gallery when
I saw Zachary step outside.

"Eugenie? Are you all right?" Phillipe reached for my arm. "What is the matter?"

I stared at him wide-eyed. What could I possibly tell him? But how could I stay and continue this dance knowing what I did?

"I must . . . I need a bit of air."

"Of course you do." His hand now cupped my elbow. "You are frightfully pale. Come, we must find your mother."

"No." I held my ground as best I could. "I don't wish to upset her, and I will be fine, really." I gave him a weak smile. "If I could just rest for a moment in the salon."

"Come this way, my dear." Phillipe thought he was leading the way though actually I made certain we went toward the green salon, with its door onto the garden. He was reluctant to leave me, and wouldn't until I begged him to find Mammy and send her to me.

The moment the door closed behind him I was off the settee and through the glass-paned doors. My slippers crunched on the crushed shell walkway as I raced toward the gallery overlooking the garden.

He stood silhouetted against the light pouring through the ballroom doors, a tall, solitary figure, leaning against one of the pillars. The stark white of his tight uniform pantaloons contrasted sharply with the dark blue of his tunic.

Though his face was in shadow I could tell he stared at me as I approached. "Mademoiselle de Valliers," he said with a stiff bow before turning toward the door.

"Wait." Lifting my skirt I moved up the stairs, trying to ignore the distant tone of his voice. Even when I'd rejected him, he'd never spoken to me as if he didn't care. "You know my name." That gave me some bit of pleasure.

"Yes." He glanced over his shoulder. "I requested the information from one of the gentlemen in attendance."

"You did?" I knew I was smiling as I took two more steps. "I thought you wished to dance with me."

"I was also told who your father was . . . and the reason for tonight's ball."

"My betrothal," I said, my voice low. I was beside him now and he turned to face me.

"Yes, your betrothal." He lifted his chin, twisting it slightly to the side. "I do not know what kind of game you play, Mademoiselle, but I assure you— "

"This is no game." I reached for his hands. "You must believe me."

"I assure you," he continued as if I hadn't spoken, "I do not care to be used as a pawn in a chess game to sabotage relations between French and Americans in this territory."

"You think I would do that?" My eyes widened in disbelief.

"I think that standing here as we are puts us both in compromising situations." Dark curls sprang loose as I shook my head, but he only continued. "I think your fiancé would demand satisfaction, and rightly so, if he saw us. And I think you know that well enough."

"I don't care." My hands tightened about his.

He was quiet a moment and I could feel the tension radiate from him. When he spoke his voice was low, and his hands were free. "Perhaps your betrothed's life means nothing to you, but I assure you mine has deep meaning to me."

"But I would never hurt you."

Liar. *Liar!* The word screamed at me as he shook his head and walked away. How could I say such a thing when I had done nothing but hurt him? I had proclaimed my undying love for him. I had sworn on that love to meet him beneath the oak in the garden . . . to run away with him and start a new life together. But I had been too afraid, too weak, too selfish, to keep that promise. Even when he confronted my father, worried I was detained against my will, I cowered in my room, refusing to see him.

Looking back, I couldn't imagine what possessed me to do such a thing. I had loved him. *Did* love him. But the idea of giving up my wealth, my position, the good will of my family, had caused me to betray his trust.

My very life had been lived as atonement for the pain I'd caused.

But he didn't know that. Somehow or another he didn't recognize me as the woman who betrayed him. He didn't even recognize me as the woman he loved.

What had changed?

Fifty years ago it was *he* who pursued me. *He,* who despite the stares of those in attendance, danced with me. He who hung on my every word. The Zachary I knew would not dare to suggest that I meant him any harm, that my motives where anything but pure . . . that I loved him.

But things had been different then. I hadn't rushed out to see him in the hallway or thrown myself shamelessly at him on the secluded gallery.

Things were different now. It was fifty years and another lifetime ago. I was an old woman, a dead old woman, and this shouldn't be happening. I didn't understand any of it.

Slowly I walked back through the garden. Mammy was sitting by the door. She glanced up when I entered the salon.

"Where ye been, child?" Monsieur Riene done sent me to check on ye. Said ye was feeling poorly. And no wonder. Your feet and hem are all damp with dew. What ye doing out in the garden all by yourself?"

"I wasn't alone." I swallowed. "Mammy, I need for you to tell me what's happening." My eyes pleaded. "I know that you know. I saw the dancers. Heard the chants." I stepped closer. "I know that you did this to me."

Four

"I don't know what ye talkin' 'bout, Miss Eugenie."

"You're lying!" Hysteria bubbled up in my veins. "I know you have something to do with this. You've put a spell on me, haven't you?" I lurched toward Mammy. Even in my darkest days when life had seemed an endless parade of gloom, I'd never struck a servant. But now the desire to do so was near uncontrollable. It was as if the itch were upon me, sending my hands flying in ways not intended.

Mammy stood her ground as did I, arm lifted, ready to strike. And then her eyes, those dark pools, as bottomless as the swamps, caught mine. I felt frozen. Sounds came to me. The frantic wheeze of my own breathing, the wild pumping of my blood. But for those I might have been a statue, hewn from cold, lifeless stone. Unable to move.

"Eugenie!"

It was my father's voice that shattered the haze surrounding me. I whirled and the expression on his face told me what he must have seen. I could only imagine how wild my eyes must be, how pale my flesh.

"Father." The sob came from deep in my chest. "You don't know what she's done to me."

His glance strayed toward Mammy and I saw them exchange a look that frightened me even more.

"Whatever it is, Eugenie, I'm certain we can take care of it tomorrow." He stared pointedly at my hand and I realized it was still above my head, poised to strike. Self-consciously I let it drop to my side.

"It is time for the announcement, Eugenie."

"What announcement?"

"Your betrothal . . . to Monsieur Riene."

My father's voice was low and calm as if he expected the slightest thing to have me running from the room screaming.

But that wasn't going to happen. I took several deep breaths, trying to force my features into a docile expression. I could not allow myself the luxury of hysteria. They would all think me insane. A glance toward Mammy assured me that she would never tell them the truth.

I would be put in an attic room, like my Aunt Felise, never to be spoken of in polite society. Tucked away and forgotten.

"Of course, Father. The excitement of my betrothal has me so I barely know what I'm about." And *I* called Mammy a liar. The betrothal meant nothing to me. Nothing. But it was convenient. And though doubt still shadowed his expression, my father smiled and offered his arm.

And so we walked down the long wide hallway toward the ballroom. People chatted and laughed, violins spun melodies, and candles glowed. There was no need to look about for Zachary. I knew he wasn't there.

The rest of the evening followed in a trancelike haze for me. I assume I acted appropriately. I was learning to take my cues from the reactions of others. My mother. My father. Even Phillipe seemed pleased with my performance as the toasts were made with my father's finest champagnes.

It was a harmless charade I played. At least that's what I told myself. I would not marry Phillipe in this life anymore than I had in the last. At least I didn't think I would. But so much was out of my control. So much.

But that was hardly a new sensation. My life, my real life, not this figment of some devil worshiper's imagination, had always been played at the whim of others. But at least then, Zachary had loved me.

He'd told me so the first time I gave myself to him. With the heavy moss forming a lacy curtain, we'd lain beneath the wide branched oak and bared our souls as surely as our bodies. And he swore to me that he'd loved me since the first moment he saw me.

The thought had warmed my heart even on the bleakest days of my life. I wouldn't even have that memory this time. For it was obvious Zachary thought me . . .

What did he think? That I was forward, indeed.

And treacherous. Me? The idea was laughable. I
cared nothing for politics, or for anything but
Zachary.

I sent Mammy away when she came to help me
ready myself for bed. There were still questions
that I wanted answered. But I sensed this wasn't
the time. I was tired and needed to think. And
sleep. Oh, how I needed to sleep.

But though I lay in comfort, slumber was long
in coming. Perhaps it was the circumstances of
my life. Or perhaps it was the rooster, whose
shadow I could see on the magnolia branch outside my window, and whose constant crowing in-
vaded my dreams.

I dreamed last night that I was dead, the satin-
lined coffin closed about me. I woke with a start,
my heart beating as if to drums, my skin
drenched with sweat. Jerking aside the mosquito
netting, I rushed to the mirror. Was it the old
Eugenie, or the new, that would stare back at me
wide-eyed?

But I knew without seeing the reflection. The
old Eugenie's body creaked with aches. The new
had pains only in her mind.

So, I was to be given another day.

Scary as the prospect was, a bit of excitement
stirred through me. Another day of life. I
glanced toward the window. The cock was gone.
The sky was bright.

I would use this day, this gift, to see Zachary.
Perhaps if I explained. No. There was no expla-

nation I could give that would be believed. But if we met again, and spoke of things we once discussed. His family in Virginia, his desire to settle on land to the west.

"Ye look to be feelin' better today."

I turned slowly, schooling my expression. Mammy may have practiced witchcraft on me, but she was also the one person who had understood my love for Zachary in my other life. Without her help I would never have been able to rendezvous with him.

I needed that help again.

She didn't question my need to be out in the carriage, nor the direction I ordered the driver to go. She said very little as we rode along, and for that I was grateful. Thoughts of seeing Zachary again filled my head. Still, I couldn't quite meet Mammy's eyes for fear that she'd catch me in their web again.

Something inside me feared that by the sheer force of her stare boring into me she could transport me back to the dead where I belonged. Though I knew it was but a matter of time till that happened, I didn't want to go now.

Not far from the Cibildo with its archways and wrought-iron balconies stood a smaller building. Zachary had pointed it out to me once in my other life. Soldiers guarded the entrance to where the American consul lived and worked. Most citizens of New Orleans, at least those of French descent considered their presence a bother . . . or so my father maintained till the day he died.

It didn't matter that he, along with most of his

friends, despised Clement de Laussat, the French prefect who governed the city. Father thought the man tactless and arrogant and there was a general fear that he would free the slave population. But he was French.

The transfer of the city to the Americans had not taken place yet. I remember well the day it did, December 20, 1803. I had already refused Zachary and lived to regret it. With unaccustomed fervor I forced Father to take me to the ceremony, hoping to catch a glimpse of Captain Hamilton. I didn't.

But that was in the future . . . or past . . . depending upon one's point of view. For now, New Orleans was officially under Spanish rule, though the die had been cast to put it momentarily into French hands, then American.

But I have never been one for politics.

"I want you to deliver this to Captain Zachary Hamilton." Without further comment I thrust the note I'd quickly written and sealed into Mammy's hand. She looked up but I glanced away before our eyes could meet. Only after she climbed from the coach did I let out my breath.

Each minute seemed an eternity. I kept my attention fixed on the paneled door wondering if Zachary would come. When he did, stepping into the bright sunlight, his golden hair shining, I could hardly contain my joy.

But obviously he could.

His motions were swift, his expression grim as he climbed into the coach, settling in the seat opposite mine. He pulled the door shut and studied me a moment in the filtered light.

"I don't understand what you wish from me, Mademoiselle de Valliers."

I had known his love and perhaps after rejecting him, his contempt, but only recently his indifference. That was perhaps the cruelest rub.

I faced it now with what I hoped was a confident smile, but my hands were damp and I feared my chin would start trembling when I spoke. "I wish nothing more than a bit of your time."

His green eyes narrowed. "My time, Mademoiselle? You will excuse me if I find that an odd request coming from one of New Orleans's French aristocracy."

When I said nothing . . . what could I say . . . he continued. "Does your betrothed know you are here? I assume the announcement was made last evening?"

"*Oui,* it was. And no, Monsieur Riene does not know where I am. Nor does my father." I recalled how he thought I might be some ruse to embarrass the American consul.

"So you've come unchaperoned except for the servant. Who is she?" Zachary lifted the rolled blind aside with one finger. "Your mammy?"

I could only nod. He dropped the shade, cutting off the sliver of light, cocooning us again inside the coach.

I could tell he was not as oblivious to me as he tried to pretend. His gaze strayed to my mouth. I licked my lips, wanting the feel of his molding mine with an almost physical ache.

Yet when it came, when he leaned over the space separating us to press me back against the leather squabs, his kiss was all consuming. Nothing like the first kiss we had shared in my garden those many years ago.

His tongue pushed and prodded, forcing its way into my mouth, as his hand closed over my breast. He had touched me there before, of course. We'd made love as often as we could that other autumn, but his touch had never been so demanding, so carnal.

When he pulled away his breathing was harsh, but his expression wasn't. He stared at me, searching my face as if he might find some eternal truth in the curve of my cheek or the slope of my nose. His thumb was gentle as he wiped away a tear from beneath my eye.

Then he sat back. "You have my deepest apology," he said before pushing out the door and leaving the coach.

I tried to stop him, but reaching for him seemed so futile. Besides, what could I really say or do?

"Gracious, that was one angry man." Mammy heaved her bulk into the carriage, swaying the conveyance as she did.

"We both know he has every right to be," I countered, knowing I tread upon dangerous territory. But I didn't care. Nothing was working out as I wished.

At least she didn't argue with me. Mammy had

the good grace to simply sit quietly, her dark eyes impassive, filled with none of the intense fervor I'd seen in them before.

At a signal from me she tapped the coach's roof and we started along the muddy street. Neither of us spoke, and when we reached the house on Royal Street I went to my room, telling Mammy to leave me in peace.

But there was no peace.

I spent the afternoon and early evening gazing out the window to the garden below, remembering how it had been during those years before I finally left New Orleans to live the remainder of my days at Belle Maison. It seemed as if my living hell was beginning again.

I couldn't bear it.

We ate *en famille* and neither my father or mother seemed upset when I excused myself using fatigue as my reason. I think they thought me on the verge of madness, a reflection not too different from my own. I've no doubt if they could hurry my marriage to Phillipe along they would. Anything to get me gone. Memories of my aunt must have been sharp edged.

Well, I was about to accede to their wishes. Not to marry Phillipe. That was the one mistake I hadn't made in the past, and didn't intend to make this time.

But it was obvious Zachary wanted no part of me. Or perhaps he did, but it wasn't love that drove him. Being near him, knowing that he felt nothing for me was perhaps more painful than the years I'd lived regretting turning him away.

I could not, would not, continue this. Certainly all of them now long dead— Zachary, Phillipe, my mother and father— certainly they'd had their revenge upon my soul. God had had his laugh.

The house was dark when I made my way up the attic stairs. I wasn't certain which of the servant rooms was Mammy's, so I simply followed the drums pounding in my head. My mouth was dry but resolve squared my shoulders as I gripped the brass knob. Beneath the door spilled enough light to tell me many candles burned inside. And I could hear chanting.

My blood ran cold as I slowly opened the door.

Five

"You're where ye don't belong, child."

"Don't you think I know that?" I pushed further into the slant-ceilinged room, wondering when Mammy would turn to face me, hoping I could hold my fear at bay long enough to say what needed to be said.

Memories assailed me. Memories of my death. It was all here. The sickly sweet scent that seemed to permeate my skin. The flickering candles, some short and squat, the others standing tall like sentinels. And Mammy, dressed in flowing white, her head bound in red. The chanting had stopped and the only drums were those in my head. But my mind's eye could almost see the shadowy figures of dancers. The imagined weight of the blanket covering my face made me suck in the heavily perfumed air.

Lurching forward I grasped the back of the only chair in the small room. I was glad I had when Mammy finally turned. I may have fainted dead away, or at least run from the room, screaming hysterically, except my fingers wouldn't pry loose from the chair back.

She was grotesque. Rice powder or something

white lightened her skin. Her full lips were painted red. But it was her eyes that captured me. Dark as ever, bottomless, yet dull and lifeless.

I might have been sucked in by them if not for the sound of the rooster outside.

"Did you hear that?" Momentarily forgetting my fear I rushed to the window, jerking open the heavy curtains that blocked out the night.

"Of course."

"No one else does. I've asked. My mother, father . . . other servants. They all act as if I'm mad when I speak of the rooster's incessant crowing," I said, inexplicably relieved that at least she heard it too. But when I glanced back over my shoulder any relief I felt evaporated like mist over the bayou.

A chicken lay on the narrow cot, its white feathers bloodied. Its neatly decapitated head was on the blanket. I stared, wishing the grisly vision would disappear. Wishing too that I wouldn't be sick.

"You had no business coming here," Mammy said.

"To this room, or this time?" I took a step forward, forcing my attention away from the feathers and blood. "I know that it's your doing." I swallowed down bile. The room was very warm. Mammy's skin was slick with sweat and I could feel dampness beneath my breasts.

"What has happened is for a reason."

"A reason?" My eyes clashed with hers and I quickly glanced away. There seemed no safe place in the room to look. "Is the reason to torture me?" I disliked the shrill sound of my voice but seemed unable to calm myself. "I want to go back."

"The decision is not yours to make."

"Aha!" With all the conviction of an avenging angel, I stepped forward. "Then you admit you did this. That you cast a spell on me. That you hurled me back in time to relive my life, when I should be lying peacefully in my grave. Dead." With each word the quiver in my voice became more noticeable, till in the end I was sobbing.

"Most of your life was spent nearly dead. Ye should know better than to covet it."

What was she saying? I had lived my life. I had. Perhaps not as I would have wished, but still I breathed and ate, slept and noticed the changing of the seasons through the window of my room.

I swallowed, deciding it best not to examine my life too closely. Instead I turned my attention back to Mammy. It was difficult to believe that this was going on in the attic of our town house. That Mammy dressed herself in an outlandish costume and used her bed as a slaughter yard for chickens.

I thought of what my mother would think if she knew and a bubble of laughter started in my throat. I thought of standing in the midst of it as I was, and the humor quickly dissipated.

"Are you a witch?" Somehow I hoped if I could explain away what was happening it would stop.

But Mammy's only response was to turn away.

Her renewed chanting was punctuated by the cock's crowing.

I considered running below stairs, waking the household, my mother, my father, the other servants. I could bring them up here and show them what she was doing. But somehow I knew that was futile. As futile as my position in this life.

Skirting the bed I reached for Mammy, grabbing her stout shoulders. "Why are you doing this to me?" I shook her, rattling the small bones she held loosely in her cupped palms. She didn't resist, but waited for my frustrations to drain away. Then she turned her lifeless eyes on me.

"It is not I that does this to ye, but ye to yourself."

I don't remember leaving the attic. I must have for I sat upon my own bed, knees drawn up beneath my chin, my body trembling. The scent of dead chicken still clung to my flesh and I wonder if the rooster's call was to his mate. Foolish thinking on my part, but no more foolish than living one's life over again. There seems little doubt that that's what I'm doing.

Today I asked my father for the date, pretending when he looked at me askew to only want a confirmation. He told me it is the year of our Lord eighteen hundred and three.

I wonder what Father would have done if I explained some of the happenings to take place in the next fifty years. Not believe me, I'm sure. I could be persuasive. There were advancements I kept up with. Perhaps if I explained some of them in detail . . .

That is *if* I spent my time thinking of those details rather than pondering Mammy's last words to me.

It is not I that does this to you, but you to yourself.

What did she mean? And why should I believe anything she says? Except that I do. Somehow I believe her words hold the key.

I simply am not sure to what.

I don't know what to do with myself.

My mother has sent word to my room that I'm to go visiting with her. The notion holds no appeal, though neither does sitting alone in my room.

Common sense dictates I abandon the thing I really wish to do. Chasing after Zachary only seems to make matters worse. I doubt he would even come to the carriage to see me again.

So I sat, preferring as appears to be my lifetime trend, to do nothing, rather than forge ahead. Mother is angry, but that is hardly a new emotion, and I know both she and Father will be furious when I tell them I won't wed Phillipe.

I barely hear the knock on my door for the rooster's constant crowing. If I but had that bird in hand I'd be happy to wring its neck. Perhaps I'm becoming a witch like Mammy, except that she doesn't look like a witch at all. In the light of day as she stands in my room, it is impossible to recall how grotesque she looked last night. I didn't send for her this morning, preferring to listen to Lily's endless chatter as she dressed me, rather than face Mammy.

But it appears I have no choice.

Mammy stood there a moment in the doorway staring at me, and I tried not to fidget. Is this the moment when time will again have no set form? Will I go hurtling forward toward the grave where I belong?

"Do you wish to speak with me, Mammy?" I hated being the coward, being the first to look away from her stare, but I seem to have no choice.

"He wants to see ye."

"Who . . . ?" I began, only to break off my question at midpoint. I knew who. My heart began pounding and I pushed to my feet, surprised my knees held me. "Where is he?"

"The courtyard, behind the carriage house."

We'd met there before, in that other lifetime that seemed more distant as every day passed. I ran from the room, my silk slippers padding quietly on the steps. No one was about, for which I was grateful. Mother had yet to return from her visits, and Father was off somewhere, discussing politics, no doubt.

I paused for neither shawl nor bonnet as I left the house through the salon doors leading to the garden. It was a glorious day, one of autumn's finest, with the sun bright and warm, and the air clear.

Scents assailed me, roses and moist earth, forcing away the sickening smells of last night. Overhead a squawking formation of snow geese headed for their wintering in the bayous caught my eye.

And reminded me I no longer heard the rooster's crow.

But I had no time to wonder at that. Zachary awaited me, and though I had no idea what he wanted, seeing him again was all that ruled my mind.

I nearly ran around the side of the carriage house, so anxious was I. But something held me back. Perhaps it was the memory of his face when I rushed at him during the ball. Whatever, I slowed my pace to a sedate, ladylike walk, hands folded neatly in front, head lowered, but not so lowered that I couldn't see him. He stood near a magnolia, the large shiny, green leaves forming a perfect backdrop for his golden male beauty.

He bowed. "Mademoiselle de Valliers."

"Captain Hamilton," I replied with a curtsey. If he preferred formality, I could answer in kind.

"Thank you for meeting me here. I realize it's a bit unconventional, however I thought it best to—"

"I understand the need for discretion, Captain."

That brought a hint of a smile, the shadow of dimples. Then he sobered, facing me with earnest green eyes. "I have come to apologize for my behavior yesterday. It was reprehensible."

"No more so than mine has been," I countered.

"But I treated you . . . well, not like a lady, and for that I'm very sorry."

"Perhaps I didn't act very much like a lady."

"Why is that?"

He stared at me as if I were some puzzle he couldn't figure out. I could explain everything to him, of course. But then he would look at me as if I were mad. I decided to remain an enigma.

Shrugging my shoulders I moved toward the iron filigree gate at the back of the garden. "Do you believe in fate, Captain Hamilton?"

"That our life is predestined for us from the time of our birth?"

"I don't know when it begins," I said. "Truthfully I'm not certain I can explain it, but— "

"It seems as if I was destined to meet you." He'd fallen in step beside me, pausing now when I did. "Actually it seems as if I've known you for a very long time," he said.

He had no idea. "And have you . . . liked me during this very long time?" I queried, glancing up at him through my lashes.

"You're teasing me," he said with a chuckle. "And who could blame you? I'm certain if you said such a thing to me I would— "

"Think me insane?"

"Hardly that." He turned his body to face mine, and smiled down at me. "Do you think you can forgive me for my behavior?"

"Oui. It is forgotten."

I sensed that he planned to leave. Not that he wished to, but that he thought it best for me. My hand fell on the sleeve of his tunic.

"Tell me of your family, Captain Hamilton. It must be difficult being so far from home."

"It is at times. I'm from Charlottesville, in Virginia. My father was a general in the American army during the late war."

"Was it predestined that you become a soldier too?"

"Yes," he laughed. "I suppose you could call it fate. The reason I'm here anyway. President Jefferson is a friend of my father's. He has a great interest in the Louisiana area and suggested I might come down as the American consul's *affaire de charge*."

"But you don't plan to make the military your career." The lift of his brow had me adding, "Do you?"

"Actually what I'd really like to do is settle to the west. I grew up on stories of the land beyond the Blue Ridge. A man can make his own destiny there."

His eyes lit up as he spoke and I wondered if he remembered at all that he'd asked me to go with him. In that other life.

Then his gaze caught mine and I knew he was thinking of the possibility. He would not ask. It was too soon. But he did bend down and kiss me. Softly. On the tip of my nose, then my lips. His arm came round my back and I melted against him.

Six

"Oh, Zachary." My arms wound about his neck, my lips opened beneath his. His tongue, smooth and sure, plunged into my mouth. His feel. His scent. His taste. He overwhelmed my senses.

Fingers that had long remembered the rough silk texture of his hair, luxuriated and entwined, buried themselves deep. I never wanted to let him go. Never.

He was back in my arms where he belonged.

His lips moved on mine, nibbling at the corners, then slowly, reluctantly pulling away. I couldn't help the whimper that escaped my throat.

"Mademoiselle de Valliers, I am sorry."

"Eugenie." My voice was as breathless as his. "Call me Eugenie."

"Eugenie."

The sound of my name on his lips was musical.

But neither that nor my arms could hold him. He pulled away, running ten fingers through his rumpled hair, then down across his face. He seemed to fight for control, gaining steadily just as I lost mine.

"Mademoiselle de Valliers . . . Eugenie, please

don't cry." His hand cupped my chin. "I would not hurt you." He paused, concentrating his attention on using his thumbs to brush away my tears. "The mistake is all mine. I should not have come here."

"No." I bit my bottom lip. Anything to stave off the tears that flowed down my cheeks. "Do not say that. I wanted you to come."

This admission appeared to leave him torn. I thought for a moment that he would kiss me again, and longed to feel his lips. But he didn't.

Instead he stepped back, taking away the warmth of his hand. "I should go."

He had turned on his heel before I was able to find my voice. "That would be the easiest way, wouldn't it?"

The narrow-eyed look he gave me over his shoulder made me raise my chin.

"Easier would have been never to have seen you."

"But it's too late for that, isn't it?" I countered.

"I'm not a man to dally with other men's wives . . . or even their fiancées."

"And you think I offer myself as someone to *dally* with?" He had never implied such before, but I had not pursued him that other time. Had never thrown myself so boldly into his arms, or kissed him with such unrestrained ardor.

He stared at me a moment, then closed his eyes. "I don't know what to think."

I appreciated his honesty at least and decided to press it. "Then tell me how you feel."

His laugh was quick in coming. "How I feel?

Like I'm on the very edge of a mountain." His eyes captured mine. "And I'm about to take a step forward."

"Do you wish to take that step?"

"Yes."

The deep tone of his voice vibrated through my body. I relished the feeling before speaking. "Perhaps the mountain is not as high as you think." I took a deep breath, then moved to the magnolia tree. With one finger I traced the contours of a leaf, following the progress with my eyes. "I will never wed Phillipe Riene."

I felt his presence behind me. His hands molded my shoulders, his breath whispered against the curls on the crown of my head.

"Don't make such rash statements, Eugenie. No good can come of this."

"It isn't a rash statement. It's a fact." As only I knew. "And I think as much good can come of this as we want." I could feel his heart beating against my back.

"Hell, Eugenie, if all that mattered was how much I wanted you. . . ." With a groan he pushed away from me, and though the day was warm, I felt a chill pass through me.

"Zachary, I—"

"Miss Eugenie. Miss Eugenie!"

We both looked toward the house as my name was called.

"I have to go inside. My mother must have returned from her visits."

"Yes, of course." His expression was unreadable. "I will—"

"Meet me tonight," I blurted out. "Here."

"Eugenie, I don't think—"

"I shall be here," I called over my shoulder as I started along the crushed shell walkway. "At midnight."

If he answered, I didn't hear him. But then I could hear nothing save the infernal drums that began beating in my head. That and the rooster.

By the time I reached the garden my skin was hot and my heart pounding. I didn't need the sight of Mammy to remind me how fleeting this second lifetime was, but she was there anyway, watching me with her dark, dark eyes.

"Why are you taunting me this way?" I called out when I saw her standing on the brick stairs leading into the house. "If I'm not to have him, then why did you tell me he was here?"

"Miz Bernadette's back and wants to see ye."

"I don't care," I began, then stopped. There was no sense sparring with Mammy. She'd made it clear she would tell me nothing. I swept up the stairs, passing her without meeting her eye. When I reached the top, I paused. "I would appreciate it if someone would quiet that rooster," I said.

A foolish remark, and one that elicited no response from Mammy. If the rooster existed at all, it was in my mind. And it was Mammy, with her chicken feathers and chants, who had put it there.

That night dinner was a festive affair with over a dozen guests, including Phillipe. He was atten-

tive. I tried my best not to draw attention to myself.

Mother caught me as I entered the house that
afternoon and commented upon my flushed appearance. She looks at me askance when she
thinks I don't see. I know it's Aunt Felise I remind her of.

Not that the comparison hasn't occurred to me
as well. Did Aunt Felise hear drums pounding
and cocks crowing, and think she lived again? But
I cannot allow them . . . anyone . . . to think me
mad. Pasting a smile upon my face, I moved toward my father and Phillipe.

"There's to be a ceremony within the month,"
I heard my father say. "The Spanish are formally
relinquishing Louisiana to the French."

"It only clears the path for the Americans to
take control."

"Do you think that will be so terrible?" I asked
Phillipe, as I stepped between him and my father.

"Of course I do."

"Eugenie, you forget yourself. Besides, this is
hardly a topic for you to discuss," my father said.

"Excuse me, Father." I lowered my eyes but not
before noticing Phillipe's indulgent smile.

The evening seemed to last forever. I spent my
time trying to ignore the crowing cock, which, as
usual, no one else seemed to hear, and thinking
about Zachary. What was he doing now? Was his
mind in turmoil, trying to decide whether or not
to come to me tonight?

· He would. At least I hoped he would. It was
difficult for me to judge what would happen any-

more. I was living my life again, but not everything occurred exactly as I recalled. I know it's because I don't act exactly as I did before. I try. But a lifetime of knowledge is difficult to ignore.

Very little of my dealings with Zachary are as they were. I've been much too forward. No wonder he thinks me someone he can touch and kiss with such passion. But I don't mind, for my desire for him is boundless, and he's falling in love with me again. It may not be exactly the same as before, but it's there nonetheless.

Because we are destined for one another.

The thought was bittersweet. How could I think of such things when my life was over? Neither the cock nor the drums nor the deep, dark pools of Mammy's eyes would allow me to forget that. But if I knew for certain that Zachary loved me, I could meet the hereafter with a happier spirit.

And I would explain to Zachary why I could not go with him. This time I would.

Mammy knows I plan to meet Zachary tonight. I can see it in her eyes. Those dark orbs make the hair on my arms stand out. She tries to act as if I don't know of her chickens and bones. But I do. I only hope and pray I can convince Zachary to love me before she decides to send me back to the grave.

But I have sent her away. Though it is not yet midnight I creep from my room and down the wide stairway. This making my way in the darkness is becoming familiar.

The drums are beating in my head, but I notice the noise fade as I make my way toward the back of the garden. This time I brought a shawl for the evening holds a chill.

He waits for me.

The moon gilds his hair silver as he stands beside the gate. My heart leaps with excitement and my pace quickens. In that other life I faced the first time I met Zachary alone at night with childish fright. This time I know what to expect.

Or do I?

Even in the dim light from the moon I can see the worried expression on Zachary's face. He doesn't take me into his arms but stands rigid and aloof, looking every inch the soldier he is.

"I came to tell you . . ." he began, then paused. He shook his head then stepped forward, lifting my chin with the crook of his finger. He grinned, and the light of his smile warmed my heart. "As foolish as it sounds I came to tell you I wasn't coming."

"Oh?" My eyes met his.

"I told you it was foolish." He took my hand, lacing his fingers with mine and led me to the wrought iron bench beneath the oak's spreading, moss-festooned branches. We sat, side by side, our hands still entwined. "My arguments are sound though," he said. "If anyone should find us together like this, your family would be outraged. Your fiancé— "

"I told you I shan't marry him."

"But he visited you tonight." When I turned my head to look at him, he continued. "I rode by earlier. Even toyed with the idea of coming to your door."

Zachary stretched his long legs out when I laughed. "So you think that humorous? But I contend it no more outlandish than this." He raised our joined hands.

"My father would not understand."

"My point, exactly." He sighed. "Do you think I don't know how we Americans are viewed in this city? They call us Kaintucks. Our every move is watched."

"It must be difficult."

"Sometimes," he admitted. "Usually I ignore it." There was a pause. "But I can't now."

"Because of me?"

His fingers tightened. "Because of you."

Seven

"I wish I could, you know."

"Could what?" I looked around at him, trying to make out his features in the moonlight . . . trying to commit them to memory.

"Call on your father. Ask to court you."

His words were like a balm on my troubled soul. "I too wish that possible." I sighed and he unlinked our hands, stretching his arm around my shoulders and settling me to his side.

"I've been thinking since this afternoon."

"How you would avoid coming here tonight?" I teased, turning my face up toward his.

"Well, that did occupy some of my time," he said with a chuckle and a quick peck on the end of my nose. "But mostly I tried to figure a way out of this."

"Not coming tonight would probably have been your easiest solution."

His arm tightened. "We both know that wasn't possible."

"I know." Fate . . . or Mammy . . . had ordained that we meet again . . . and suffer again. I leaned back against his shoulder, breathing in the woodsy, erotic scent of him, wishing I could keep him from being hurt. His heartbeat lulled my senses.

I was startled when he sat straighter.

"Resigning my commission is an option." He hurried on before I could stop him. "I had thought to wait until the spring to do it, after the United States officially received the territory. But I could do it now."

His offering was as wonderful this time as last. I could only stare at him, savoring the moment.

"As a private citizen, my every move won't be dictated by the consul . . . or the army. Even so, because of your father's feelings about Americans there will probably be a scandal." His voice lowered. "One hurting you more than I, I'm afraid."

I should tell him now. Tell him that anything but fleeting happiness between us was impossible. I'd let it go too far already.

But the truth was so . . . so unbelievable.

And I couldn't bear for him to look at me as if I were mad.

"Zachary." I laid my hand on his cheek. "You mustn't do anything rash," I said, echoing words he'd spoken to me.

Even in the near darkness I could feel his eyes probing mine. "Is this a game to you? A flirtation with forbidden fruit that you will tire of soon?"

"No!" Panic filtered into my voice. How could he think such a thing? He was the most important person in my entire life. "Zachary, please." My fingers slid behind his neck. "You must know that I would give anything, my very soul, if we could be together."

He leaned forward, drawn by my admission to press his lips to mine. And I, through the haze of desire, wondered if that was exactly what I'd done. Had I somehow sold my soul for this fleeting chance at happiness?

Soon though, even that weighty question seemed to lose its importance, as my body and mind responded to Zachary's kiss. It was all consuming . . . and over much too quickly.

His breathing rasped against my neck, his words vibrating through me. "It would be better if you were but flirting, adding yet another conquest to the string of hearts you've broken."

Had I broken other hearts? There were suitors, of course. Suitors turned away when my father decided upon Phillipe. But none of them had seemed too forlorn. No, it was only Zachary's heart that I was destined to truly break.

For it was only Zachary's heart that offered me true love.

"Those others," I began, "were more infatuated with the idea of Eugenie de Valliers, than the woman I am."

"Then they were fools," he said, pulling away enough so I could see the grin on his face, the dimples denting his cheeks.

"Were they? Then do you think you know me so well?"

"I know you're kind, and loving, beautiful . . . and passionate." His lips brushed mine.

"Perhaps *you* are the heartbreaker," I said, my head lolling back, allowing easy access to my throat as euphoria seeped into my veins.

My eyes opened when he pulled away.

"I shall never knowingly hurt you, Eugenie." He took a deep breath, and stood. "Which is why I shouldn't be down here with you."

He was going to leave. I could feel it, taking his leave for my own good. Even as I pressed myself against his back, I could feel it.

"Eugenie." He turned, cupping my shoulders and holding me apart from him. "I don't know how it has happened so quickly, but I have fallen in love with you."

"And I love you," I said. "I always have."

This time when I melted into his arms I knew there would be no turning back. At first, when I realized my life was replaying itself, I thought his forgiveness was all I sought. Then I hoped only to hear the magical words that meant his heart was mine again. Now I knew there was more I wanted. Selfish, selfish me.

I want to share our love as we did before. To know again the splendor of soaring in his arms.

And he wanted me with the same fiery desire. It was as if the levee holding the surge back, broke. His mouth left mine, forging a path down my jaw and lower. Heat scorched through me wherever his lips touched.

And his hands, those strong sure hands that could be so gentle, now pulled me beneath the sheltering arms of the moss-curtained oak, our own special sanctuary, shadowed even from the shimmery moon.

"Eugenie."

My name on his lips sent tremors down my

spine. I stood transfixed, wanting him more than life itself as my gown skimmed over my head. His knuckles brushed the tip of my breast through sheer cotton and desire tightened my body. I raised my arms and the chemise drifted to the ground.

I should be embarrassed, standing before him, naked but for the stockings he knelt to strip off. Perhaps the other time, all those years ago, I was. But memory fails me.

I know only now. Only the erotic fire of his tongue.

My hands ride his broad shoulders, wanting to feel the skin beneath the wool tunic. And then I am clutching fistfuls of fabric, my breath coming in ragged gasps. I would have fallen to the ground if not for his firm grasp on my flesh. All through me the throbbing pulsed. Mindless. Erotic. All consuming.

It was so long since I'd felt the soul-searing pleasure. So long since I'd felt one with him.

Before the tremors released me, I slid down his body. Beneath the oak the smells of dark earth mingled with the musky scents of two people in the throes of making love.

His uniform was a barrier neither of us could abide. My fingers were as frantic as his to un-loosen the buttons and tear aside the tunic. His boots and pantaloons were next and then we were both gloriously naked. He lay on me, his weight pushing me down in the spongy grass-covered ground.

"I don't want to hurt you," he whispered in an echo of years past.

"Just love me," I answered. "Love me."

The pain was sharp and quickly gone, and then he was inside me and we were one. As always, it was new yet familiar.

His mouth molded to mine as the movements of our bodies surged deeper and stronger. Time as I knew it stood still.

Our souls joined. All appeared right with the world. And this moment, lying in my beloved's arms, seemed worth any price.

Except I feared it wasn't.

My heart still pounded with excitement as Zachary rolled to his side, cuddling me to his chest. "Are you all right?" he whispered, his voice breathless.

"Yes, oh, yes." I brushed my lips across the wiry hair that covered his chest. "It was more wonderful than I ever knew."

"I should have waited, taken you in a fine bed . . . on our wedding night."

"Shhh." I leaned up, my finger pressing against his mouth. "Beneath God's handiwork, this magnificent tree, is all the splendor I need. As for the other—"

"I'll speak to your father tomorrow. Surely he will—"

"No!" The vehemence of my word had me sitting up. "No, please. You don't know him. He will not allow us to wed." I turned my face away from the eyes I knew searched me in the dark. "He won't."

"I can't just do nothing." Zachary raised on his elbows. "Not after tonight."

"You needn't feel responsible simply because—"

"Damnit, Eugenie. 'Tis not about responsibility and you know it. I love you. I want to be with you."

"And I with you," I said, propelling myself toward him as I blinked back tears. "We will find a way. But please . . . wait."

His arms wrapped around me and I could feel the pressure of his mouth on my hair. "I'll wait, if that's what you want."

"It is."

"But not forever, Eugenie. I can't wait forever."

But he had. And Lord help me, he would again.

I forced that thought from my mind as we were there beneath the wide-flung branches, sharing dreams and hopes. He wanted us to wed and leave Louisiana. "We can go to Virginia if you like. Charlottesville is no more than a village, but Richmond is growing."

"But I thought you wished to go west," I said as I ran my fingers across his chest. I could not stop touching him.

"It was a dream of mine, but now . . ." He tucked his chin to look down at me. "I'm not sure it would be fair to you."

I wanted to say I would follow him anywhere. That I had learned my lesson . . . my lifetime of lessons. But he spoke of fairness, and the guilt I had kept at bay swamped over me. I was not fair to him.

With each word, each touch, I drew him further into the web of believing we could have a life together. I fed his desires. I fueled his hopes. Knowing all the while it could never be. Knowing he would be disappointed when whatever spell that held me in this sphere of time thrust me back.

Even now I could hear the drums. Reminders that this existence was not real.

Why did I do this to him, the man I professed to love? Selfishness. A need to be near him.

Yet even as I chastised myself, my fingers curled more tightly about him. "I don't want to leave you," I whispered.

"And I don't want you to go." He finger combed a twig from my hair. "But you must. I didn't realize how late . . . or early it was." He pushed us both to sitting.

"What do you mean?" I accepted the chemise he handed me.

"The rooster. Don't you hear it? Could it be morning already?"

My blood ran cold. "You hear the rooster?"

"Who wouldn't? The damn thing crows over and over."

"But you can't. Only I can hear it. Only I understand what it means." I yanked on my underclothes, then the rumpled gown, pushing his hand away when he tried to calm me.

"Eugenie? What is it?" As quickly as I, he pulled on his clothes. "Tell me, sweetheart."

"I can't. Not now." My feet slid into my slippers. "I must return to the house."

"But when will I see you?" He started to follow me along the crushed shell walk. "Eugenie?"

"Soon." I tossed over my shoulder as I ran. "I shall contact you soon."

My feet kept time to the drum beat and crowing cock as I ran toward the house. What had I done? Dear God, what had I done?

Eight

"What have you done to him?"

I burst into Mammy's room, grabbing her by her shoulders as she lay on her cot and shaking. My breath was coming in painful gasps, partly from my mad run up the three flights of stairs, but mostly from the terror that seemed to keep tightening in my stomach.

Terror that pounded through me as surely as the drums beating in my head.

My skin felt too tight for my body and I feared I might explode; shatter into a thousand pieces. Was this to be my ending then? My punishment? I could bear it. I could. As long as Zachary was spared.

But he wouldn't be. I knew it from the moment he heard the cock. He'd entered my world. The madness of it.

And it was Mammy's fault.

My fingers tightened, digging into her dark skin and still she only stared at me. In the moonlight slanting through the attic window her face looked very black against the white sheet.

"What have you done to him?" I repeated, trying to hold onto my anger. But it was difficult when she did nothing but look at me a with blank eyes.

My fingers forfeited their grip.

Pushing myself off the cot I paced the short distance to the door and back. I had to remain rational. That was my only chance of staying sane. My glimpses of the other side were frightening.

Forcing myself to be calm, I sat upon a rickety chair, the only piece of furniture in the room besides the cot. I took a deep breath. "Please, Mammy," I began. "Captain Hamilton does not deserve. . . ." Tears filled my eyes and I brushed them away. "What will happen to him?"

When she didn't answer I felt my body slump forward.

"I know I'm being punished for . . . for rejecting him. For the life I led. I know that. And I accept it. I do. But Zachary . . ." Fresh tears spilled forth. "He has done nothing."

Her silence was maddening.

"It is my fault, I know. I should have let him alone. But I wanted his touch so." Turning my head I stared toward the small square of silvery moonlight. Beyond the window the rooster crowed incessantly. And now, because of me, Zachary heard it too.

"You must do something," I insisted. "Undo what has been done, for God's sake!"

"His fate is in your hands."

"What?" I hadn't expected her to speak. My hands scrubbed at my wet cheeks. "What did you say?"

"Your fate is also your own."

* * *

She would say nothing more and I tired of trying to force her. What she said was gibberish. I have no more control of my destiny than . . . than a moth dancing about a flame. Tempted by the light I drew nearer, repeatedly asking for one more moment of basking in the warmth, only to be drawn in and destroyed.

I'd known from the moment I awoke to relive my life that my fate was to plunge into the candle's flame. I lived in this time only by the whim of one of hell's demons. The drums and crowing rooster that rarely gave me peace were proof enough of that. At any moment this devil would tire of watching me flit about and end his cruel jest.

It was my fate and I was resigned if not happy. But Zachary knew naught of this. He did not deserve this.

My only hope was that somehow Mammy was right. Could I hold the key to my fate? To Zachary's?

A scream, loud and compelling pierced the early dawn. I twisted to see one of the cook's helpers staring at me, her eyes wide above hands clasped to her mouth.

"What's wrong? Stop it." I pushed to my feet, only to have her cry out again.

Doors opened all over the house. Several servants raced from rooms in the attic. From around the curve of the stairway I saw my father, followed by my mother. Father was tying a silk dressing gown and carrying a brass-handled dueling pistol.

They all converged upon me where I stood at the foot of the attic steps, grasping the banister.

"What in the hell is going on here?" My father's question was directed at me.

"Eugenie?" My mother's voice was full of concern as she approached. Then her back stiffened and she turned to the servant who was offering a blabbering account of how she'd come out of her room to go to the kitchen to start peeling potatoes for breakfast.

"I didn't see her there 'til I was near on top her 'cause I didn't have no candle. I don't usually need one ye know 'cause I come this way every mornin' but . . . I thought I seen me a ghost, and I just started to— "

"Hush up, Sully," my mother snapped. "Mammy, bring her to her room." With that she turned and led my father back down the stairs.

I didn't understand what all the fuss was about until I caught a glimpse of myself in the cheval mirror in my room. I did look like a ghost. An unkempt ghost. My skin was pale, my hair in wild disarray. Absently I lifted my fingers, pulling a twig from the tumbling mass of curls. My gown, soiled and wrinkled hung on me, unfastened, with one shoulder drooping.

How I managed to become so disheveled was no mystery. Why I allowed myself to be found in such a state was. I glanced toward Mammy who stood, her hands folded over her stomach, her expression as devoid of emotion as when I burst into her room earlier.

"I will know the meaning of this behavior, Eugenie."

It was my father. He'd managed to clothe himself and now faced me, dressed as if ready for a meeting with other planters. The purplish, red hue of his face was the only sign of his anger.

"Where's Mother?" I asked. Not that I truly wished to know. But I hoped the extra time would give me a chance to come up with some explanation other than I sat on the stairs and became lost in thought.

"She will be here shortly. At the moment she's very distressed."

As was I.

"You have acted strangely since the day of your betrothal ball. Oh, don't think your mother hasn't told me of your actions. They border on inexcus— "

"I don't wish to marry Phillipe," I heard myself blurt out.

"What? What are you telling me, girl?" His face was an even darker shade of red.

"I don't wish to . . . I won't marry Phillipe Riene."

"It's inconceivable to me that you're saying this." He twisted away and then turned back. "Do you have any idea what you *are* saying?"

"What *is* she saying?" My mother, still dressed in a voluminous dressing gown, closed the door behind her. Spotting Mammy she signaled for the black woman to leave the room.

"No! Mammy stays. She's the reason for—"
Sanity slammed into me. What was I about to
tell them? The suspicion in my parents' eyes was
unnerving enough without confirming their
fears. I was not mad. I had to remember that.
"Do what my mother commands, Mammy," I said
with a nonchalant motion of my hand.

"Where were you? You look as if you've rolled
in the dirt."

"She's refusing to marry Phillipe," my father
informed her. He obviously considered that more
important than where I'd been, or what I'd been
doing.

"Not marry Phillipe. But the betrothal agreeant
has been drawn up and signed. The ball . . . everything. . . ."

"She will wed him, Bernadette."

"I won't." Contradicting my father took all my
strength and I fell back into a chair.

"Eugenie, you must stop this immediately." For
once my mother's expression showed some emotion. "Edmund." She turned away from me to
face my father. "You don't think she could be
like—"

"I'm not insane!" I said, pushing again to my
feet. "I'm nothing at all like Aunt Felise," I insisted with enough vehemence to have them both
staring at me wide-eyed.

My father simply turned and opened the door,
summoning Mammy who was still in the hallway.
"Get her dressed. We will leave for Belle Maison
after we've broken our fast."

"No. I don't want to go back to the country,"

I called out. But the only one to hear me was Mammy. And she only stared at me with those dark eyes that knew all . . . and told nothing.

Perhaps this was for the best.

It's been a fortnight since I was brought back to Belle Maison. My time has been spent mostly in solitude, though I join the family for some meals in the dining room. We sit across the wide expanse of polished mahogany and make polite conversation. I must be fairly adept at hiding my true feelings for tonight Phillipe is to join us. Mother and Father must have decided I'm not mad . . . and that my punishment has been severe enough.

I can't decide what I shall do. Should I risk banishment to my room again, where the only company is the incessant beat of drums and my memories? Or should I play the obedient child? Whichever, my resolve is firm. I will not marry Phillipe.

And I shall always love Zachary.

But there has been no word from him, nor do I expect any. Because of my forward behavior our affair surged ahead much faster than in my other life. There was no long courtship, clandestine or otherwise. This time I forced myself upon him before he was sure of his feelings.

I know he swore his love to me, but I think . . . I hope that was in the passion of the moment. Far better for him if he can leave here. Go back to Virginia, or to the west and forget me. And break free of the crow of that cursed rooster.

But that was not to be.

I saw Mammy staring out the window of my room, the front window that overlooks the alley of moss-draped oaks. I was sitting near the garden window, trying to stay as far from her as possible. I didn't like being around her for she frightened me, her presence reminding me of how tenuous my life was. Yet I couldn't help rising as she continued to watch. My feet seemed to have a mind of their own, drawing me toward her till I too searched the late afternoon scene before me.

It wasn't until I'd stood thus a few moments that I noticed a single rider astride a magnificent black stallion galloping toward the house.

"Zachary."

Pushing away from the windowsill I turned, then raced from the room. My feet scarcely touched the ground as I flew down the stairs. I was on the wide veranda by the time he rode onto the circular drive and in his arms as he leaped from the horse's back.

"Eugenie." He crushed me to his chest, lifting me till my toes only skimmed the crushed shells.

His kiss was passionate, possessive, and I reveled in the feel of him. The taste. I had him back with me. Where he belonged. The drums were gone. All I could hear were his whispered words of love.

"I asked about you everywhere."

His mouth left mine to trail a path along my jaw and my flesh burned.

"I missed you so much."

His teeth tickled my earlobe and my insides melted.

"Why did you leave me?"

The answer to his question hit me and my blood ran cold. Slowly my hands cupped his face, holding him away from me. "You shouldn't have come," I said, feeling the ground beneath my feet for the first time.

"I know it will be difficult but we can work everything out. I resigned my commission," he said. "Your father has to understand that we love each other."

"It's more than that," I argued. "There are things *you* wouldn't understand. Things even I don't understand."

"Whatever it is we'll deal with it. Nothing is more important than how we feel about each other. . . . Eugenie?"

I had turned away, unable to face the expression of disappointment on his face once he realized my reluctance.

"Eugenie, what is it? What's going on?"

"Yes, Eugenie, perhaps you owe us all the answer to that question."

I didn't have to look toward the veranda to know who stood there.

My father and Phillipe.

Nine

"Father!" As I turned to face him I expected the aristocratic expression of disdain. What I didn't foresee was the pistol pointed in our direction.

"Step away from that man, Eugenie." This directive came from Phillipe. And I looked at him, my eyes pleading.

"Take the gun from him, Phillipe," I begged. "Don't let him do this."

"You heard your betrothed, Eugenie. Now come here."

"I will not." I nearly screamed the words. "How dare you try—"

"Eugenie." It was Zachary's voice, much calmer than mine, as he stepped in front of me.

Before my frightened eyes he strode toward the verandah, pausing near the bottom of the steps. His bow was formal. "I am Zachary Hamilton, late of the United States army."

"I know who you are." My father nodded toward Phillipe. "We both do. Now leave my property at once."

"Monsieur de Valliers, if I could just have a few minutes of your time—"

"You, sir, shall have nothing that belongs to
me. Not my time . . . or my daughter."

"But Monsieur de Valliers, I love your daughter
and she— "

"No!" The metallic click of the pistol being
cocked echoed through my head, dispelling the
rhythm of the drums. I lurched forward, trying
to throw myself in front of Zachary.

But he was quicker than I. Before I could
shield him, Zachary was up the stairs, facing my
father, looming over him. He reached for the pistol, encircling the barrel with his long fingers,
and pried it from my father's hand.

I could barely breathe for fear my father would
squeeze the trigger. But he didn't, whether forced
by a sense of decency over shooting an unarmed
man, or simply overpowered by Zachary's presence, I don't know.

Zachary tossed the pistol aside. It skidded on
the grass, coming to rest against the fence post
and I let out my breath. Zachary was still staring
at my father, his eyes narrowed when I scrambled
up the steps.

"Get off my property! Get off my property, I
say. You and your kind may take over Louisiana,
but this is still my land." My father's face was
red and flecks of spittle spotted his mouth.

"Zachary, please." I touched his arm, feeling
the tension in his muscles beneath my hand. He
glanced down at me then and I could see the
anger he tried to suppress.

My father, of course, made no effort to hide
his wrath. And Phillipe's features were contorted

by the same degree of ire. Nothing would be solved this way, of that I was certain. I just wished I were as sure of what to do.

"I think you should go." I could tell my words took Zachary by surprise. His stare now shifted to me, and it was incredulous.

"This is it then? You are sending me away?"

"No, no, of course not," I countered. But I'd done it before. "Nothing has changed. I love you and I always will. But I need to talk with them." I spoke as if my father and Phillipe were not mere inches from my side. "I need to make them understand."

"We'll both talk to them."

"The hell you will! Now get off my property." My father reached for my arm but I shrugged him away.

"He won't listen while you're here."

Zachary audibly expelled a breath. "Eugenie, he isn't going to listen at all."

"He will." At least I hoped he would. Somehow, here in the sunshine, Zachary by my side, the pounding of the drums a distant memory, I felt empowered. "You must trust me, Zachary," I said, my eyes pleading with him.

His gaze met mine and his love and warmth flowed through me. Then his attention shifted toward the two men filled with impotent rage, standing close by.

"I can't leave you here with them."

"He's my father, Zachary." I thought of him as I'd known him last in my other life . . . old, frail, helpless. "He won't harm me."

"For God's sake, Eugenie, he pointed a gun at you."

"At *you* and he didn't shoot it," I reminded. "Please, it's the only way I can do this." My lower lip trembled. "The only way."

Even then, convincing him hadn't been easy. In the end he'd walked purposely to the fence post and picked up the pistol, shoving it into the waist of his buckskin breeches. He mounted in a fluid motion, then leaned down toward me.

"I'll be back tomorrow, Eugenie."

"I'll be waiting."

"And I'm taking you with me then, whether or not you've convinced him." He glanced toward the verandah where my father and Phillipe stood in stony silence. "To stop this foolishness."

I swallowed, only able to nod in response. For tomorrow when he came I would have to tell him the truth. Then it would not be my father keeping us apart. Zachary would not want me. But there was no other way.

But I had to know if I'd already harmed him beyond hope. My fingers reached up, grabbing his thigh. "The cock," I questioned. "Have you heard it crowing?" Did its strident shriek intrude upon his every waking hour like it did mine? Was he already marked?

He raised a brow and smiled, his dimples deepening. "A rooster, Eugenie? I usually hear one in the morn."

"That's the only time?"

"The only time, Eugenie."

My fingers loosened with relief.

He leaned lower. "Are you certain you will be all right? You look pale."

"I'm fine . . . will be fine." His lips brushed mine. "I will see you tomorrow."

"The first day of our new life together," he said. "I love you."

"I love you," I called, but he'd already pressed his heels to the stallion's flank. Between the pounding hooves and the beating drums he may not have heard me. The idea that he hadn't bothered me, but I consoled myself with the thought that he already knew. He had to know.

When I turned to face my father he was gone, slamming his way through the front door. Phillipe still stood on the verandah and I decided to speak with him first. I felt twinges of guilt about him, as I had in that other life. Though I didn't love him, and doubted he loved me, he was a guiltless pawn in all this.

"Phillipe," I said as I climbed the stairs to the wide porch. "I am sorry."

He stared at me, his expression one of contempt. "Your feelings are no longer of any concern to me."

"That may be, Phillipe. However, it was never my intention to hurt you like this."

"As I suppose you didn't plan on becoming that American's whore."

Anger and shock made the blood drain from my face, but I lifted my chin and walked inside. I had nothing more to say to him.

My father met me at the doorway to his library. He carried the twin of the dueling pistol Zachary took.

"What are you doing?" My hand trembled as I reached for the gun. "Give it to me."

"Go to your room, Eugenie."

"I will not." Until meeting Zachary, I'd never spoken with defiance to my father and I could tell he was shocked. But he would have to get used to the notion that I would no longer follow his words blindly. Whatever happened with my life . . . and I knew that any moment could be my last on this plane . . . I would not reprise my role as the mindless maiden I had been.

"We need to discuss this, Father. I am not marrying Phillipe."

"As if he'd have you now. My God, Eugenie, have you any idea how utterly common you looked in that man's arms?"

I whirled about to face my mother who'd come up behind me. "I love him, Mother," I said, but I was beginning to understand that meant nothing to either of my parents.

My mother confirmed my feelings with her next words. "You don't know what love means, Eugenie. You have insulted a fine man . . . a wealthy man . . . who would have given you anything you wanted. I've come to think you are like your Aunt Felise."

"No." My heart beat in rhythm to the drums. "No, I'm not mad. I'm not. I only wish. . . ." The drums were beating so loudly now I couldn't think. What did I wish? Zachary. I wanted Zachary. But he was lost to me too. He would not love me once he knew the truth about me.

"I think you should go to your room, Eugenie."

"No." I backed away from my parents who were now standing side by side to confront me. "I don't want to go to my room." The rooster crowed and the drums beat and my head pounded. I could feel dampness sheen my face, as I took one step back, then another. "I won't go to my room."

And in the end I didn't.

It was to the attic room they took me. The attic room where Aunt Felise had lived out her life.

While I stood in the corner near the front window servants bustled about brushing aside sheets, transforming ghostly furniture. A bed emerged and a dresser. A chest and chifforobe still holding outdated and elegant clothing worn by my aunt. Even though she'd been insane, she was still a lady and expected to attire herself as one.

Even as she spent endless days alone in the attic room.

I tried not to think of her, of what her life was. Yet as I stood there I could hear the thumping on the attic floor, the haunting screams at night. And I recalled what relief I felt when she died.

But that wouldn't be my fate.

For I was already dead. And I wasn't mad. Somehow I would have to convince them, my mother and father, that I was as sane as they were.

But they didn't come to see me that day. And I probably couldn't argue my case too well anyway. The noises pounded in my head till I thought my skull might explode. I sat as still as I could watching out the window. Watching as darkness rolled in from the bayou, enveloping the land in eery night.

Dinner was brought to me on a silver tray, and I ate only to keep up my strength. When the servant left I heard the unmistakable tumble of the lock, and that sound joined the pandemonium in my brain.

I slept fitfully, waking often to the cock's crow. The spell seemed so intense now, I had trouble separating reality from fantasy. But I know that Zachary will come and he will stop them from torturing me. He must.

The truths that I must reveal to him weighed upon me like a shroud. But I owed him that. Owed him that a lifetime ago.

The day was cold and rainy, with a wind that whipped the moss about the trees. A draft coming from around the window chilled me, but I stared through the panes anyway. Watching for Zachary. He will come. I know he will.

Yet for all my assurance, I still jumped up, hugging myself for joy when I saw him ride up the lane. He seemed not to notice the inclement weather and tears of relief clouded my eyes as I knocked on the rain-marbled glass.

"Zachary!" I called his name again and again, willing him to look up toward the gabled roof.

When he disappeared beneath the verandah overhang panic set in and I looked about for something, anything, to use. Aunt Felise's cane caught my eye and I rushed to grab it. Pounding. Pounding on the floor as hard as I could.

He must hear me. He must.

But minutes passed and I heard nothing but my own futile attempts to battle the drums. When I raced back to the window, I wasn't surprised to see Zachary mounting his horse.

The cane seemed to have a will of its own as I brought it back over my shoulder then thrust it through the window. Glass shattered, flying everywhere, mixing with the rain. But though I screamed his name, Zachary didn't look my way.

But he did reign his horse to a stop just as I heard the key turn in my lock. "Zachary!" I screamed, then screamed again from pure fright.

Mammy stood in the doorway, holding the skeleton key in her hand. She extended it toward me, the brass glowing softly, as I stared at her in shock.

"The choice is yours, Miss Eugenie. It has always been yours."

Ten

I stared at Mammy as if in a trance. For a moment I couldn't remember what I was doing in the attic. Why was I holding Aunt Felise's cane? Then suddenly my mind cleared. My head whipped toward the window, then back. Rushing toward her I threw myself in Mammy's arms. "Oh Mammy, you found the key. Thank you."

"Ye best get goin' child if ye plan to catch your man." Her eyes narrowed. "That is, if that be what ye want to do."

"Of course it is," I answered, racing back to the window. "This is the choice I should make." The wind blew gusts of chilly rain in through the shattered pane, but I didn't care. "I'm coming, Zachary," I yelled and waved frantically when he looked up toward me.

I passed my mother on the attic stairs and paused only long enough to hug her. "Don't be angry with me. I love Zachary. My life would be nothing without him." As I continued down the stairs what I'd just said echoed in my head. My life would be nothing without Zachary. They weren't just hollow words. Somehow I knew it as fact.

Which was silly.

I was just so excited, so happy to have escaped before Zachary left. He threw open the front door just as I passed the landing. I nearly flew down the stairs and into his arms. He was wet and I didn't care. Cold, but I'd warm him.

His kiss was like a homecoming.

"Your father said you didn't want to see me." He whispered the words against my throat as his arms tightened.

"How could you think that? Not going with you would be the worst mistake I could ever make."

"Eugenie!"

Turning I faced my father.

"You will not leave with this man. I will not allow it."

"Nothing will keep me from going with Zachary. Nothing in this world or beyond."

"Mmmmm."

"Are you sleepy?"

"No," I sighed, snuggling closer to the warm body lying beside me on the mattress. "Just feeling . . . wonderful."

Zachary's chuckle vibrated against my breast as he took the taut tip into his mouth. When I was no more than molten desire, squirming beneath him, he lifted his head and stared down into my eyes.

"It *is* late, Mrs. Hamilton . . . or should I say early." Dawn's first streaks painted the sky a pale pewter beyond the window. "Perhaps we should try to get some sleep."

"Oh no you don't, Mr. Hamilton." I reached between our bodies, closing my fingers about the part of him that belied his professed interest in slumber. "You, sir, need to finish what you started."

He laughed again, as did I. But soon neither of us could do anything but feel. His kisses intoxicated. His touch scorched a path over my flesh. When we came together, our bodies straining, when the pleasure peaked, it was as always, as if our souls united.

My head rested on his shoulder, my arm draped across his chest. And though drowsy from a night of making love, I couldn't stop touching my new husband. We were married a fortnight ago in Natchez. Now we lay in a wide tester bed in Zachary's house in Charlottesville. In less than a month we'd be leaving for the west.

"You aren't sorry, are you?" Zachary tucked his chin, kissing the top of my head.

"What? That I left Belle Maison and married you?" My tone was incredulous. How could he think such a thing? Yet when I shifted to stare into his face I could tell, even in the grainy light, that he was serious.

My palm cupped his cheek. "No, Zachary."

"I will work hard to carve out a world for us . . . but I can't give you what you had at Belle Maison. Or what Phillipe could provide for you. At least not at first."

"Oh, but you can give me so much more, Zachary. So much. It frightens me to think what might have happened had I not chosen you and your love."

"You'd have been a lot wealthier."

"Not in the things that count." I pushed up to brush my lips to his and his arm tightened around me. Outside the sky paled and from somewhere in the distance came the strident crow of a rooster.

"What is it?" Zachary rolled to face me as my body stiffened.

"Did you hear that?" My mouth felt suddenly dry.

"What? The rooster?"

I could only nod as Zachary pulled the blanket about my shoulders.

"It's morning," Zachary said with a chuckle. "And we've hardly slept at all."

I turned my head to look toward the window. "It is, isn't it? Morning of a new day." I smiled. "That's all the rooster's crowing meant."

Zachary grinned. "What else could it mean?"

Suddenly I felt foolish. "I don't know. It's just . . . well, for a moment it seemed as if there was something I needed to tell you."

"What?" Zachary brushed a curl off my forehead.

"I can't remember." I laughed self-consciously. "Isn't that strange?"

He shrugged one muscled shoulder. "You'll think of it sooner or later."

"Perhaps. Or maybe I just wanted to tell you that I love you. I always have. And I always will."

Zachary settled me into the shelter of his arms. "That's the only thing I need to know."

About the Author

Christine Dorsey lives with her family in Midlothian, Virginia. She is the author of over ten Zebra historical romances, including her Blackstone trilogy: *Sea Fires, Sea of Desire,* and *Sea of Temptation,* as well as her MacQuaid brothers trilogy: *My Savage Heart, My Seaswept Heart* and *My Heavenly Heart.* Christine is also the author of a novella in Zebra's Christmas anthology, *A Christmas Embrace* and Zebra's June Bride anthology, *A Bride's Desire.* Christine's newest historical romance, *Splendor,* will be published in February 1996. Christine loves hearing from readers and you may write to her c/o Zebra Books. Please include a self-addressed stamped envelope if you wish a response.

The O'Madden

by

Lisa Ann Verge

One

The time had come to find a mate.

Maeve fisted her cloak closed as she reached the height of the gentle slope. A bonfire snapped on the worn stone and hazed smoke into the dusky sky. The village girls clasped hands and raced in drunken circles around the All Hallow's Eve fire. Maeve lingered in the fragrant shadows of the thin edge of the woods, searching the faces of the men through the wavering heat.

A girl screeched across Maeve's path, her fair hair streaming. A young man seized her by the waist and sent her skirts flying as he swept her up over his shoulder. The couple's high-pitched laughter dissolved in the shadows beyond the roaring glow.

"Glenna," Maeve said to the woman beside her, as her fingers dug into her cloak. "I must have been daft to come here, to think of doing this."

The fairy-woman sank her walking stick into the earth and clasped gnarled hands over the hilt. "It was your choice to come to the Samhain fires, so far away from home."

"I'm not footing the blame on you. But look at them." Maeve frowned at the young men jostling around the flames, vying to be the next to leap through the fires. "A full month's spinning says there isn't a one of them older than five-and-ten."

"A young man's passion flares, then dies just as quickly." The old woman cackled. Her lined face collapsed into folds of humor. "Are you sure that's not what you're wanting from this night?"

"Glenna, this is no matter for teasing. I'm nigh five-and-twenty, I'll be invisible to all of them."

"Be patient, my Maeve. The evening has just begun, and you've not yet seen the whole herd. Soon the youngest of them will be paired off and snoring somewhere in the bracken." Glenna leaned into the stick and rubbed the ache of her back. "As will you, daughter of my heart, as will you."

Heat crept up Maeve's cheeks. Her turnip-gourd lantern banged against her knee as she snapped away from Glenna's side. She walked the line between the shadows and the light, not knowing which nauseated her more: the hungry glances cast toward her from the light, or the languorous, throaty laughter rising here and there from the shadows of the woods. She would know both intimately, before the night was through.

So it had come to this, she thought, sweeping her cloak out of the way as another couple hurtled past her into the embrace of the woods. So it had come to searching for a mate by the light of a foreign village's All Hallow's Eve fire. For sure, she wouldn't be getting the loving she'd imagined in her foolish youth. Tonight, in the embrace of one of those red-cheeked boys, she'd expect no slow, patient tutoring. She'd be lucky if she managed to lure him far enough away from the fires for a bit of privacy before he hiked up her skirts and had his way with her.

Stop complaining, Maeve, things could be worse.

Aye. Much, much worse. She could have been forced into a marriage to an old man, or a hated one, or an enemy. Few women realize the full of their romantic dreams. The only thing that made her different from other women was the mantle of duty that lay heavy upon her shoulders. So she would choose one of these boys. At least the deed would be quick and silent. So she would lay with a stranger this night. At least, she thought, scanning the crowd, she could select the man who would touch her so intimately.

She peered around the edge of her hood. A haze of smoke crackled up from the bonfire. Ashes drifted down like black snowflakes. The feathery bits clung to tunics and smudged across young shining faces. So many young faces. Such high-pitched giddy laughter, the laughter of children being tickled too much; the over-bright eyes and jerky, prancing movements of hounds suddenly unleashed.

Then she saw him.

A blond giant of a man. Standing at the outer edge of the circle of light. While she watched, a fire-leaper hurled through the flames, collapsed into a ball and tumbled into the giant. A flock of women descended upon the boy to quench the nip of fire with their skirts. The giant backed out of the way and grinned—the slow, lazy grin of a man who knew exactly what was going on beneath the flap of all that wool.

A hot blast of air flapped open the edges of her hood and singed her face, already grown warm. This was no soft-cheeked boy. He made some sidelong comment to his companion and raked his hand through his hair. The uneven tawny ends brushed the short cape stretching across his wide shoulders. Bristle darkened the line of his jaw. Hooking a thumb into his studded belt, he spread his legs wide and laughed at his companion's response.

She could not hear his laughter across the blaze of the flames, but she sensed the vibrations of that rumbling as if they trembled through her own body. Beneath the cover of her cloak she ran a hand down her belly, down to the drape of her belt across her hips. An odd sensation spiraled in her abdomen, a slumbering movement of blood and loin.

A branch snapped beside her. Maeve knew it was Glenna without tearing her gaze from the man. Glenna had a scent about her. Years of making the herb-potions of her livelihood had tanned her skin with the sweet perfume of crushed greenery and fresh wildflowers.

Glenna made a low murmur of approval. "There's a fine bit of manhood."

Maeve trailed a tress of hair off her face, watching the strength of his hands as he palmed a cork out of a bladder of ale. "Do you know him, Glenna?"

"He's not from these parts. I'd remember such a sight as that, even if I were stone blind." Glenna shuffled into the light and squinted toward him. "A traveler, by the looks of those boots of his. I'm after thinking he's one of the pilgrims my cousin Eira said were sleeping up at the monastery tonight."

A traveler. A tall, strong-armed, barrel-chested stranger. Here today, gone tomorrow.

She couldn't have dreamed up a better choice.

"Look at that face, Glenna." Maeve couldn't seem to stop looking at it, at the easy drift of a smile across his lips, at the humor in his eye as he watched the antics of the villagers. "That man is good Irish stock, no doubt of that."

"He appears Irish enough with that hair and those light eyes. But there's no knowing the blood of him by his face, Maeve." Glenna tugged the tail of Maeve's hood until the cloth crumpled onto the young woman's shoulders. "Go on now, child. Speak to him. Do you think a man like that will be standing around the Samhain fires without a woman for long?"

Glenna's walking stick lodged between Maeve's shoulder blades. Maeve stumbled forward. An uncertain shame rippled over her as the light fell warm upon her face. She'd traveled far from her own home for an opportunity like this. She'd spent months thinking about it, planning it, deciding on the thing. Yet with all her careful plans, she'd always skipped over this part in her

mind—hoping that when the time came, she'd
know just what to do to entice a man to her side.

Now she stood as frozen as a statue on a nook
in the church. The unfettered glee of younger
women, more experienced women, swirled all
around her. Maeve knew she wasn't hard to look
at, but she'd never used her face or her figure
in such a way as she needed to use it now. The
finest-honed bow and the sharpest arrows were
useless in the hands of the untrained. The walking stick wedged between her shoulders again,
and she found herself nudged into the midst of
the madness.

The fire breathed its own hot wind, lifted the
ends of her hair and swept the dark strands
across her face. He was just a man, she told herself. Finer of figure and face than she'd ever
dreamed of, when she'd dared to dream of such
things. And he knew nothing of her, nothing of
her secrets, nothing of the significance of this act
they would commit tonight, if she could find the
courage to cross the distance that separated them.
Here, for the first time in all her life—and probably for the last—she could be Maeve the *woman*.
And nothing else.

She let the power of that knowledge suffuse
her; she let it give her strength.

His brow furrowed as if he sensed her watch-
fulness. He cast his gaze around the clearing. Despite the curtain of ashes raining between them,
despite the shimmer of heat and the dart of excited young bodies, despite the roar and cackle

of the fire and the shriek of voices—their gazes met, and locked.

The sleepy swirling tightened to a fist in her abdomen. A gasp stole the breath from her lungs.

In that moment of delicious shock she suddenly understood why the priests turned a blind eye to the doings on the hills of Ireland on All Hallow's Eve. How strong this power, how fiercely it gripped her. An ancient, pagan ceremony, full of a licentiousness that the people dared not confess come Sunday. An evening, so Glenna had told her, when the veils between this world and the Otherworld thinned to mist. Anything was possible in the edge between light and darkness. A woman could hide a lifetime of secrets in this crack in time.

She felt as if she'd tumbled into that crack, for in this moment as their gazes locked nothing existed—not the sweep of time, not the blaze of the fire, not the dry rustle of late autumn leaves in the trees. Nothing but the fierce intensity of the merge of their gazes, and a strange sort of yearning which parched her throat.

He blindly nudged the bladder into his companion's arms. The giant's tunic hung to his knees, but there was no hiding the thick-thighed power of his stride as he made his way through the heat and the throng. Excitement set her body to trembling. The man was all height and breadth and heaving muscle swelling beneath the tight sleeves of his tunic and the wool of his hose. She was not ignorant of male beauty. She knew many a laborer who prided himself on how big a calf he could heave upon his shoulders, and she'd seen many of her own people sweating in their *braies* in the fields in the heat of summer, their broad backs slick and gleaming with sweat. But none so tall, none so straight-backed . . . none so lean with muscle as this man slowing to a stop before her.

He bore a man's face, well-used. His nose sloped crooked, as if he'd broken it more than once in his lifetime. A scar cut a path through one brow, and another through the stubble on his chin. Blue eyes gleamed at her. The skin around them crinkled as he disarmed her with a smile as boyish as that of any of the young men hurtling through the fire.

"I was warned," the giant rumbled, "about creatures like you."

Her skin tingled, for he had a deep voice that brought to mind lazy mornings and entwined limbs.

"Beware the spirits of the dead, I was told." He reached out and captured a tress of her hair rising aloft by the fire's wind. "And watch out for the fairy-women, who slip out between the veils this night to bewitch human men."

Maeve felt her smile widen. It was a common enough thing to say on this night. Fairy-women were said to be beautiful, lissome creatures, and she supposed many a young man used that knowledge to find his way into a girl's good graces. Yet his words brought a flush of pleasure to her cheeks, a flush that made her feel as foolish as a young girl. *This* Maeve hadn't heard the likes of such words ever in her life.

"Here I was thinking you look like a man of common sense." Her voice rushed husky through her throat. "Why would someone warn you of so common a thing?"

"Where I come from, this night is for mischief." He stretched her hair across his hand and let it slip out of his grip like silk. "For young masked men to hurl themselves through the dark streets and frighten any who dare to linger about."

"We'll have enough of that, too." She tilted her head at him, as she'd seen a dozen young women do when talking to their men. The gesture exposed her neck, made her feel vulnerable. "You've no fires?"

"None," he said, tilting his head to the wildness of the bonfire, "like this one."

It was on the tip of her tongue to ask what strange kind of place he came from that didn't celebrate All Hallow's Eve with fires. He spoke with a clipped sort of Irish, not the musical lilt of her own people, but a true, easy Irish nonetheless. She didn't want to know whence he came. It was clear enough he was Irish, and that was all that mattered, she told herself. In the end, she supposed it would be best that they know as little about one another as possible.

"It seems you need someone to take you in hand," she murmured. She swung up the hollowed-out turnip lantern she clutched by a leather thong. "Did no one give you a lantern?"

He rolled one massive shoulder. "Who needs a lantern with that moon and this fire?"

"Don't be losing it. You need it to ward off the dead who walk this night."

"I'll share yours."

The air she sucked into her lungs rushed tingling through her blood. "Then it's a bit of luck for you that you found me."

"More than a bit of luck. I was told there's magic in this night, and now I know it's true."

Aye, what a fine man this was. Look at the way he looked down upon her, his eyes twinkling with humor, enough to make a woman forget herself, forget duty and obligations and the power of ancient curses.

Her lips trembled into a smile. "Don't you have a tongue full of pretty words."

"What's closest to the heart is closest to the lips."

"Aye," she mused, "and ale-talk gets weaker with the night air."

"You wound me, woman." He clutched his breast with a work-hardened hand. "Haven't you struck me enough with your beauty?"

"Beware the love at first sight which happens in the twilight."

"Life would be a boring thing," he said, "if a man took such care."

Then he thrust his hand past her cheek and into the fall of her hair, and she reeled with the sensation of those callused, work-hardened hands curling against her scalp. He smelled of wood-fire smoke and sweet ale, the warm scents of a man's hard body.

"As thick and black as a cloud of soot." His fingers brushed the nape of her neck, stirring the wispy hairs. "Be you fairy or not, it's good to find a woman here who doesn't look like she just put away her teething-blocks."

"I could say the same for a man," she said, breathlessly, "who doesn't look like he just rose from the muck of his mud-castle building."

His smile stretched warm. "What's your name, my rare Irish beauty?"

Maeve. . . . She swallowed the word, and it stuck in her throat like a chicken bone.

"My name," she said, around the lump, "is Maire."

"Maire, eh?"

She met those blue eyes as a fair brow lifted over one of them, as his lips curled in a mocking sort of smile, and she wondered if she were really so transparent.

"Aye, well, Maire. . . ." He placed an emphasis on her name that left no doubt he didn't believe her. "Maybe you'll tell me why you came to the fires this night."

His fingers wove magic along the nape of her neck, curled around the wispy hairs and brushed the sensitive skin under the sweep of her hair. With every twist of his finger that strange sensation twisted tighter in her abdomen, reminding her exactly why she'd come here— to submit herself under the physical power of this blond giant of a man.

To mate.

Yet she couldn't just tell him that. She couldn't look into those crystal blue eyes and let the man know that she was willing to lay under him as freely as any laundress at fair-time. The words wouldn't come, she could barely form them— she did not know them. Glenna must be cackling from the shadows now, seeing her as wordless as old Sean who had lost his tongue to English cruelty.

She opened her mouth to say something, anything. His lips silenced her.

He tightened his fingers in her hair to fix her in place under his kiss. The shock jolted through her body. The turnip-lantern splattered to the ground. The prickle of stubble razed her cheek, her chin— a caress both gentle and rough, like the lick of a cat's tongue. The spark of shock bolted through her and left her limbs throbbing. Her bones melted to the consistency of warm thick honey. She swayed into his warmth, into the hard wall of a chest so wide and so strong a woman could lay a world full of troubles on it and he'd never feel the weight. He tasted of fresh yeasty ale. His skin smelled of salt-sea breezes and exotic spices. Cinnamon. Ginger.

As soon as it began it was over. The world spun around his face as the hot breath of the Samhain fires coursed between them.

"You have lips of milk and honey, little Maire." He traced the curve of her lower lip with a callused thumb. "Better to have silence, than to spoil them with half-truths."

Her lips swelled as tender as a bruise. That open blue gaze roamed over her face. She felt as translucent as the waters of the Nenagh stream, which gave no cover to the roll and clash of the pebbles on the river-bottom.

"The tale says I've now imprisoned myself with a fairy's kiss, and I'm lost to all my kith and kin." He loosened his grip in her hair, and trailed a finger down her neck. He nudged her cloak aside, curled his hand around her arm, and slid his fingers down to her own hand. "They say the Otherworld is full of youthful pleasures. A place where time stops. A place where a man and a woman can live a lifetime in a day."

He waited and watched, his hand curled in hers. She felt herself caught up, as if she stood waist-deep in a river during spring flood, when the first wave of mountain water gushed down from the hillside and swept her feet out from under her, buoyed her along in a current too swift and too fierce to deny— no hope of catching an overhanging branch or feeling the crush of the river bottom scrape the soles of her feet. Her body coursed with a roiling brew of fear and excitement, with the giddy exultation of being pushed along in the strong hands of a greater power.

She never imagined it would all be as easy as this.

She swept up the turnip-gourd. Her fingers tightened over his. She swiveled away from the light and headed toward the beckoning shadows

of the thin woods, past Glenna's silent figure, as
still and as solid as an oak tree.

Away from the blast of the fire, the night air
snapped as crisp as chilled cider. The forest floor
crackled beneath her feet as she wound her way
through the trees. She tugged the giant in her
wake. His hand, thick-palmed, tough with many
a day's honest labor, lay hot on hers. Soon she'd
feel those hands on her flesh, on places no man
had ever touched, and muddled thoughts of forbidden bedtime fantasies set her breath hitching
in her throat.

She let her mind roam, knowing there would
be no stopping it now. Here, at last, she could
set that secret part of herself free. In these woods
redolent of oak-spice and rich, crumbly earth,
she'd know the love-secrets which glowed on the
faces of the village girls the morning after Samhain; she'd finally feel the touch of a man who
didn't look up at her with his features carefully
modulated with respect. In this crack in time with
this looming hulk of a stranger she would know
a taste of Paradise.

Strangely, she felt no fear as she tugged him
beyond the woods, to the rise of another hill.
She'd felt no fear the moment she'd looked into
those honest eyes, and felt the touch of his hands.
No shiftless tinker, this one. No foul-breathed
laggard. The roll of those muscles spoke of a life
spent in honest labor. The easy smile on that
rugged face spoke of a man with a sense of humor, a man who knew and accepted the frailties
of humanity and even admitted a few of his own.

God's gift, he was. Lord knew, she'd deserved one, for the fate she'd been doomed with. She'd feel no shame if she took a full measure of pleasure in the night to come.

The voices and the laughter of the Samhain fire dimmed. She led him over the rib of the hill, to another height cleared by the fell of an ancient oak. Ivy seeped from the decaying log, where lightning had cracked it open. The lush grass lay like fairy-hair, sheened by the moonlight in silver.

When she and Glenna had arrived in this village yesterday, Maeve had spent a good hour before dusk roaming these hills. She'd discovered this sheltered place, and in the cold-hearted way she'd planned this whole evening, she'd decided that she would head here with whomever she'd chosen for her mate. She had wondered if she would actually make it this far, or if her mate would press her down behind the nearest gorse bush and have done with it. In her cold-hearted way, she told herself it didn't matter, so long as the deed was done.

Now, somehow, it did matter. It pleased her, that this giant had followed her so silently. It spoke well of the man, that he had the patience to wait for his pleasure.

She nestled the turnip on a bed of ivy. The flame flickered as tallow oozed out of a cut in the gourd. A gust of wind swept across the clearing, setting the flame to flickering.

They had so little time.

He let go of her hand and trailed to the edge

of the hillside. The moon pearled the slopes of the rolling land, and inked the shadows of the shallow valleys a deep blue. A sliver of stream silvered its way across the darkness like a still bolt of lightning. On a distant hill glowed a spark of orange— another village's All Hallow's Eve fire.

"Well chosen," he said. "You know these lands well."

She cast her gaze down, letting him believe what he will.

"A man might think," he continued, "that you've led me through the veils to *Tir na nOg.*"

"A woman," she whispered, "might think you believe in the illusions of a child's imagination."

"This place is no illusion." He lifted his hands to his hips and breathed in deep the crisp autumn air. "In my life, I've never seen such a land of peace and pleasure and Otherworldly beauty."

She peered past him, to the landscape cast in the moon's glow. "Are the fairies playing tricks on you, with you seeing castles in common pasturage?"

"You've lived here all your life. You don't know how uncommon such a place is."

She gazed over the landscape, thinking aye, the moon cast a veil of silver upon the hills, but surely the sight was as simple as grass. She found herself wondering again what kind of place he came from that he found such beauty in tilled fields and sod huts. She pushed the curiosity from her mind as he turned and cast his web of enchantment upon her.

"We've traveled far afield of hearth and bon-fire, lass."

She hoped the sheen of the moon would not reveal the darkening of her cheeks.

"A man might think you don't fear the creatures of this night," he continued. "A man might think you've bewitched me, only to turn into a swan or a white cow come morning."

She turned her face away, for he tread far, far too close to the truth. How strange it was that this rough-handed giant knew of the gentle side of the old Irish tales, when most men spoke only of the legends of gore and war: The Fenian warriors, the bloody feats of Cu Chulainn, the lost honor of King Cormac.

She gestured to the flicker of the turnip gourd. "I have the lantern."

"That will long sputter out by the time we're done."

"By then," she whispered, "I will have you to keep me safe."

She couldn't believe such words had left her lips. Yet there they shimmered between them, sparking a gleam in his eye, curling a smile up one side of his mouth. A smile that spoke of intimate knowledge, as if he'd danced this dance a thousand times before— and savored each subtle move. She began to tremble, from much, much more than the cold.

"Fairies don't shiver." He swept open his cape. "Come. I've room enough in this cloak for two."

He folded the cloak around her like great black wings, and she found herself pillowed in a burrow of warmth, she found her nose pressed against the dagged edges of his brushed shoulder-cape, her head swimming with the scent of cinnamon and ginger.

"No fairy, this," he muttered, splaying his hands across her back. "I feel the heat of your blood." He buried his nose in her hair. "Mmm. Clean, womanly. Sweet."

His lips trailed down her temple, over her cheek. She turned her head to meet his mouth, but he avoided her throbbing lips. His mouth trailed over her eyes, her brow, down the other side of her face. His lips trailed a strand of her hair, damp from his kisses, across her eyes. She turned her face again, seeking those lips. He captured her upper lip in his mouth, then pressed his forehead against hers.

"You're a rare feast, little fairy." He brushed a tress off the corner of her lips. "I'll taste the full of you before the night is through."

He sucked on her trembling lip as his words drew a world full of pictures in her head. Her breath hitched in her throat. Her body trembled, trembled, she couldn't seem to stop it— the warmer she became in the cocoon of his cloak, the more she trembled, as if she were shaking off some brittle shell to reveal the creature within, this foreign, sensuous woman who pressed close to this man's body as if she knew exactly what she wanted when she only had the vaguest idea.

He trailed one hand down the length of her hair, beneath the fall of her cloak, into the hol-

low of her back, which was strangely aching and
tender. Everywhere he touched swelled tender
and over-sensitive, rising to the merest brush of
those callused hands. She flattened her own
hands against him— such a solid wall of chest,
she could feel the hammer of his heart beneath
the layers of wool and flesh. She trailed her fingers up, up, over the swell of those bulky shoulders, to hang onto them while the rest of her
body shivered into jelly. Still he teased her with
kisses, still he teased her lips as they swelled ever
more tender.

When she could bear it no longer, she gripped
his face, guided his lips toward hers, and kissed
silent his husky, knowing laugh. Kissed him quiet,
kissed him until he kissed her back, until a trill
of urgency shimmered between them.

He banded his arms around her, and lifted her
from the ground. "We can have it like that, fairy-
woman, if that's your pleasure this night."

She had only a moment to wonder what she'd
unleashed when he strode back toward the fallen
log and the flickering spark of the turnip-gourd,
with her breasts crushed against his chest and
her legs dangling beneath the sweep of his cloak,
and her face level with his, looking into those
eyes turbulent and intense, only a shadow of humor remaining on those lips.

Then the world tilted, the bare boughs of the
trees swung into her vision and the flax of the
grass gave beneath her back. He swooped down
upon her like a great black bird, and his cloak
fluttered down to encase them again in warmth.

The weight of him pressed down upon her. He thrust his thigh between her legs, to lodge it against the warmth and heat of her core, to lodge it in a place that shot sparks through her body.

This is what she had expected of the night: the swift eager press of hands on her body, the rushed tugging of laces, the hot breath of a man's mouth on her lips. The heat and weight of a man's body pressed upon hers, the hardness of the ground beneath her back. He'd offered her the tenderness she'd thought she would crave, and now she thanked God and the stars that he'd given her instead this hungry eager mating.

What she hadn't expected, was that she would *want* this, as fiercely as the man moving atop her.

Aye, she wanted. She ached for the full of his body on hers. She yearned for the slap of bare flesh against bare flesh. She hungered for the taste of the stubble of his cheek. She sought his tongue, to fill her mouth. He thrust his hand beneath her kirtle and scraped his callused palm over her breast. She arched up to fill his hand, even as she thought— *this is madness, this is madness.* The liquor of the night coursed through her blood until she was drunk on it and the taste of this man, the spice-smell of him. His hands razed over her aching body. *Is this it, then, the hungry lust that animated all those young people by the fires?* Somehow she sensed this passion was more than that— much, much, more— that the yearning that yawned between them, the passion that flared so hot upon the touch of their skins, was a far greater force, a far deeper force, and she knew when the loving was over it wouldn't leave dry, dusty ashes— such embers could never be so easily extinguished.

Crazed, disjointed thoughts flew through her mind. A man shouldn't have hair so soft, so smooth-silky. How sweet the grass smelled, crushed beneath them. Oh, what was he doing, scraping his fingers up her leg, over her knee, beyond her thigh? His pouch dug into her hip— she wanted it gone, so she could feel his hips against hers. His fingers splayed over the joint between leg and hip, and even as heat rushed over her skin, she found herself opening her legs, she found herself arching up for whatever he would do.

What he did launched a cry from her lips, made her squeeze her eyes shut against the blinding white light of the stars. She dug her fingers into the bulk of his back and sucked chill air into her lungs only to breathe it out like fire. A sound rumbled in his chest and suddenly he was tearing at something, shifting his weight off her only to shift it back on her again. With one tug he hiked her skirts to her waist and she felt the brush of his hose against her naked thighs, and she felt something else— the hot throbbing root of him, as he hiked her knees up past his hips and lodged it against the part of her which needed it the most.

No thoughts of duty kept her stoic now. No doubts, no hesitation. All that existed in this silvery clearing was Maeve the woman, the man she'd chosen, and this passion she'd never known herself capable of until now.

She cried out at the first thrust of his hips, a shout of exhilaration launched to the trees and the sky. She arched up to meet him with the second. He said something, an exclamation muffled in the sweep of her hair, then buried himself in her again. She squeezed her eyes shut and buried her face in his shoulder, breathed in the scent of him, and with each movement of his body against hers, she traveled farther and farther to exotic places, launched to distant lands bright with freedom and promise.

A long time she lay under him. As slowly as a feather drifting down from a tree-top nest, she floated back from the milky sweep of stars to the coolness of the silvery clearing. The tallow candle in the turnip gourd sifted blue-gray smoke toward the tree tops.

He filled her with his firm warmth, still. He lifted his face from the pillow of her hair and gazed at her through half-lidded eyes.

"Aren't you a strange one." He traced the curve of her cheek. "So full of secrets."

"I'm thinking," she mused, a bubble of laughter rising in her throat, "that there's not many secrets between us anymore."

"True. There is at least one less." His finger trailed to her lip. "What kind of place do you come from, that a man hasn't lured you into the grass before now?"

She started.

"You should have told me, lass. I mistook your innocence for eagerness."

"I don't know what you're talking about."

"You've a look as cool as ice, but a body as hot as fire. I couldn't tell by looking at you that I was the first man you've lain with." The finger trailed down her jaw, over her neck. "Had I known, I would have been more gentle with you, lass."

Maeve felt her blood run cold. Glenna had told her men take their pleasure and pay little mind to the pain it inflicts upon the woman. Glenna had told her that a man wouldn't even notice the loss of her maidenhead— he'd roll over and snore when the thing was done.

"You're . . . you're not supposed to notice such things."

One brow cocked in a wretchedly alert face. "I'm not?"

"You're supposed to grunt and have the thing done with, with no care for the woman."

"Someone has been filling your mind with foolishness." Laughter rumbled in his voice. "Is that what happened here tonight?"

"No."

The word slipped out before she could catch it. Well, there would be no hiding it, not while she lay under him with his body still locked in hers, with the flesh of their loins hot against one another. She'd enjoyed the mating, and what of it? She'd certainly waited for it long enough.

"Obviously," she said, "I chose well tonight."

"Aye, and all that remains is why."

Why. The reasons swarmed in her head, whirling up a lifetime of quiet anguish. Oh, how she'd love to tell him all, how she'd love to spill the secrets of her heart to this man in the darkness of this cool night, in the intimacy of their joining. She had so few people to talk to about such things. She'd spent a lifetime holding her troubles in her heart, searching for answers alone. At least tonight, she could be the Maeve of her dreams; the Maeve who had choices.

But of all people who walked the earth, this man was the last one she could tell.

"No." He pressed two fingers on her mouth as she sucked in a breath to speak. "I don't want to know, not yet."

"Aren't you a strange one," she whispered, "asking and then stopping me."

"There's a whole web of reasons, I see them spinning in your pretty eyes. But I'll be damned if I'm leaving you yet."

An owl hooted from the woods. Night creatures crackled through crumbling leaves. The night was still dark, sheened only with the breath of the moonlight.

"You're no Caer of the legend," he murmured, "doomed to change into a swan the morning after Samhain. You're too hot-blooded for that." His eyes blazed a bright blue as he lowered his lips to hers. "Let reason," he growled, "wait until the daylight."

He touched her again, but differently this time. He anointed her with every brush of his fingers. He christened her with every teasing hot-lipped kiss. With trembling breath she laughed softly with him. With wide-eyed wonder she ran her fingers under his tunic, on the bare tough flesh of his abdomen, through the crisp hair of his solid chest. A world of wonders opened to her in this crack of time, and she learned greedily, eagerly, like the Caer of the legend he'd spoken about: forced to live a lifetime in an evening, before the break of dawn turned her into a swan.

Under the cover of stars, Maeve threw away all sense. She opened her heart and her body to this gentle giant of a lover.

The moon slipped across the open sky, then sank behind the black lace of the bare trees. Night dew settled on the grass like fairy's breath then crystallized into a glittering veil of frost. When Maeve blinked her eyes open, the first rosy fingers of dawn curled up over the eastern horizon.

The giant moaned in his sleep and shifted. She stilled. In the pale blue light, his hair hung over his brow. For all the crookedness of his nose and the nicks that scarred his face, in sleep he looked as tousled and careless as a boy. She backed out from under the edge of his cloak, into the chill slap of morning.

Never before had she so hated the song of the lark.

His voice rumbled from beneath the covers. "Don't wander far."

She looked down into the blue brightness of one eye, squinting open against the light. Her lips swelled tender. She forced them into a smile.

"I won't," she whispered.

She waited until he closed his eyes, until he turned his head into the crook of his arm. Still she waited, staring down at those broad shoulders, the thickness of one thigh hiked up outside his cloak, memorizing the color of his hair, the slope of his back, the smell of him, the hundred thousand impressions of an unforgettable night.

She swiveled one heel into the grass. She headed through the fencing of trees as hot tears blinded her. When she'd walked far enough away, she fisted her skirts and began to run.

At least, she thought, choking on a sob, *this poor fatherless child will have been conceived in love.*

Two

Garrick kneed his mount through the last shelter of the forest, into the wide rolling lands of Birr. The tavern-keeper in the last town had told him the castle of Birr stood just beyond these woods. Garrick narrowed his eyes on the hills of green, on the haze of a mist still clinging to the crook of the valley, on the bow-backed cattle lowing on the slope.

No sign of a castle.

It had probably disappeared into thin air, he mused. Just like that fairy-woman of Samhain.

He curled his hands over the reins. The horse tossed its head in resistance. He told himself that a castle couldn't run away as easily as a fleet-footed young woman. He told himself that a castle couldn't hide on open ground. He scanned the landscape. These wide misty valleys, these musical forests . . . he had scented the magic in them the first day he set off from the stinking, narrow streets of Wexford to seek his fortune. How clear the air, how quiet the land. How easily one could dream up fairies who lived under ferns and drank dew from foxglove blossoms. How easily a man could be lured into enchantment by a dark-haired beauty on All Hallow's Eve.

Garrick shook his head free of foolishness. The pilgrim who Garrick had traveled with for the first leg of this journey had told him he'd been bewitched; and that Garrick would have no rest until he shook himself of the memory of her. Garrick twisted his lips into an uneasy smile. Forget. Forget night-black hair like silk in his hands, forget skin the color and smoothness of country cream, and eyes as gray as morning mist. Forget husky, uncertain laughter. Forget the moist heat of her beneath him in the dark of night.

Nay. He'd find her. If he had to seek the doors of the Otherworld, he'd find that woman who had writhed beneath him so passionately on All Hallow's Eve. For two days he'd searched, and no one— no one— had ever seen her or knew her name. She'd sailed off to places unknown like the ships in Wexford harbor, leaving him on the docks staring into the seamist like some sailor's forgotten wife. But he would find her nonetheless. He would find her, as surely as he would find the Castle of Birr and claim it as his own.

He kicked his mount westward, on a trail no wider than a cow-path. The flaxen waves of a harvested wheat field came into view, then, in the distance, the blades of a mill. As he curved around another hillock, another building came into view: a tumbled-down square donjon of stone, planted by a winding sliver of a river.

A scattering of sheep nibbled at the stubble in the field by the path. Garrick spied a young boy sleeping with his hood pulled over his eyes. Garrick pulled his horse to a stop and called out to him. The boy started up from his crouch— then stumbled to his feet when he saw Garrick. The boy's clothes hung off his bones.

"That castle, up ahead," Garrick called out. "Could that be the castle of Birr?"

"Yes, m'lord. And the village, too, if you'll be wanting to know."

Garrick sank back in the saddle. His lips twisted in a wry smile. Well, will you look at that, he thought. A damn sorry sight it was. The wooden roof hung off the building, and the stones looked as green as pond scum with the veneer of lichen clinging to them. It looked as if ten years or more had passed since a man put his back to fixing the stones on the wall encircling it. A clutch of huts sagged under the hang of dirty thatch just outside the wall, and trailed along the valley next to the cut of a narrow river.

Garrick rubbed his jaw as a smile spread over his face. What a fine trick his great English lord of a father had played. In that lofty lord's mind, a son who was nothing but a by-blow from a summer night's dalliance with an Irishwoman deserved no better than this. What the damned aristocratic fool would never understand was that to Garrick, this was the finest pot o' gold of all.

Better than digging another man's turnips, Garrick thought. Better than sweating under the casks and bales and boxes of the docks of Wexford. He had expected no better, for land obtained by a ruse grown so thick and so old.

"Tell your people," Garrick said to the boy, "that the new lord of Birr has arrived."

The boy clutched his hood as he shot past Garrick. The boy's bare feet flew as he sped across the field to the first thatched hut. Garrick rolled his shoulders and straightened on his mount. The fine woolen clothes he'd had made in Wexford before his journey itched him now, not as loose and easy and simple as the shirt and *braies* he was accustomed to wearing in all kinds of weather. They hung on him as awkwardly as his new title, but he straightened his shoulders under them nonetheless.

Women scurried out of the huts, spindles and pots still in hand, to watch through lowered eyes as he passed. What a bony, sunken-faced tribe, he thought, dirty in threadbare clothes no dockworker would be seen in. A young girl scratched in the dirt, a bowl of wheat and a crushing-stone lolling beside her. Her mother snatched her hand and yanked her to her feet as Garrick nudged his horse up a shallow rise, through the rock-pile fence, to the square tower of the castle of Birr.

The villagers followed him at a distance, like nervous hunting hounds behind a brutal master.

"I'll take your horse for you, my lord."

The boy he'd spied sleeping in the stubbled fields held out a dirty hand. The boy spoke in uncertain English. The language lay heavy on his tongue. A good set of lungs, Garrick thought, for all his thinness. And fleet-footed as the red deer Garrick had spotted in the woods through which he'd passed.

Through *his* woods. Garrick wondered if he'd ever get used to the idea.

"The old master used me as a stable boy when it pleased him, my lord." The boy's hand dipped to his side. "I . . . I know the way of tending horses . . ."

"Better than me, no doubt."

Garrick dismounted and tossed the reins to the boy. It had been a long journey, and Garrick still hadn't callused his thighs to the sway of the beast's gait. He stilled the urge to rub his backside. The crowd stood silent behind him; he sensed the weight of their stares. He planted his hands on his hips and stared up at the old square tower. At his home.

Three stories to the tower, though what the third floor looked like with that roof collapsed in on it was another question all together. Good, thick rock, beneath all that ivy and lichen. The boy led his horse behind the castle, where Garrick caught a glimpse of a number of outbuildings—stables, henhouses, and storage, no doubt.

Then the door squealed open on querulous female voices. Two women burst out into the courtyard, arguing. The younger, twisting her hands in her apron, whirled around to face him—then stumbled to a halt.

"You."

Garrick stood for a moment, too shocked to take in the tumble of all that dark hair, the startled gray eyes, the skin the color of the richest cream. His first coherent thought was that she was as beautiful in the bright of day, as she had been in the shimmer of the moonlight.

"You," she repeated. "What . . . what are you doing here?"

"I could ask the same of you."

He stared. He couldn't believe his eyes. It was too fine a coincidence. She stared back at him, a mirror of his own shock, her mouth hanging open like a fish. No fairy, this. A fairy didn't wear a ragged old apron, or walk about with flour staining her brow. A fairy's cheeks didn't flush dark with surprise. A laugh threatened in his chest. She was human, flesh and blood, and whole, standing before him. After all that searching. . . . she stood here before him, obviously a part of his castle, of his manor. Fate had thrust them together again.

He laughed. The sound bellowed off the walls. "Aye, woman, it's good to see you," he said. "I'm the new lord of Birr."

He strode to her, and threw out his arms to bury her in his embrace. He needed to feel the full of her against him, to fill his hands with those generous hips, to bury his face in that hair, to prove to himself that this wasn't another trick of the magical Irish countryside.

As he neared, panic lit her eyes. She dipped her head and fell into a curtsey at his feet.

Her voice came out breathless. "I am Maeve, my lord."

"It's about time I learned your real name, Maeve."

"And I, yours," she said in her throaty alto, an

edge entering her voice. "We did not expect you quite so . . . soon."

"The day is full of surprises."

"I've kept this house in your absence," she said, rising to avoid his outstretched arms. "On behalf of the people of Birr, I welcome you . . . my lord."

Cagey, she was. As nervous as a squirrel, standing there fisting her skirts in her hands. She had secrets, this one. He'd known it on All Hallow's Eve. Now every nerve of her sang with them; now her gaze darted beyond him, to the crowd standing silent behind him. He was of half a mind to destroy her pretense here and now. After all, she'd left him lying alone on that hill on All Soul's Day, feeling as daft as if the fairies had stripped him of his soul, with only the turnip-gourd and memories of fire as proof that he'd lain with someone that night. For her mischief, he should punish her with kisses. Already he savored the price.

His hands itched to feel the silk of her hair, his body burned already with the want of her. He'd found her—a rich thing, that. He'd found her when he wasn't even looking. His grin widened. He wondered what the wench would do if he reached out and pulled her against him, if he tasted those honeyed lips again. He sensed that she would fight and claw and scratch like a trapped stray cat. She was arching her back as if she were caught in a corner.

Color drained from her face. Her wide gray eyes pleaded with him, and took the edge off his lust. Garrick let his hands drop to his sides. Aye, the woman had secrets, and he didn't know the first of them. He wasn't the sort to play on a woman's terror. He would wait. He would play her game for a time, and see how it settled.

He was feeling generous. After all, he'd have her again. This very night if he had his way of it.

"Won't you come in, my lord, out of the cold?" Her chin raised, she turned toward the door and scraped her palms down her apron. "You must be tired after your long journey."

"It wasn't the journey that wore me out."

"You'll have to take your ease in the hall," she said, thrusting open the door. "We practice economies here when the lord is away, and use very little wood."

Garrick dipped his head beneath the rounded arch of the door. The great hall was littered with reeds and hung with worn, faded tapestries. A pitiful spark of a fire crackled in the huge fireplace, where a gaggle of women fluttered down to their seats as if they'd raced across the room at the sound of his step by the door. The room, devoid of furniture, echoed with voices and the clatter of spindles.

"Had you sent word ahead," Maeve said, "we would have had your chamber prepared properly— "

"I have no doubt you can prepare it for me, Maeve. *Properly.*"

"Someone will see to it. It might take some time. Most of the servants are home threshing the grain or tending to the slaughter. I'll have to summon them—"

"Don't hurry. I'm sure I'll find all the comfort I need in you, Maeve of Birr, as long as you're not planning to disappear."

Maeve's footsteps clattered against the stone floor as she strode toward the fireplace. "Was your journey comfortable, my lord?"

"Exceedingly," he replied, watching the twitch of her hips. "But I was delayed about two days' ride from here. Searching for a fairy-woman I met on All Hallow's Eve."

"Sorcha, don't be standing there staring with your mouth open like a trout." Maeve tugged a spindle from the woman's hand and speared it into a basket of wool. "Go to the kitchens and fetch some ale and bread for our lord. Surely he expects a better welcome—"

"She just disappeared with the coming of day," Garrick interrupted, "without a word of reason."

"Forgive me, my lord, for saying so," Maeve continued in a breathless voice, "but a man who frolics about those wretched fires on a spirit-night gets no more than he deserves."

"Oh, I got much more than I expected."

"Then surely you shouldn't be asking for anything more." Maeve hiked a basket of wool onto her hip. "Mona, have done with that sewing now. Is the master to sit so far away from the fire while you loll there basking in its warmth?"

"I told myself I'd find her," he continued. "I spent two days looking for her."

"For a fairy-wraith?" Maeve footed another basket away from the hearth. "Easy, my lord, or my people will think you're bewitched."

"I am." He shouldered his cape. "I'm thinking she was no fairy. Though she was as beautiful as one."

Maeve waved a white hand in the air. "Well, it's no concern of mine, my lord, such things as that."

"Maybe you know of her. She could have come from these parts—"

"It's sure I know little about the fires, and want to know even less, God be praised."

"She was not young. I'd say she was about your age."

Gray eyes flashed. She slammed the basket of wool down on the other side of the hearth, away from the flames. "Well, thank you very much for marking me a spinster."

"And she had hair as dark as soot. About as long as yours, as well."

"Isn't that a common thing—what would you be knowing of the color of her hair in the dark of night?" Maeve turned on two girls staring at him with open curiosity. "Eibhlin, Flanna—what's our new lord going to think, with work to be done, and you two as idle as doves in the cote?"

"And eyes as—"

"Will you be wanting to see the lands?" she interrupted, rising to a fine Irish ire. She brushed past him. "There's not much to them, and by the time it's done, your food will be here to keep that tongue of yours busy."

The girls clustered just by the servant's door

sucked in a collective gasp and skittered back as
Maeve strode to the servants' entrance as swift
and straight as an arrow. Aye, he thought, a smile
widening. He'd teased her sore, but what of it?
By sunset he would soften her ire into something
else.

He followed her at his own leisurely pace, wink-
ing at the girls who fluttered about like so many
butterflies as they cleared up the woman's debris
by the hearth— loom, spindles, baskets of wool
and mending— staring after Maeve with undis-
guised surprise. He caught the door Maeve
shoved open before it closed in his face, then
trudged out into the mud of the field.

"This," she said, thrusting out a long, white
arm to a sagging wreck of a building, "is the
henhouse. Those are the kitchens. That," she
continued, thrusting out the other arm, "is the
stable. And this," she said, trudging into the coolness of a open building, "is the hay barn."

He followed her into the dim building, which
smelled of cow and the sneezing perfume of
green hay. She paced the length of the building,
whirling up clouds of chaff which had settled on
the floor from a recent threshing. She peered up
toward the second story, gleaming with piles of
hay. Satisfied that the barn was empty, she turned
to face him and whirred up a cloud of chaff.

"Now that we're alone," she said, "you can
have done with this mockery."

"I'll agree with that." He hiked an elbow on
the door of a milking stall. "But it's you who has

explaining to do. It was you who played the Samhain trick."

"A brazen one you are, to ride into this place and call yourself its lord."

"No more brazen than the woman who lay with me under the moonlight on All Hallow's Eve."

Her color heightened. Her hand shot to the laces of her tunic as if to hold them closed. "That's not what this is about."

"Isn't it?"

"No." She scanned his clothes, all the way down to his dusty boots. "It's about you, posing as the lord of this place and riding in as bold as can be— "

He slid his elbow off the door. "Posing, am I?"

"Don't play the mockery on me. I know who you are."

"You don't even know my name."

She thrust out the flat of a palm and shook her head. "I don't want to know."

"Garrick." He crossed the distance that separated them and seized that hand. "Garrick of Wexford, your humble servant, who has done nothing these past days but think about this— "

He pulled her to him. Their bodies slapped together. He buried his hand in her hair and forced that lovely face up to his. He stole the kiss he needed. It all came back to him, the fresh, sweet smell of her, the soft cloud of her hair forming a dark curtain against the world. The taste of her, virgin and innocent and hot-blooded, firing his own blood to the boiling point. The give of ample hips against his loins, the kind of lust that only comes to a man once in a lifetime, if he has luck about him.

She struggled in his grip and pulled away. He released her. She shook her head and skittered deeper into the darkness of the barn, then thrust her forearm against her mouth.

"Don't."

"You want it as much as I do, Maeve."

"That doesn't matter. It doesn't matter what I want." She wiped her mouth and buried her arm in her skirts. "It was best, leaving you. I never thought you'd come after me."

"A man is never satisfied with one taste of heaven, *a stór.*"

"A man is supposed to *want* such a thing." She paced unevenly in the dimness, running her fingers through her hair. "Men dream about such women, who leave them willingly after such a night."

"There are nights, lass, and then there are *nights—* "

"Don't be talking like that." Her voice was breathless, uncertain. She dropped her hands and wrung them in her apron, spotted with oil. "This cannot be."

"Nothing is impossible. Nothing." He took a step toward her. "You shouldn't have run away from me."

"Isn't it time that a woman ran away from a man?" she retorted, stumbling over a pail set by a milking stall. She swept it up and hugged it to her belly. "When always it's the man running away from a woman after he's had his way."

"Did you hear that rubbish from the same person who told you men grunt and have done with it?"

She hung the pail into a peg lodged in a pole, then leaned her forehead against the wood. "Why couldn't you be," she murmured, "like other men?"

"Why couldn't you be," he retorted, "a woman who clings and demands more than a man could give? I searched for you for two days. Two days, Maeve. I thought I'd lost you."

"You don't know me."

"I know more about you than any other man."

"Aye, maybe of my flesh. Maybe of my spirit, but you know nothing of me, of my place here in this castle—"

"Now that I've found you, we'll have time enough for that."

He strode behind her, then curled his arms around her. She did not resist. Her hair smelled of hay and sweet summer grass. The memory caused a rush of blood to heat his loins—the memory of a woman as innocent as she was passionate, as open and loving as the warm rich earth of Ireland.

He'd had women in his life. Whores who worked the quaies of Wexford. Some as hard as nails, others soft-hearted despite the wear of their work. He'd kept one of his own for a while, a mite of a girl with big brown eyes, but the warmth he'd felt for her was like that of a distant young cousin. The time came when he stopped laying with her and set her up instead in a laundress's establishment, so she wouldn't have to ply her wares on the docks where a woman aged too swiftly. His experiences were with work-hardened women, pleased to be having a man who took some pleasure in pleasing them. Not with a sensuous innocent who touched him with wonder in her eyes; not with a woman of such soft hair, of such sweet scent, of such mystery.

He'd wanted Maeve the minute he'd spied her across the heat of that All Hallow's Eve fire. It was if she'd been standing there waiting for him for a lifetime. Now he found her here, on his own lands. The coincidence was far too unlikely. If he hadn't seen the surprise in her own eyes, if he didn't sense her resisting him, he'd think the whole thing was a ruse. It wasn't. He was never a man to question the gifts of fate.

"We were fated to meet, Maeve."

"Don't talk to me of fate." She pressed back against him, and curled her fingers over his forearms. "We had an evening . . . Garrick. A moment in the time between the times. I'll treasure it for a lifetime. But the world goes on."

"Are you married?"

"You know I am not."

"Then all that matters is that you are free— "

"Marriage is not the only thing that can bind a woman."

"I'm the lord of this place now. I can snip any ties that bind you."

"Stop." She pushed out of his arms. "You're talking foolishness, crazy foolishness. Mayhaps a fairy did steal your senses that night, to set you on such a ruse. How long did you think this mockery could last? You didn't even bother to thicken the ruse by speaking English."

"I'm staying, Maeve." He rolled his tongue over the word. "It's good to know the taste of your real name."

"The people will suspect any day now. Look at you. You rode in without a single servant to attend you, on a horse that has seen stronger days. How long did you think you could do this," she argued, "before the real lord of Birr arrived?"

A shadow crossed his thoughts. Well, what did he expect? The Earl had granted him this land, but no gold to wrap his bastard son in the silken trappings of a nobleman. "Is it so hard to believe that I'm the lord of this place?"

"You're talking nonsense. Aye, you've flattered me with the ruse, more than I ever expected, but you must be going on. Aye, aye, tis true, we've had no lord here for many a year— praise be to God— but at the breath of a whim the Earl could decide to send another of his wretched sons-in-law to suck the life out of this place—"

"He sent a son this time."

"I've never known such boldness." She planted her fists on her hips. "He has no sons."

"Aye, he does. A bastard son." He pounded his chest. "Not worth much to a great English earl, but enough to warrant giving me this place, if for no other reason than to stop my Irish mother from badgering him in the English courts."

Her eyes widened. Her fists slipped off her hips.

"Yes, Maeve." He trailed his gaze over her, over the body he'd loved so thoroughly that night, over the face drained of color. "He has recognized me. I'm lord of this place. A lord," he said, "who needs a wife."

Yes, he thought, the moment the words left his lips. All his life he'd been scorned for his impetuosity. It had sent him, once, on a journey to the wilds of Wales when he'd been offered a place on a merchant ship. It had launched him on this voyage to a lordship, to a manor he knew nothing of running, to a life of husbandry he hadn't a clue how to manage. Always, luck had shown him a smiling face. How bright it shown this day. What irony, that they both be virgins in their own way, and they each would relieve one another of the burden.

"Be my wife, Maeve."

He stepped closer to her and reached for her hands, but she skittered back until she slammed into the wall of a milking stall.

"You're . . . you're English."

Her face contorted as she spoke the word. *Ing*-lish. As if it were something slimy slithering over her tongue.

"The Earl is. My mother is as Irish as they come."

"You— you lying— you deceived me— " She clutched her belly, then cupped a hand over her mouth, sidling along the milk stall until she shouldered into the wall of the barn. "My God . . . my God."

An unfamiliar wave of shame rippled over him.

He hadn't asked to be the by-blow of an Earl. She didn't seem the sort of woman too proud to take a bastard to her bed.

"I asked you to be my wife," he repeated. He'd never asked a woman such a thing. "I'm asking you to be the lady of Birr."

She tore past him, stumbling in the chaff. She whirled to a stop in the light of the doorway.

"Never," she cried, her dark hair wild. "*Never* will I be an Englishman's wife."

Maeve stumbled across the fields. Mud splashed under her skirts, soaked her hose, hung heavy on the hem of her tunic. The woods loomed ahead, bare-branched and gray in the midday light. She barreled toward them, seeking the home of her youth, where all was simple and plain.

She had lain with an Englishman. An *Englishman*. All her plans lay in shards of ruins around her.

It was Glenna's fault. Glenna should have known, she had that power. A fairy-doctor was supposed to know such things, she was supposed to sense it with whatever magic she possessed. Glenna was supposed to guide her away from such catastrophes, Glenna was supposed to see that all worked out right. Glenna had led her to that village, Glenna had said that this was the best place to go, for the plans Maeve had made. What good was a fairy-woman if she couldn't protect the people who came to her from the very calamity they feared the most?

Maeve broke into the woods and stumbled from tree trunk to tree trunk, tearing a path through the crinkled layer of autumn leaves. When Maeve had first seen him standing in her yard her heart had swelled— *he's come back for me, he's come for me*. She'd even thought for a flicker of a moment that she could touch him again, she could kiss him again, she could even lay with him again, before he went on his way. She thought— what a coincidence, that he would find her after all the lengths she had taken to disappear. Perhaps fate would smile upon her, perhaps he would be the man she *could* marry: an outsider, a strong and brave Irishman who would accept what and who she was. How brave he was, how unbelievably brash, to come here masquerading as a lord when by the fires of All Hallow's Eve she'd seen the dirt of Ireland staining his broad worker's fingers.

An *Englishman*. All those silly dreams had shattered like rich cathedral glass in a storm.

Glenna's wattled hut hugged the base of a gnarled giant of an oak tree, which sheltered the ivy-choked thatch with muscular boughs. Maeve hurtled toward it and shoved open the door.

"Glenna!"

The door slammed open, then squealed in the silence. The wood of the walls seeped the scent of boiled herbs, the pungency of dried summer reeds. The ashes of a fire lay cold in the hearth.

Oh, where could she be? Maeve pressed the

butt of her hands upon the trestle table. It was far too late in the season for Glenna to be herb-gathering, and Maeve had passed her cow chewing some grass, its udder already emptied. Wasn't it like Glenna, to flutter off when Maeve needed her most?

Maeve whirled out of the hut, then planted herself on the stump of a stool just outside the door. Many a day in her youth she'd sat by Glenna's feet as Glenna curled on this tree stump, twisting her fingers around the spinning as she twisted her tongue around a tale. Here, Maeve had grown to womanhood. Here, Maeve had learned of the old Irish tales, the history of her people. Here, in this clearing under the rustle of this oak, she'd been taught her life's duty.

A cruel twist of fate, this was. More cruel than all the others. But sitting in this clearing where she'd spent so many years of her childhood injected a measure of icy calm in her wild tumbling thoughts. A measure of the same unforgiving ruthlessness that had sent her on a journey halfway to the sea, to another village's Samhain fires, where she had chosen an Englishman. An enemy.

She had chosen unwisely.

She closed her eyes against the memory, against the tears. Why, why, of all the men racing around the fires that night, did she choose this one? The memory rose, warming her from the inside out. It was as if they'd been drawn together by some Otherworldly force, it was as if in that sweet night they'd lived a lifetime. There was too much magic riding the wind on All Hallow's Eve. Now the mischievous creatures of that night laughed at her, gleeful in their wretched cruelty, piling curse upon curse. Waiting to see what she would do.

She had no choice. Maeve pulled her cloak closed against the whistle of a hollow wind. This Englishman must leave Birr, like all the others before him. As quickly as possible, before he did any more damage. The curse was specific and clear.

She rose from her seat and headed through the fencing of trees, hating the cruel fates who hung her with such duties, hating those who would now force her to drive off the man she loved.

The man whose child, even now, might be growing in her womb.

Three

Garrick stumbled out of the castle into the cold slap of morning. Muttering under his breath, he yanked his cloak closed against the chill. Pale pink clouds fingered the eastern horizon, driving back the deep blue of twilight. His footsteps crunched across the hardened earth. The air rang with an inhuman caterwauling which had torn him from an uncomfortable sleep while stars still glittered in the sky.

He rounded the castle. Through crusty, sleep-salted eyes, he saw a milkmaid shriek across the yard and vault herself through the open door of the kitchens. He planted his fists on his hips and snorted out a frosted breath. Cows. A dozen of them, trailing in an uneven line out from the hay barn. He'd never known cattle could make such an annoying wail. Then again, he'd never known cattle.

He trudged across the yard. One of the cows turned its head and rolled an eye at him. He slowed his pace. The closest he'd ever gotten to a cow was a tepid pail of milk his mother bartered for with the red-faced farmer who drove it into Wexford every morning. Stupid-looking beasts. Bigger than any he'd seen driven through the town of his youth. It was the bulls one had to beware of . . . wasn't it?

Garrick edged around the portal into the musky shadows of the barn. He skidded through something wet, stubbed his foot on a milk pail and sent it tumbling across the carpet of chaff. Milk splattered across the ground.

At least, he thought it was milk. He crouched down. The smell of it wafted up, musky and warm. He trailed a finger through the fluid pooling in the shallows of the hard earth, then frowned at the liquid clinging to his fingertips.

"It's green today."

Maeve swept in, her black hair a cloud against the spill of the morning light. Four servants, banging pails against their knees, skittered around Maeve, bobbed at the sight of him, then rushed to crouch down beside a cow.

"Aye, as green as the hills," Maeve mused, planting her fists on her hips and staring at the milk seeping into the dirt floor of the barn. "At least it isn't blood-red. That gave us quite a scare last time, it did, with us not knowing if it were some sort of bloody flux. Well, we'll have to milk the cows anyway, else they'll stop making milk altogether."

He ran his thumb over his fingers to spread the fluid off his hand. The green clung to him like tar. He knew milk wasn't supposed to be green—he wasn't so ignorant of husbandry. But his groping, sleep-fogged senses settled on something more visceral: the bright-cheeked woman standing over him, clear-eyed, clear-skinned, and radiating energy— the woman he'd not seen since she'd torn out of this very barn yesterday, spurning his marriage proposal.

"I trust the cows didn't interrupt your slumber, my lord." Maeve strode past him as he rose from his crouch. She slid back the bolt of the opposite door and pushed it open. Morning light swept through the barn. "The girl who usually milks the cows ran off without a word this morning. By the time we realized the cows weren't being milked, we'd already sent out another milkmaid who knew nothing of the curse. Gave her quite a scare."

His mind registered only one thing. "The curse."

"Aye. It has begun again." She leveled him with a gray-eyed stare. "I'll send a girl to buy some milk from the villagers. They'll have enough to spare, for now. Unless you have a taste for cursed green milk."

She swiveled on a heel and disappeared around the edge of the portal. Garrick moved to run his fingers through his hair but caught himself. He stared at his splayed hand, rubbed the fluid on his cloak, then stepped out into the growing light. He caught sight of Maeve, striding straight-backed toward the henhouse.

He razed a forearm across his whiskered face. He let his gaze trail over the twitch of those generous hips as at least one part of his body stirred from its slumber. Aye, Maeve. . . . It had been a sleepless night for more than one reason. Now he'd woken to discover her behaving as if a marriage proposal was as common an occurrence as cows giving green milk.

He strode into the pen and clacked the gate closed behind him. Her shoulders flinched at the sound.

"So," he began, leaning back against the loose post of the hurdle. "What is all this about a curse?"

"Don't be telling me you didn't know." She flung open the doors to the henhouse. One door squealed over in the dust and hung askew by a single leather hinge. "Didn't your father see fit to warn you?"

The birds burst out, cackling in mockery. The Earl saw fit to visit his by-blow once a year or so. Garrick remembered the ruthless scrubbing, the snipping, poking, and prodding of the day before the Earl's yearly arrival much more vividly than the fleeting moments of the Earl's critical perusal. Garrick remembered the way the Earl's man had shoved the documents of the transfer of these lands into his mother's hands— then galloped away, peering nervously into every dark alley of that part of Wexford that rarely saw such a rich, fat mark.

"The Earl," he said drily, "was remarkably unforthcoming on the details of this manor."

"Then you don't know about The O'Madden."

"Who?"

"The O'Madden." Maeve shooed the last of the hens into the yard. "The person destined to break the curse, and drive the last Englishman off this land."

Garrick straightened from the post. Aye, he could stomach a tumbled-down wreck of a castle. He could stomach a tiny glitch of a village, a bow-backed herd of cattle. Those things could be changed and improved; a manor could grow. But he'd had no inkling of a land contested.

"A pity," she mused, swiveling to enter the henhouse, "that the Earl didn't value his bastard son enough to warn you, before you trotted off to your new manor."

"These lands are mine now." Garrick braced himself in the portal. His, indeed, by whatever ruse. "Any man who contests my hold will have to deal with me."

"Steel is useless against a widow's curse." She slipped a basket off a hook just inside the door and slung it over her elbow. "I see I'll have to tell you the full of it."

"It's nigh time you told me the truth about something, Maeve."

She flinched. Her gaze skittered away as she thrust her arm into a nest and groped for eggs. "I never lied to you."

"Didn't you . . . 'Maire?' "

"I had my reasons for that."

"Aye, and its those reasons I'm still seeking. No—" He raised a hand as she opened her mouth to speak. In love and warfare all was the same: There were times to attack, and there were times to retreat . . . if only to find better ground for another assault. "No more lies, Maeve. You'll

tell me when you want to, that's the way of
women. I've more patience than most men. Tell
me of this O'Madden instead."

She had the dignity to blush. She rolled an egg
into her basket. "It's a common enough story.
Every lad in the village knows it."

"I'll be hearing it from you."

"For sure, I'm getting to it, where's that patience you just bragged about?" She snapped her
skirts as she swiveled to the next nest. "Before
the English came, more years ago than I care to
remember, these lands were ruled by the O'Mad-
dens. Their appointed leader was called The
O'Madden."

When Garrick was a boy, the Earl had paid a
priest to teach Garrick his letters. The priest had
had a penchant for the bloody history of the English in Ireland. Now the voice of that priest-tutor
drifted back to him, amid the fidget of forced lessons on fine Saturdays. Garrick vaguely remembered some talk of The O'Donnells of Tirconnel,
the O'Neills of Ulster, the Maguires of Ferman-
agh— heads of the great clans of the Irish in the
lands outside English control. Over the years, the
English had tried to destroy them, and the loyalty
of their people. The English had, for the most
part, failed. The blood of the tribal clans ran deep.

Later in life, it had amused Garrick that the
Irish priest had taken English coin to teach a
half-breed whelp lessons in warfare, with a de-
cidedly rebel slant.

"The last O'Madden," she continued, "built
this castle when the English threatened, nigh

thirty years ago. He was sure a stone castle would hold out against them. But when the English came to conquer, the O'Madden lost the battle. He was brutally murdered for rebelling."

"Are you thinking of giving me a lesson in the history of Ireland, Maeve? Such a story is common enough."

"Nay, herein lies the history of Ireland, Garrick of Wexford." Her fine-boned features twisted into a scowl. "The cowardly English were so frightened that another O'Madden would rise to take the dead one's place, that they took all of the O'Madden's sons and hanged them on the trees of the yard." She rolled an egg into the basket as her voice lowered with fury. "They say the youngest cried for his mother as they dropped the rope around his neck. He was scarcely three years of age."

Garrick stilled. Maeve thrust her hand into another nest, and turned her face away from his. Her arm trembled.

He swiveled a heel in the mud of the yard, only to find himself facing the bare-boughed trees scattered around the castle, only to find himself imagining those branches hung heavy with the most bitter fruit.

"So many years," he said, not believing the words even as they came out of his mouth, "can twist the truth into something it never was."

"Does it assuage your conscience to think so?" She gripped an egg tight in her fist. "Thirty years is not so long. Some still live to bear witness."

Words stuck in his throat. He couldn't deny
he'd heard worse stories. He couldn't deny it ever
happened. He knew little of the Earl, and nothing of the Earl's father, who had probably been
the one to order the atrocities. But he wasn't so
much a fool to denounce his own blood, at least
not in public, to one of his subjects who wanted
nothing to do with him.

"The English," she argued, placing the egg
with exaggerated care into her basket, "are remembered for what they've done."

"You made that clear enough yesterday."

"Aye, I suppose I did." She swung around to
the other side of the henhouse and thrust her
arm into a nest. "Take it as a blessing, my lord,
that I didn't hold you to your word, accept your
proposal, and mix your proud English blood."

He stifled the flash of anger. He still wanted
her as his bride, but he'd be damned if he'd let
her know that now. He wasn't a proud man, but
he had enough sense not to put himself up to
be rejected two days in a row. "You shouldn't
judge a whole of a race by the sum of its rotten
parts."

"Have you no mind for the Statutes of Kil-
kenny? The English can't marry the Irish, it's forbidden without royal dispensation." Her skirts
snagged on a nail. She yanked on them, trying
to pull them free. "You're not even supposed to
be speaking the Irish, yet I've not heard a word
of English out of you yet."

"I've never had much of a mind for the King's
rules."

"That's the Irish in you then." She pulled her skirts free on the sound of a tear. "There may be a bit o' hope for you yet."

"Aye, but will that hope be with you, Maeve?"

"Don't be talking like that."

"Seems to me, we've got more than a bit of talking to do about All Hallow's Eve."

"Wasn't it a moment ago you were talking of patience? Aye, a man has the patience of a child. The less said about that night, the better, by my way of thinking."

"What is it, Maeve?" he asked as she headed out of the pen, toward the kitchens. She shouldered by him so close that he caught a scent of her; sweet green hay and sunshine. "Afraid to poison your good Irish blood with that of an Englishman?"

"Don't you be turning my own words against me." She brushed her gaze over him as he fell into pace beside her. "How was I to know who you were? You sent no notice that you were coming. And you're a strange one. You're not like the others, mincing and prancing about in silks and stinking of perfume."

"The English don't treat their bastards as generously as the Irish do."

"You have this manor, isn't it enough for you?" She slung the basket of eggs to her other elbow. "Blood will show true, my lord. Blood will show true."

"I'll take that as encouragement, Maeve my girl, since half of mine is Irish— "

"Don't be calling me that." She crushed her

skirts in her fist and stepped over a rivulet of sewage water trailing from the back of the castle. "I'll not be your anything but your servant, for the time you're here."

"I'll be here until I'm buried under the dust."

"Is that what you're thinking?" She stopped mid-yard and glared at him. "Did you sleep well last night, my lord of Birr?"

"Now there's a question." A tress of that soft, dark hair trailed across her brow. He resisted the urge to tuck it behind her ear. "I would have slept better, had I a hot-blooded, silver-eyed woman in my bed—"

"No doubt you can find a woman willing to do your bidding for the price of a few coins, we're a poor enough people here." Color crept up her cheeks. "Though not even the most starving woman would sleep in that bed of yours for a night. Are you going to pretend that you didn't hear the footsteps?"

Garrick shrugged. Last night, he'd been awakened three times by the sound of someone stomping above his chamber. Each time, he had climbed the only set of stairs to the third story of the castle. By the light of a tallow candle, he'd peered over the ruin of the roof opened to the light of the stars. He'd found no one. Not a living soul. The floorboards were so rotted with weather that he hadn't dared to clamber across them, lest the roof cave in onto his room below.

"She haunts the place," Maeve said in a hushed voice, clutching the basket to her side. "She won't rest until justice is done."

"That castle is haunted by birds and neglect, no more."

"It's haunted by the wife of The O'Madden. The widow who cast a curse upon the land."

There was a saying among the Irish, one he knew well. *Shun it as you would shun a widow's curse*. Not even a priest's curse carried as much potency as that of a widow betrayed.

"The mother of those poor murdered children. Did you think any Irishwoman could remain silent about that? She cried for justice. She even fasted at the Earl's door." Scorn curled her lip. "But the Englishman ignored her. I could pity him for his foolishness, for his ignorance of our Irish ways, if ever I could pity an Englishman. She died fasting at his door. A widow's curse was no better than he deserved for such shame."

"So," he said, "she cursed the milk green."

"She vowed," Maeve continued, narrowing those silver eyes at him, "that there would be no prosperity in these lands until the last Englishman was driven out, and an O'Madden of pure Irish blood ruled at Birr."

"You said that all her sons were killed."

"Aye."

"Then she cursed the land forever."

"Only when the English are here does the curse start up again." Maeve tilted her chin. "When the English lords abandon this place, everything returns to normal. Now that you're here, the curse has returned."

"There are worse things than green milk."

She fished an egg out of her basket, then

dropped it at his feet. The jelly splattered on his boot and wobbled a bright robin's-egg blue.

"The last lord of Birr left after a week." Maeve swiveled away and headed toward the kitchens. "I'm told he saw blood oozing down his walls on All Hallow's Eve."

"More likely he drank too much ale during the revels."

"Not a single English lord has remained on this land," she argued, "for more than a month. I've no doubt I'll see your back soon enough, and praise be the day."

He watched the twitch of her hips as she headed toward the kitchens. Twenty-four hours he'd been here, and already he knew he'd found what he'd spent a lifetime searching for. The woman *and* the place. It wasn't often a manor fell into a dockworker's lap; it wasn't often a man found his match by the fires of Samhain. He'd be damned if he'd give either one of them up.

Aye, Maeve, you'd like to be rid of me, and of all that happened on All Hallow's Eve. You'd like to forget it, even though the memory shimmers between us every time you meet my eye. Even though I see the pulse racing in your throat, I feel the heat of your body across the distance; I sense your presence before you even come near. You'd like to forget the fierce magic of that night; you'd like to pretend that we aren't fated for each other— but we are, Maeve, we are.

The woman and the place both held mystery. They needed nothing more than a man of determination to crack them. He wondered how great a length she would go to, to be rid of him and whatever unspeakable secret she held to her heart.

He raised his voice to carry across the yard. "It'll take more than green milk and ghosts to get rid of me, Maeve."

She slung the basket off her arm. Her face was pale in the darkness of the portal. "Time will tell, my lord. Time will tell."

Maeve frowned into the churn, then ran a hand through the milky mess of curdles clinging to the sides. She sucked her finger into her mouth and frowned. The sourness burst on her tongue as if she'd bit into an unripe apple.

"Well, there's nothing to be done about it now." She wiped her hands upon her apron and met the wide frightened eyes of two young servants. "Don't be staring at me like that. It isn't the first time the butter hasn't come on the milk, and no doubt it won't be the last. Go to old Aislinn, and ask if she can spare a bit of her butter." Her eyes narrowed on a thought. "And take one of the furs on the lord's bed as compensation. It's sure he has no need of that mountain, and won't miss one or two."

The girls skittered out, and bumped into another woman bustling into the kitchens from the castle.

"They are here, my lady," the servant whispered. "They're coming up the road now."

"Well, don't be telling me." Maeve tipped the churn on its side and hefted a foot on it, to roll it across the dirt floor. "Go and tell the master—it's him who'll be receiving the tribute this year."

"He's not here. He's off doing something again." The servant wrung her hands. "I heard Seamus say the master was off to fix the hurdles on the sheep pen, if you can believe that."

Maeve frowned as she bumped the churn over the threshold into the open yard. Last week, he'd fixed the thatch on the barn. Three days ago, he'd fashioned a new hinge for the door of the henhouse. Yesterday, she'd come upon him cutting back the ivy which had begun to send roots into the castle mortar.

That man had lived in this castle for two weeks. Already, he'd dripped more sweat into the earth than all of the other English lords combined.

"If you don't mind me saying so, my lady," the servant whispered, "he's a better man than the others. Strong and hard-working. And he doesn't snap and order us all about like the others." She paused. "A pity he's English."

"Yes. He's English." Maeve granted the woman a glare as she heaved the churn upright. "Mind you remember that, today, when he accepts the tribute and steals the life from all of us."

Maeve strode toward the sheep pens, jarring her heels with every step. Black clouds scudded across the sky, threatening another day of rain. A crafty one, this lord. For the price of a bit of sweat, he wins the admiration of a people used to brutal, unfeeling masters. How quickly their loyalty drifted. She kept wondering when he would give up this mockery, and start acting like

the lord he was, instead of the rough-handed,
hard-working Irishman she'd lain with on All
Hallow's Eve.

She stumbled over her own thoughts. She
mustn't resurrect that ghost again, it must lay
dead and buried in her heart. She'd lain with an
illusion that night. She must think of the evening
as no more than that. Oh, so she still shivered
with hot pleasure every time she heard him laugh
in the mead hall. So she still felt her body melt
every time he came near these past weeks, to ask
her some simple question about the running of
the castle, or to tease her with that look in his
eye. She was a woman now, and knew what kind
of pleasure a man could give. The kind of pleasure *this* man could give.

She faltered to a stop as she caught sight of
him on the other side of the sheep pens. He'd
discarded his cloak. It lay in a careless heap over
one of the hurdles. A splotch of sweat stained
his tunic dark between his shoulder blades, and
trailed in a point down the length of his back.
A tumble of wood lay on the ground, a chaff-
flecked axe lodged in one of the logs. He strad-
dled the fence, wrapping rope tight in the joint
between hurdle and strut.

Her throat parched. Aye, she was like a woman
who had had her first taste of wine and now
struggled with the thirst of a drunkard. How
greedy could she be? She'd had her one night of
loving, that was all she had asked from the Fates.
She hadn't wanted this— she hadn't wanted to be
faced each day with the cheek-burning memory

of a night she'd vowed to bury. She hadn't wanted to see the strong, bulging arms which had held her so tight; or the powerful thighs which had razed so intimately between hers. And why, why did they have to belong to such a perfect, hard-working man, an English lord she could never, ever have?

"I know you haven't come to fetch me for dinner," he said suddenly, sweeping the rope under the strut again. "A man might think you've come to keep me company, Maeve."

She flushed as he sidled her an eye. So she'd been staring, aye. Well she was made of flesh and blood like any other woman, and the powerful giant working the wood and rope before her was as fine a sight as any on such a cloudy morning.

"Have done with that," she said. "The Lord of Birr has far more important duties than fixing a fence this day."

"There's a ditch outside the walls that needs to be cleared, and a roof to be put on the castle if we're to keep the third floor from collapsing into the second—"

"Such is the work of tenants, not the work of a lord."

He stretched the rope tight, using the full of his weight. "There are times, Maeve, when I think you'd rather I let the whole place fall apart."

"I'd rather," she retorted, trying in vain to ignore the bulging of his thighs and his arms, "you'd leave the place altogether."

And leave me in peace, leave me with memories and no more— nice, safe, controllable memories.

"Get that idea out of your mind, Maeve me girl, I'm here to stay. And I'll set this place to rights if it takes years to do it. It's been long enough since this place saw a man's hand."

She frowned. It had been longer than he suspected. She and her people had been too busy tending to their daily needs of food and shelter to put any work into the castle. The other lords of Birr had done nothing to improve the grounds or the outbuildings. They'd only seen fit to import their own comfort into the castle, and waste as much of the land's wealth as possible, however fleeting their stay.

"You are the lord of this place," she said. *For now.* "It's no concern of mine what you do with it."

"Is that why you're scowling and snapping at me whenever I pick up a hammer?"

"If I scowl, it's at a man's foolishness. What do you know about such things as this?" She waved a hand at the fencing, at the bulk of the knots between hurdle and strut. "You're probably making everything worse— it'll all fall apart at the first storm."

"I've some experience picking other men's turnips and thatching other men's houses and loading boxes on the docks of Wexford."

An odd pedigree for the son of a lord, even for a bastard son. But Maeve was beginning to realize that this was no ordinary man, no ordinary Englishman. Had he been so, she'd never would have chosen him from the crowd at the Samhain fires.

"A man's got his pride," he said. Garrick made one final yank on the rope and let his sharp blue gaze trail over the green hills of Birr. "But for a few lessons in Latin, I took nothing from the Earl until he offered me this." He settled that unsettling gaze upon her. "Tell me now, Maeve, how's a man to give up the chance at a piece of land of his own?"

"Land taken with children's blood." She wrapped her hands in her apron for warmth, she wrapped her heart in bands of steel against his words. "You should have done with this now— you're lord of the place. You'll probably hurt yourself with all this heavy work."

"A fine thing that would be, to have you as nursemaid."

"I'll be no nursemaid to you, Garrick of Wexford. Now come down off there."

"For my housekeeper, you have an odd habit of giving orders." He softened his words with a half-smile as he settled his weight on the hurdle. "Give me a reason to come down, lass, and you won't find me lingering up here for long."

"The tenants," she said, ignoring the gleam in his eye, "have come to deliver tribute."

"Tribute?"

"Aye." She gripped her elbows against the cold. "The rents they owe you for the privilege of living and working on this land. They are waiting for you. Are you going to keep them standing in the cold?"

He leapt off the hurdle with a graceful bunching of muscles and wiped his open hands on his tunic. "That wasn't the reason I was looking for, but it'll do. For now."

She turned away and headed toward the castle. He fell into step beside her, with that lanky, easy stride. There was no escaping him. Always, always he found his way to her, walked beside her, breathed down upon her so she could smell the ale on his lips, or the remnants of pepper sauce from the midday meal, and looked at her with those clear blue eyes that knew all her secrets. In the castle she'd worked in all her adult life, she felt like a mouse under a cat's eye.

"You look fine today, Maeve my girl. The air has put color in your cheeks."

"Mind you keep your eyes on the counting of the tribute." She fisted her hands in her skirts. "I'll not have it said later that the people have cheated you of your due, because you didn't have the sense to keep your eyes where they belong."

"It's a hard thing you ask of me, to set my sights away from you. Like asking a man to stop basking in the sun. Or, rather, the moonlight."

"Have done with your foolishness."

"For three weeks I've been a patient man. How long do you expect me to wait, Maeve?"

"When God made time, he made plenty of it, Garrick of Wexford."

"Aye, well, castles are built stone by stone I suppose. But the rope is fraying, Maeve, my patience is growing thin." They wandered around the barn, and took the path around the side of the castle. "What, exactly, is my tribute?"

"You don't know that, either?" She sidled him a glance. "How do you know you'll get the full of it?"

"I've full faith in you, Maeve."

She frowned, and wished for a flash of a moment she'd had the courage to cheat him out of his due. Too late now. The men waited in the courtyard. And she supposed he'd find out, sooner or later, what his true tribute was.

"Only a few things." She pushed a lock of hair off her shoulder. "One out of every three calves born. A fifth of all the grain."

"A fifth?" He nodded. "Generous."

"Someone has to pay for the luxuries of this manor." She stepped over a drainage gully he'd cleared last week. "From every tenant you get two hens. One fifth of their wool. One third of the flax harvest."

His pace faltered. "Is that all?"

"Oh, no." Her chin tightened. "Let it not be said that the people of Birr do not pay fine tribute to their lord."

"Maeve— "

"Two lambs out of every five born were added to the rent due with the last lord." They swept around the corner of the castle. "That, and three pieces of gold."

May as well have asked for a chunk of their hearts, or the lives of their children— it all adds up to pretty much the same. Maeve surveyed the crowd of villagers as they came even with the castle door. A lamb, loose from its brothers, clattered bleating across the paving stones. Calves bumped against one another, lowing in the cold. A farmer clutched a coarse sack battering with trussed fowl. Other men bowed under the weight of sacks, their bony arms bare under the ragged sleeves of their tunics.

Aye, think of this, she told herself, fixing her attention on the people wearily weaving their way up from the village to congregate in the yard. Think of this, she told herself, watching the villagers heave their meager wealth at the castle door. Think of this, the next time your woman's body weakens to feel a strong Englishman's embrace.

She turned, to find Garrick standing with his legs braced, a scowl marring his features. He hefted meaty, work-hardened hands on his hips. Those clear blue eyes scanned the crowd. It struck her that though he didn't wear the clothes of a lord, right now, standing so big and so fierce before these people, he had more of the demeanor than any of the milky-faced aristocrats who had been in his place before.

He ran a hand through his hair, and palmed the nape of his neck. "This is my tribute?"

Her eyes narrowed. She recognized that look of disgust. So the calves were thin this year, and the sacks lighter than usual. Early rains had ruined part of the harvest. *This is all they have, Englishman, and you'll take it. You'll suck the lifeblood out of this land as your predecessors have done before you.*

"It has been a bad year," she said, forcing her chin high. "This is all they have for you."

"Hell."

Garrick's scowl darkened. He dropped his hand from his neck. Maeve bit back a surge of anger. So the man was disappointed. So was she. She had expected better. God knows why, but she'd expected better from him.

"Seeing you lack someone to keep accounts," she said, holding her tongue still, "I can offer the services of— "

"Tell them," he interrupted, "that this year they may keep their tribute."

Words died on her lips. A ripple of sound trembled over the crowd. She blinked up at him, sure she'd heard him wrong.

"Tell them," he continued, "that it is my gift to them, for years of loyal service."

Four

A light drizzle misted the ground by the time Garrick wove his way back from the sheep pen to the looming silhouette of the castle. His palms burned from stretching thin thongs of leather across hurdle and strut, and seeped here and there with pinpricks of blood where he'd taken slivers of the fresh-cut wood into his skin. It wasn't as strenuous work as hefting bales of wool, or cages of Irish wolfhounds, or unloading casks of French wine off the docks of Wexford—but it left his back aching nonetheless with the soreness of muscles well-spent.

He startled a bevy of women as he strode in through the back door of the castle. Any other day, he would laugh at their surprised expressions. But not after what he'd done today. He'd been here at Birr long enough to learn his place—and it wasn't the servant's entrance. Old habits were hard to break. It was time for him to remember that he didn't have to earn the bread he put into his mouth, not anymore. He had to be careful. After all, he had secrets of his own—dangerous ones that had to be kept.

He climbed the stairs, and leapt past the third

one which, he'd noticed, had long lost its mortar, then he pushed open the door to his chamber.

A fire crackled high and hot in the fireplace, illuminating the brilliant tapestries which draped the walls. The golden light shimmered off the silken draperies of the canopied bed, and cast shadows amid the tumble of pillows and furs. His lip curled as he shuffled his way through the rushes, smelling vaguely of some sweet herb. It was no wonder they all hated the English so much. Every lord before him had taken the food from their children's mouths, turned it into something as cold and dead as silks and gold, and draped this very bedroom with it.

It was no wonder *she* hated him so much.

The door burst open and two girls bobbed in, their arms stretched with the weight of pails full of steaming water. They waddled past him toward the hearth.

"I've ordered a bath for you." Maeve followed the girls in. Linens hung from her shoulder. A basket swung from her arm. She moved aside as a man rolled a wide, cut barrel through the door, slid it through the reeds, and tipped it upright in front of the fire. "I thought you might need one, my lord, after all the hard work you've done today."

He hazarded a glance to her, but she avoided his eye. She nodded to the men who slipped back down the stairs, then she bustled about, laid the linens on a stool by the fire and rifled in her basket as the girls poured in the water.

"I've found some good soap left over from

when the last lord was here." She waved it under her nose. "Too fine stuff for any of us to use, but worthy of you."

He slid his hands to his hips and narrowed his gaze at her, wondering if she was being sarcastic. Wondering what was so damn important in that basket that she wouldn't lift her head and catch his eye. The servants finished their pouring, clattered up their pails, and skittered across the room. The door clicked shut behind them, leaving him alone in his bedroom with Maeve.

"Don't be standing there as dull as a cow," she said, sifting something into the water. "The water won't stay hot forever."

He raised a brow at her. It was custom for the woman of the house to bathe any visitors, but that was a privilege Maeve had dodged from the very first. Now he wondered what mischief she was up to, lingering about over his bath, and ordering him in.

"Are you going to stand there staring at me until I grow old and withered? It's not as if I haven't seen you without your *braies.*"

He smiled then, not so much at what she said, but at her own expression after the words left her mouth. As if she couldn't believe she'd said them aloud.

"A bath is welcome, Maeve."

"No doubt it is, with the way you're wearing yourself out fixing up the place."

"I've worked harder than this for the taste of bread."

"You should be hiring some of the villagers to

do this." She tossed a vial back into the basket. "They'd welcome the work, and their labor wouldn't cost more than a few calves come slaughter-time."

"Is that all?"

"If I told you that price was generous," she said, raising her face to his, "you wouldn't even know, would you?"

"No." He set to the ties of his tunic as he let a smile slip across his lips. "I have to put my trust in you, Maeve."

"It's a fool who trusts an enemy."

"You're no enemy."

She had done well enough since he'd been here. She ran the estate with a strong and even hand. All the servants looked to her for guidance. And though she proclaimed she hated his English blood and wanted to drive him off, not once had he seen her do anything to harm the manor itself.

"Hire some good men, then." He set to his belt and tossed it across the bed. "I need several to help me mend the roof of this castle."

"You know that it won't make any difference." She jerked up as his belt slid off the bed and clattered to the floor. "All your work— it's futile."

"There's nothing futile about a good, strong roof."

"The curse won't go away by you fixing things," she argued, casting her gaze down as he fisted his tunic off his back. "The milk will still come out green, the eggs blue, the butter won't come in the churn, oatcakes will still burn in a cold pan. And bought loyalty never lasts."

He rolled the tunic in his hands. Caked mud flaked onto the reeds. "Is that what you think I did out there today?"

"That was a foolish thing you did today." She planted the basket at her feet and crossed her arms across her breasts. "With the cows giving green milk and the hens laying eggs we can't eat, how are we going to survive over the winter? You have servants to feed, and yourself, and the livestock, as well. Did you think of that, when you so blithely refused the tribute?"

He tossed the tunic on the bed and frowned. This woman knew more about his own estate than he did. Perhaps he'd condemned the people of this castle to a season of starvation with an unwitting act of foolish generosity.

Hell. What did he know of running an estate? He knew how to thatch a roof, how to mend a fence, how to heft the bales of hay so they fit tightly amid the rafters of the hay barn. But he didn't know a damned thing about raising cattle or feeding two dozen servants over the winter. He swept his gaze over her, over that cloud of dark hair and those pale, fine-boned features, and wondered why she didn't just marry him so he could let her run the place as she'd obviously done all these years.

"There's cattle on those slopes." He sat on the edge of the bed and footed off one of his boots. "They're mine, aren't they? And the sheep?"

"You've got a big enough herd for a lordship of this size."

"Time comes to thin the herd." The other boot clattered to the floor. "Or is the meat cursed, as well?"

"I haven't the faintest idea."

"We'll see to it then." He ran his fingers through his hair then planted his palms on his thighs. "The villagers need that tribute more than we do, that was plain enough to see. We'll make do this winter."

"I suppose," she said softly, "we will."

Something in the husk of her voice drew his gaze to her. She'd uncrossed her arms, and as he watched she pressed her palms against the cloth of her apron. She looked up at him with eyes he'd not seen since Samhain Eve. Eyes of molten silver, full of unguarded emotion.

Something deep inside him stirred to life; the slumbering hope he'd held still, for the sake of this woman.

"Ah, Garrick." Her gaze dipped, then rose again, shining with pride. "For all its foolishness, it's a fine thing you did this afternoon. A fine, fine thing."

He basked in the warm glow of that soft gaze. His insides turned over. Something shimmered between them, a gleaming thread of hope and expectation— so fragile and uncertain that he was afraid to move, even to speak, lest the vibrations of his words shatter it. Looking at her reminded him of an Irish wolfhound which had come free of its cage one day, upon the Wexford docks. It had taken hours for him to corner the sleek hound. When he did, the creature had looked up at him with the same mixture of fear and skittish expectation, the creature's body had quivered with nervous wiry strength, as if with one move on his part, the hound prepared to bolt.

Finally, he nodded to the bath lofting fragrant steam between them. "I'm thinking," he murmured, "that the bath is big enough for the two of us, Maeve."

"Not for you, my lord." Dusky lashes dipped over those silver eyes. "Don't I know that well enough."

Her words emboldened him enough to rise to his feet and take a careful step toward her. "There are times when a man and a woman can take the space of one."

"If you'll be wanting a woman," she whispered, "don't you be asking me to find one for you."

"Aye, Maeve, you know it's you I want."

"Don't, Garrick."

"Haven't we waited long enough, lass?"

"Don't wait for me, Garrick. For this thing between us . . . must never be. Even if I did see the finer side of an Englishman this day." She trailed her fingers across the rim of the tub. "Perhaps it's best you see to your own bath tonight."

"Don't leave."

"I must."

Her chin high, Maeve crossed the room. Garrick watched her stiff back, silently willing her to stay, silently willing her to stop and turn and come into his arms. He curled his hands into fists, forcing himself not to run after her; for in such things as this, a woman must come of her own will.

He took one step toward her anyway. She curled her hand over the handle of the door. She pulled.

Nothing happened.

She pulled on the door again, in vain.

He stilled as he watched her take the handle in two hands and give it a good yank.

The door didn't budge.

"Maeve?"

"It's locked." She blurted the words, louder than necessary. "No. It can't be. The lock is on this side of the door." She yanked again. "It's stuck."

"It can't be."

"Don't be telling me what can't be," she argued. "It's stuck."

Garrick watched as she struggled to pull the door open. The warped, scarred old door didn't budge. It didn't make any sense. The bolt had long rusted still, and it lay on the inside of the door. The door couldn't be locked from the outside. In addition, it opened inward, making it impossible to prop the door closed from the narrow landing outside. And he'd heard it squeal upon its hinges many a time since he'd arrived here at Birr. This door had been another thing he'd determined to fix over the winter.

A bubble of laughter rose in his chest and slipped out between his lips.

"A fine one you are," she snapped. "You're not even going to help me."

"I'm not going to help you leave, Maeve."

"Must be the weather." She planted her fists on her hips and glared at the door. "When the rain threatens, everything seems to stick."

"That door has never stuck. It swings open if it isn't closed tight in the portal."

"It is closed tight now."

"It is." A smile stretched across his face. "The curse can work two ways, obviously. It can work against even you."

What a strange twist of luck. Well, he wasn't a fool to let another opportunity pass him by, no matter what forces were at work. He crossed the distance that separated them, and flattened the palm of his hand on the door, right over the curve of her shoulder.

He smelled her again. Sweet summer hay, rising from that dusky cloud of hair. Grass and woman. His body hardened at the .memory, at the reality of the woman so close to him. He sensed, too, her sudden agitation, the quiver of her body against his: the plumpness of buttock, the tremble of back.

"You want me, Maeve."

"I don't."

"Is that why you're breathing so quickly? Is that why your blood runs through you as hot as mine? Is that why you stay still against me?"

"I've no place to run. And you're English."

"My worse half, I'll admit that. Is that any reason to hate a man? Because he was born on the wrong side of the bed to a father he hardly knows?"

"Yes. Yes."

"A person cannot help who his parents are, *a stór.*"

She caught her breath. He felt the surge in her, the crumbling of her will. He seized her arm, turned her around, and pressed her back against the door. A tress of dark hair trailed from the corner of her lips. Her eyes shone as large and dewy as the morning sky, filling with tears that threatened to drop off those black lashes and trail over that luminescent skin.

He fixed his gaze on her lips and knew tonight he could wait no longer.

"Brace yourself, Maeve my girl." He dipped his head. "I'm going to kiss you."

She saw the kiss coming just as she had imagined it a hundred thousand times in her dreams as she thrashed on her pallet by the kitchen fires. She wanted it with the same fierceness; she wanted it with every throb of her heart; she wanted it mindlessly, for she knew the consequences of succumbing to her secret fantasies. Yet now, standing with her back against a door that shouldn't be stuck shut, she could no more slip away from the giant's kiss than she could wish herself born of different parents.

A person cannot help who his parents are.

It was as if he knew. . . . It was as if he could understand what he didn't even know. It was as if he could understand the fate she was condemned to, for no more reason than an accident of birth.

So she parted her lips as his mouth descended upon hers. She opened her mouth and drank his breath—a hot heady brew of passion and yearning and triumph. She pressed her lips up to his and felt the raze of stubble on his cheek as he slanted his face. The softness of his shoulder-length hair tangled with hers as it slid silken past his ears. She welcomed the prison of his hands as he cupped her face. She let herself revel in the coarseness of his callused palms, in the strength of the thick joints, in the all-encompassing broadness of those worker's palms. She told herself for the hundred thousandth time that in his heart he was a man of the earth and air and wind—salt and water, sweat and muscle—as honest as the land itself. In any other time, in any other place, they could be as one, they could fulfill the inexplicable bone-deep passion they shared. They could nurse it and make it blossom into something strong and thick-rooted; a rare and hearty bloom.

She clutched the illusion to her heart for as long as she could as he blinded her with kisses. She dug her nails into the rough weave of his shirt and filled her lungs with the smell of his skin—river-rain and fresh-cut oak. She let herself drift away as he pressed his body against hers, as he flattened her between a door and himself—both things equally unyielding in bulk and strength. Her blood sizzled through her limbs and left her skin tingling as if she'd twirled naked through grass fresh with morning dew. She held him even as the first tear fell from her lashes and slipped salty into their kiss.

In the end it was Garrick who pulled away, Garrick who rained kisses upon her to taste the tears sluicing down her face; it was Garrick who brushed the hair from her eyes and made her, once again, clear of sight.

His gaze asked too many questions, and she knew she could hide the truth no longer. He deserved the truth from her, even if it meant it would destroy her.

"You must leave, Garrick."

Her words came out unrecognizable—in the husky voice of the woman she'd vowed to leave behind on the hills of that Samhain fire.

"Ten thousand ghosts or ten thousand Englishmen," he said, "could not tear me from your side again."

She squeezed her eyes shut against magic words. Fresh tears trailed hot down her cheeks.

"Stay with me tonight, Maeve."

"You must leave." She sucked in a breath, she sucked in strength. "You must leave or I am doomed, and forever this land and this people."

"Don't be talking to me of curses, not now—"

"There will be no prosperity to these lands," she repeated, "until the last Englishman is driven off, and an O'Madden with pure Irish blood rules at Birr."

"You talk like a little girl repeating her lessons."

"I am speaking my lessons, Garrick. I've heard those words every day of my life."

He wiped a tear off her jaw with a flick of his thumb. "It's time to stop listening to lessons and start living *life*."

"There will be no prosperity to these lands," she repeated, more forcefully than before, "until the last Englishman is driven off, and an O'Madden with pure Irish blood rules at Birr." She gripped the cloth of his shirt. "The curse goes away, Garrick, as soon as you and the others leave. As soon as *I* rule here, alone."

Her words gave him pause. He searched her gaze. Surprise and incredulity dawned on his face. Maeve felt her heart breaking, a sharp, spearing pain in her chest. Aye, the time had come for the truth to be known. The time had come to destroy any hope that she and this man of her heart could be one.

"Yes, Garrick." She released his shirt, and smoothed the wrinkles against his chest. "I, Maeve of Birr, am The O'Madden."

Garrick pushed away from the door, away from her. She stepped out from under the shadow of his arm and paced somewhere behind him in the rushes.

"You spoke true," she said, "when you said a person could not choose his parents. I did not choose mine. I did not choose to be the only surviving child of The O'Madden and the widow whose curse only I can break."

Garrick stood still and listened. The story came out in a flood of words. She had been no more than an infant on the breast when the English had attacked. She'd been with her wetnurse the day the Englishman seized all the O'Madden sons. The nursemaid had wrapped her in common swaddling and pretended that Maeve was her own child. The villagers, loyal even under the torture of Englishmen, had kept silent about her presence. And while the widow fasted at the Englishman's door, Maeve was sent to be raised in the woods with a fairy-doctor.

Garrick ran his hand through his hair as Maeve sank on the edge of his bed and spoke with a trembling voice. Her dark hair marked her as an O'Madden, she told him. Only in the woods apart from the fair-haired villagers could she be safe from the sharp eyes of the jealous Englishmen. Glenna had taught her the things that an O'Madden must know. Glenna kept her safe as Englishman after Englishman took on the title of Lord of Birr, until so many years passed that they all forgot about the threat of The O'Madden. Glenna kept her safe so the English would not know that one of the royal blood still lived, to fulfill the terms of a widow's curse. In the end, Glenna arranged to have her installed as housekeeper in her own castle.

Garrick knew she spoke the truth. He heard the verity in the tremble of her voice. The story explained so much: why she walked amid her people like a queen, why she didn't fear the strange goings-on in the castle. These were things that could not touch her, for she was The O'Madden. She was his rival to the lordship of this manor.

A thought came to him, hard and fast.

"You went to the fires," he said, "to conceive a child."

He turned to face her, finally. She balled her apron in her hand and wiped the cloth across her face.

"Try to understand," she whispered. "For a lifetime I've lived separate from all. I'm too well-born to take a husband amid the boys of the village. Yet my true identity has been kept a secret from all of my own rank, all the neighboring chieftains. That, too, was for my own protection, and for the safety of the manor. It was too big a risk to go to the neighboring chieftains with my true identity: I had no one to protect me but the cattle herders of the village. What was to stop one of the chieftains from marrying me off to one of their sons and conquering my lands for themselves? If that happened, there would be no O'Madden here, and the curse would continue. What man of chieftain's rank would take his wife's name?

"Yet here I was, nigh five-and-twenty," she continued, "with no hope for a husband, no hope for a son to take these lands back." She shrugged a shoulder, and in that moment, Garrick had never seen her looking so fragile, so uncertain. "I yearned, too, for a normal life. For a family. But you see, that didn't matter. As The O'Madden I'm not allowed such common dreams."

"You went to the fires," he said, "to conceive a bastard."

"Aye." She tilted her chin. "Among our people, bastards are honored as highly as legitimate sons. The son I would bear could be the hope of the future, he could raise armies loyal to him to take back this land—something I could never do. I told myself I would get myself with child, and raise a warrior."

"Against me."

"Against whosoever dared to hold against The O'Madden, the rightful heir to the leadership of this clan."

He stared at her with new eyes, and wondered how he could not have known. Look at her, so straight-backed and regal, with the stamp of aristocracy on her fine-boned features. She belonged there, perched on the edge of a royal bed. He was the usurper. Truth be known, she was of higher rank than himself. She bore Irish chieftain's blood, probably with a pedigree she could trace back to the time of Patrick. He was nothing but a by-blow of a summer night's folly.

Truth be told, even less than that.

"It was a bitter twist of fate that I found one like you, Garrick, at the Samhain fires." She swallowed a humorless laugh. "I wanted someone who would get the deed done, and forget about it, about me. Someone I would never see again."

"Nay, Maeve." He shook his head. "Such things as this never happen by accident. Luck smiled upon us."

"Luck." She buried her face in her hands. "Everything is ruined, everything, don't you see? What luck is this, that I get myself with child by an Englishman?"

Five

Maeve vaulted from the bed and strode across the room, her back to Garrick, to put as much distance as she could between herself and the words she'd just blurted.

"You really must disrobe." She trailed two fingers through the cooling bath water. "Else the water will be too cold to bathe in, and all our work will be for naught."

She seized a pile of linens off the rim of the barrel only to lay them down again on a stool by the fire; she rearranged the position of the soap and the brush in the basket. Finally, she seized a poker and crouched by the hearth, to stoke the fire now fading to a quiet crackle.

What difference did it make? she asked herself. So she had told him what she'd only just begun to suspect. She had told him far more dangerous things this night. She had handed him the power to destroy her, and thus destroy the last claimant to the very lordship he was determined to hold as his own. Perhaps in some deep part of herself she had told him the truth, so he would have mercy on her and the innocent soul growing in her womb.

She dismissed the thought as soon as it came. In her heart of hearts, she knew Garrick would never hurt her. If she hadn't known that in some deep instinctive way, she never would have trusted him with all her secrets.

His voice came, softly, far closer to her than she expected, from just over her shoulder.

"Were you going to tell me, Maeve?"

She bit the flesh of her lower lip. "I don't know." She rose to her feet and slid the poker into the pail by the hearth. "Truth be told, I hadn't thought that far ahead. You do that to me, Garrick . . . you make me do things without thinking."

"You do things to me, as well. Strange things." His voice dipped low and husky. "You make me think of the future, of plans."

"To get rid of me?" She hated the quaver of her voice. "No one would blame you, for getting rid of the woman who is destined to destroy you."

"Listen to you. Would you raise that babe in your womb to destroy his father?"

"Don't be talking foolishness. He'll be born with English blood and can never stop the curse." She hugged her arms. "Even if that weren't the case . . . I could never set him against you."

"And I could never destroy you, Maeve. Only a fool of a man would destroy his own heart."

His arms curled around her and she closed her eyes against the warm, tight embrace. She couldn't help herself. She turned into him. She pressed her nose in his chest, in the opening of his shirt so she could smell the man-smell of him, cinnamon and ginger, warmth and salt-sweat. She would forgive herself tomorrow for succumbing to him. How could she resist, locked in this room with the only man she would ever love, the father of her child, the man who she was bound by honor and duty to defeat?

"All this time," he said, his voice rumbling in his chest, "and it's the curse which kept you from marrying me."

"My people have suffered for too many years." She mumbled into his shirt. "I am their only hope. My life is not mine, it has never been mine. Except for that one All Hallow's Eve."

"Maeve. . . ." His arms flexed around her, loosened, then flexed tight again. "If I weren't English, you would take me as your husband."

"Oh, Garrick, what's the use in talking of 'ifs?' A whole world rides on such things."

"But it's true. It's my English blood that keeps you from being my wife."

"If you weren't English, you wouldn't be the Lord of Birr, you wouldn't be here, and we would never have met."

"Tell me you'd be my wife, if no English blood ran in these veins."

"Without a moment's hesitation, without a moment's doubt." She breathed in the scent of him—then closed her eyes and committed it to memory. "There. You've left me with no pride now, Garrick"

"I'll leave myself none, either." He pulled himself away from her. His gaze skidded away from hers as he turned and walked, slope-shouldered, toward the bed. "I have something to tell you, Maeve. And it's not a proud thing."

She stood strangely cold, though the fire crackled at her back. He'd pulled away from her so suddenly, she felt bereft of more than just the warmth of his body. It was as if he'd packed away the warmth of his spirit, and guarded it until he could say his piece.

He ran his hand through his hair. The firelight shimmered amid the fair strands twined along the honeyed length. His shoulders flexed uncertainly beneath the broad sweep of his shirt. He sat upon the edge of his bed, and hiked a knee upon its height. He rested an elbow on his knee and let his fingers dangle in between.

"It seems neither of us is who we expected to be." Garrick took a sudden interest in the pattern of the reeds on the floor. "It seems we both have secrets."

"Garrick?"

"Yes, Maeve. I've been keeping things from you, as well."

Maeve sank her heel back into a pile of ashes. The edge of the mantelpiece bit into her shoulder. Garrick avoided her eye. He filled his lungs with air and breathed it out in one heaving rush. She flattened her palm over her belly, sensing that her world was about to tilt all over again.

"My mother had been a laundress in Wexford," he began, curling his fingers over his ankle and hiking his leg onto his other knee. "Not an easy life, that. It paid barely enough to keep her belly full. But as she is still so fond of telling me, she was a pretty enough lass in her youth. She used her looks to earn an extra coin or two, when the opportunity arose. That's how she came about meeting the Earl."

Her cheeks warmed. She knew how the English lords took advantage of a woman's poverty. And she knew, even more intimately, how bastards came about. "You aren't the first man begotten from an Englishman's roaming eye, Garrick."

"Nor the last, no doubt." He shrugged his giant's shoulder. "And the way my mother speaks of it, it was her eye that had been roaming that day."

Maeve dropped her gaze. So he was the son of a woman of uncertain virtue. How easily he admitted it. Who was she to judge, when she, too, had let her eye roam over the assembled men on All Hallow's Eve, for the express purpose to choose a mate and sire a bastard?

"It had been fair time in Wexford, so the story goes. My mother was walking about, with a new tunic she'd 'borrowed' from amid the laundry. The way she tells the story, the tunic was big for her, and kept slipping off her shoulders with every breath. She caught the Earl's eye that day. He offered her far more than a single coin for the pleasure of an evening. My mother is a hard-headed woman, and she knew something of the Earl's past. She took his money.

"A few weeks later, she found herself with child. She wasted no time going to the Earl with the news. The Earl gave her a purse and paid her little mind . . . until my mother gave birth to me. A son. The Earl's only son, amid a dozen legitimate daughters." Garrick gripped his leg with two hands and spoke on a sigh. "But you see, there was something he didn't know."

Maeve curled her fingers into a fist against her abdomen, as a strange sort of hope swirled within her.

"At the same time my mother was entertaining the Earl, she'd been sleeping with the local butcher. A giant of a man, young and blond and strong-armed, and much admired among the laundresses of Wexford." Garrick nodded as he caught sight of her face. "Yes, Maeve. Only God knows who was the true father of that child growing in her womb. But *she* knew it would be more profitable to claim the child was the Earl's." He slipped his knee off the bed and spread his broad hands. "So I was raised as the by-blow of an Earl, even as the truth became more and more obvious. As my mother grew older, the truth faded so much in her mind that as far as she was concerned, I *was* the son of the Earl."

"Are you saying . . . ?"

"It's an old ruse, tired and gnarled and thick." He raked a hand through his hair. "As the years passed and the Earl's daughters gave him hope for grandsons, the Earl's generosity waned. My mother fought in the courts for recognition, for recompense. In the end, the Earl gave me this place to wash his hands of me. I'm no fool." He shrugged. "I took it. I know men who would do much worse, for a chance at a piece of land."

"Garrick. . . ." She took a step toward him, crushing her apron in her hands. "Do you know what you're telling me?"

"I'm telling you I'm full-blooded Irish, Maeve. Without a drop of poisoned English blood."

She flattened her hand on her abdomen, imagining she felt the throb of life in her belly. *My son won't be English. My son will be an O'Madden with pure Irish blood.*

My son can end the curse.

"Now you have the means to destroy me, Maeve." He rose to his full height. "No one knows the truth but you and me. With a word to the Earl, or to the authorities, I could have my lordship stripped from me. You could be rid of me, forever."

She trembled as the full meaning of his words washed over her. She trembled with incredulity, with excitement, with exhilaration. Her child wasn't English. Garrick wasn't English. Garrick was Lord of Birr, and of full Irish blood.

"Why would I make you leave this place," she said, her voice husky with joy, "when by doing that, I'd be all but inviting a true Englishman to take your place?"

He took a few steps closer to her, not touching her with his hands, but scouring her form with the fierceness of his gaze. "Noble blood doesn't run in these veins, Maeve my girl."

"Noble blood has brought me nothing but grief."

"Aye, but it runs in your veins nonetheless," he argued. "Far nobler blood than mine."

"It suits me fine to know you have no English blood."

"What I hold, I hold by ruse."

"And a fine ruse on an Englishman it is, I'm thinking." Her lips curved. Joy rose up in her. "Finer than any I've heard."

He reached out, tentatively, and placed a hand on her abdomen. "Our son will be an O'Madden of pure Irish blood."

"Yes." Tears blurred her vision as she placed her hand over his. *"Yes."*

"I could be his father. In name, if you'll have me."

"No child," she whispered, her throat husky with tears, "could have a better father."

"Or a better name." He reached up with his other hand and traced the line of her chin. "There's one more thing, Maeve. . . . For a man like me, of no name, O'Madden is as fine a name as any man could claim."

She sucked in a trembling breath, and met that clear blue gaze. What a strong man this was, who could proudly take a woman's name, who would wear it without doubt or regret.

"Don't keep me guessing, woman. Tell me yes."

She drew his hand around to her back, then pressed her breasts against him. Aye, such a giant. Such a warm, honest, open-hearted man with courage enough to reveal weakness without shame. She'd chosen well on Samhain. Aye, she'd chosen well.

She opened her mouth to him and tasted the breath of passion. It flared fierce and hot between them.

She pulled away and spoke against his lips. "You can have your way with me tonight, Garrick of Wexford. But tomorrow, you'd best make an honest woman out of me."

He moved to kiss her. He paused as he heard a gentle squeak whine in the room. They both glanced to the portal.

As they watched, the battered door sagged open on squeaky leather hinges.

"Come along, Garrick, by God, you're dragging your feet like a boy being brought to the barber to have a tooth pulled."

"It's not dragging my feet, Maeve." He tugged her to a stop and rolled her into his arms. "It's the sight and smell of these woods that's got me slowing down. That, and the memory of you in them, not so many weeks ago—"

"Listen to you! Did you not have your fill of me last night?"

"Nay." He nipped her nose with his teeth. "And I'm thinking of having a bit of you now, here, while the mood is upon me—"

"I told you, you've got to make an honest woman of me." She pulled out of his embrace. "And for that, you've got to meet the approval of Glenna first."

Maeve skittered away from the swipe of his hand, then laughed as he trailed her in mock sullenness through the winter woods. Though the air sang crisp through the lace of the bare boughs, she felt no cold. A warmth suffused her from the inside, a warmth born of the second night of their joining . . . a warmth born of the knowledge that there would be many nights to come, if Glenna cast her blessing upon this union.

Maeve hugged her skirts to her breast and pushed a sapling out of the path. She had little doubt Glenna would give her approval. After all, it was Glenna who had encouraged Maeve to seek out Garrick that Samhain night. How full of secrets that fairy-woman always was. She'd have made everything so much simpler, if she'd only told Maeve the truth of Garrick from the first, rather than hiding these past weeks and keeping Maeve in a state of total agony. But Glenna had always said that truth never comes easy, and a person will only believe it if she comes upon it herself. No doubt, this was another of Glenna's wise lessons in action.

Maeve frowned as she neared the clearing of Glenna's house. There had been no sight of the cow. Strange. Always, Maeve passed Glenna's old bow-backed cow munching amid the forest before reaching Glenna's hut. The cow must be pasturing on the other side of the woods, Maeve thought, though in all her life she'd never seen Glenna herd it to the north.

A cool finger of light painted the clearing with swirls of cloudy mist. Maeve quickened her step as she approached the familiar old hut. The door lay open, tilted against the wall of the house.

"It looks," Garrick said, in a voice oddly hushed, "like the house of a fairy-woman."

"I grew up here. Spent my life playing in this very clearing." She frowned at the ivy which had grown over the thatch and hung nearly to the ground, obscuring the building and making it look like a part of the oak behind it. "I never noticed how rundown it had become all these years."

"You come back here a woman today," he said, "and no longer look upon it with child's eyes."

"Perhaps that is it." She touched his arm. "Wait here. Let me tell Glenna of your presence."

Maeve ducked her head beneath the portal, brushed a dusty cobweb out of her way, and entered the cool interior. The house smelled of damp, rotting wood and the pungency of dried and crumbled herbs. Cobwebs feathered the rafters. Her feet scraped footsteps in the rug of leaves that had blown in and gathered in the corners halfway up to the roof. Bird's feet trails made designs through the patina of dust.

Maeve wandered into the hut and took a deep, deep breath. No Glenna. She couldn't even smell Glenna, that distinct smell of crushed wildflowers and fresh herbs that always hung about her clothing, that smell Maeve had grown up with, the smell that reminded her of the only home she'd ever had. And look at this place. No sign of a fire in the hearth, no sign of food, no sign of life at all. It looked as if no one had lived amid these walls for generations, though she herself had slept here as recently as a few months ago.

Something gleamed on the table. Maeve brushed off a scattering of leaves and caught her breath.

There, amid the dust, lay two rings wrought in the finest, reddest gold Maeve had ever seen. Maeve took them in her hand. They pulsed warm against her palm.

A smile nudged the corner of her lips as she stood in the hazy light, the rings snug in her hands. She'd made the right decision, she thought, as she looked around the old hut. Such a token as this could mean only one thing. She'd made the right decision. The curse was broken.

Such a gift as this was no other than a goodbye gift, from a fairy-woman who felt she was no longer needed.

Aye, Glenna. All these years, and I didn't know. You really are of fairy blood.

Maeve held the rings to her heart. It was over, it was all finally over. She glanced one last time around the old hut, and whispered a silent thanks to the mists. Then, clutching the rings, she stepped out into the sunshine, into the warmth of Garrick's smile, and opened her heart to destiny.

About the Author

Lisa Ann Verge lives with her family in New Jersey. She is the author of *Twice upon a Time* and *Heaven in His Arms*, both of which are available from Zebra Books. Lisa is currently working on her next Zebra historical romance, *The Faery Bride*, to be published in March 1996. Lisa loves hearing from her readers and you may write to her c/o Zebra Books. Please include a self-addressed stamped envelope if you wish a response.

SURRENDER TO THE SPLENDOR OF THE ROMANCES OF ROSANNE BITTNER!

CARESS	(3791, $5.99/$6.99)
COMANCHE SUNSET	(3568, $4.99/$5.99)
HEARTS SURRENDER	(2945, $4.50/$5.50)
LAWLESS LOVE	(3877, $4.50/$5.50)
PRAIRIE EMBRACE	(3160, $4.50/$5.50)
RAPTURE'S GOLD	(3879, $4.50/$5.50)
SHAMELESS	(4056, $5.99/$6.99)

Available wherever paperbacks are sold, or order direct from the Publisher. Send cover price plus 50¢ per copy for mailing and handling to Penguin USA, P.O. Box 999, c/o Dept. 17109, Bergenfield, NJ 07621. Residents of New York and Tennessee must include sales tax. DO NOT SEND CASH.